HOUGHTON MIFFLIN STEREOTYPE EDITION.

CROWS & CARDS

A NOVEL

WRITTEN WITH DILIGENCE

BY

MR. JOSEPH HELGERSON;

TO WHICH ARE ADDED

FINE ILLUSTRATIONS

BY

MR. PETER DESÉVE.

ALSO INCLUDED IS

Dictionarium Americannicum;

BEING THE WORDS HEREIN MOST ARCANE AND ALIEN
AND THEIR DEFINITIONS

sandpiper

HOUGHTON MIFFLIN HARCOURT
BOSTON • NEW YORK

SANDPIPER and the SANDPIPER logo are trademarks of
Houghton Mifflin Harcourt Publishing Company.

For information about permission to reproduce selections from this book,
write to Permissions, Houghton Mifflin Harcourt Publishing Company,
215 Park Avenue South, New York, New York 10003.

www.hmhbooks.com

The text of this book is set in Bodoni Book.
The illustrations are wax crayon.

Glossary woodcuts are from *1800 Woodcuts by Thomas Bewick and
his School*, published by Dover Publications.

The Library of Congress has cataloged the hardcover edition as follows:
Helgerson, Joseph.
Crows and cards / by Joseph Helgerson.
p. cm.

Summary: In 1849, Zeb's parents ship him off to St. Louis to become an
apprentice tanner, but the naïve twelve-year-old rebels, casting his lot with a
cheating riverboat gambler, while a slave and an Indian medicine man try to
get Zeb back on the right path. Includes historical notes, glossary, and biblio-
graphical references.

[1. Apprentices—Fiction. 2. Gambling—Fiction. 3. Slavery—Fiction. 4.
Shamans—Fiction. 5. Indians of North America—Missouri—Fiction. 6.
Conduct of life—Fiction. 7. St. Louis (Mo.) —History—20th century—Fic-
tion. 8. Humorous stories.] I. Title.
PZ7.H37408Wes 2008
[Fic]—dc22

2008013308
ISBN 978-0-618-88395-0
ISBN 978-0-547-33909-2 pb

Manufactured in the United States of America
EW 10 9 8 7 6 5 4 3 2 1
4500221879

FOR THE MONDAY MORNING LIBRARY CLUB

AND THE LIBRARIANS WHO HELPED US.

♥

ACKNOWLEDGMENTS

My thanks to Kate O'Sullivan for asking hard questions, George Rabasa for insights on writing, Tim Johnson for discussing dictionaries, Helen Kay Stefan for help with tin ears, Mike Stinocher for first driving me to St. Louis, Earl Brown for dog talk, Justin O'Connell for sharing his love of language, and Crow Dan for taking me under his wing.

Also, I'd like to thank the people and organizations that helped free up time to write this story with an artist grant. Funding was provided in part by a grant from the Minnesota State Arts Board, through an appropriation by the Minnesota State Legislature, a grant from the National Endowment for the Arts and private funders.

CHAPTER ONE

WHEN I TURNED TWELVE, my pa guessed it was time I learned a trade. Not wanting to disappoint, I told a stretcher and said I was all for it. That's when the bargaining started.

"How about apprenticing with a cooper?" he suggested.

The thought of making wood barrels all the rest of my born days left me kind of squirmy. True, there's nothing so handsome as a well-made butter churn or molasses barrel or milk bucket, but I hated slivers. Having Ma take a needle to one stuck in the meaty part of my hand made me carry on worse than a colicky baby. And since coopers are forever working in wood, well . . . So after pretending to build up some steam thinking about it, I shook my head no, all regretful-like.

"Wouldn't seem to be much of a future in it," I reckoned.

Telling Pa I was scared to death of slivers would never have worked, but bringing up the future nearly always bought me some breathing room.

"All right," Pa allowed, still sounding fresh about our talk. "How about blacksmithing?"

"Wouldn't you think I'm kind of scrawny for it?"

"It'd put some meat on your bones," he pointed out.

On goes my thinking hat again as I ground away, real serious-like, on the prospects of being a blacksmith. Of course, I already knew that blacksmithing wouldn't do either. Aside from my being a runt, which would make it hard to handle the bellows and pound the horseshoes and such, I'm awful jittery about getting burnt. And what blacksmith can do his job without a ripping hot fire?

"Wouldn't there be some dark days ahead for blacksmiths?" I asked. "What with the coming of railroads and all?"

The year was already 1849, after all, and the railroads had big plans, though I hadn't heard any talk about their doing away with blacksmithing. Lucky for me, Pa considered the smithy in the nearest town—that'd be Stavely's Landing, on the Mississippi—to be a rude and balky brute, which made it one possibility he was willing to let slip away without a fight.

"Hmm," Pa said, turning thoughtful and sizing me up with one eye, kind of squinty-like. "What would you say to work-ing in a livery stable? There's steady work there."

Well, taking care of horses and fancy carriages and such would be pretty quality, all right, but I figure Pa's up to something with this one. Everybody knows how bad horsehair gives my nose the dithers.

"'Fraid they wouldn't have me," I sighed. "Not the way I'd always be sneezing and spooking the livestock."

"Couldn't have that," Pa agreed, smiling despite himself. "Say, maybe you'd like to set your sights on becoming a preacher? Your Uncle Clayton went that route, you know."

We were talking about Pa's favorite brother, the one where my middle name sprang from and who'd baptized me in the river. I'd heard the story of my dunking many a time, 'cause my uncle got carried away with his preachifying and held me under a might long, till I was blue. Course, they got me working again, but my near miss of heaven left my family feeling I had a leg up when it came to talking with higher powers. So real careful-like, I asked, "Didn't he get swallowed up by the wilderness?"

"We don't know any such thing at all," Pa snorted. "He could show anytime."

"Sorry, Pa," I said, doing my level best to sound overlooked and dejected, "but I'm afraid I ain't heard no trumpets calling. Not yet, anyway."

"Now listen here," Pa grumbled, bearing down. "Is there anything you'd be willing to try?"

"Oh, most everything," I volunteered, hoping I sounded helpful.

"Could have fooled me."

"Wouldn't want me to jump into something without considering it real careful, would you?"

"I'm beginning to think maybe I wouldn't mind that at all." Pa wagged his head in wonder. "You're twelve now, ain't ya?" Then a knowing smile ruffled his mustache and I braced myself for the worst. "Say, how about this: maybe we could get you work as a cabin boy on a steamer."

Well, there weren't many boys along the Mississippi, Ohio, or Missouri rivers who wouldn't have given all their marbles along with a first-rate mumblety-peg* knife for such a chance as that. So I had to take her slow. First off, I grinned at Pa, on account of it was expected.

"Yes sir," Pa pressed on, probably thinking he was on the trail of something promising at last. "You'd start out low, but it wouldn't be long before you moved up to mud clerking or maybe cubbing for a pilot. After that, who knows?"

I nodded at the grandeur of it all, but pretty soon I frowned

---

*Anyone wondering what mumblety-peg is can risk a trip to the small dictionary lurking at the back of this book. But proceed with caution. That dictionary's filled with words and foreign phrases that have been dying off in these parts since the time of this story. There's no telling what kind of diseases you might catch from them.

a tiny bit, as if a troublesome thought had crept up on me. As of yet, I didn't know what that thought might be, but I hoped it would come to me quick. I was deathly afraid of drowning in the Mississippi, though it goes without saying that I couldn't tell Pa such a thing; squawking never got me anywhere with that man. Obstacles only made him more set in his ways. He didn't have a mean bone in him, but he didn't have any that were known to bend either. To change his mind, I had to come at him sort of sideways.

So while Pa went on about how he hadn't been selling wood to steamboats for going on ten years without knowing himself the names of some captains, I got busy sweating over how to tackle this one. You see, my pa's own pa had spent all his years yanking out tree stumps and starting up farms clear across Pennsylvania, Ohio, and Indiana, which didn't leave time nor money for setting his sons up in a trade. Naturally, that meant my own pa was bound and determined to see things turn out different for me. Finally, I couldn't bear his enthusiasms a minute longer and called out real desperate, "Wouldn't be much of a future, would there?"

"No future?" he cried, digging a finger in his ear like he couldn't believe what he was hearing. "Why, not even the railroads can put a dent in the future of this river and the steamers it carries. The whole West's being settled, and it's the rivers getting it done. Without 'em there wouldn't be no civilization beyond the Alleghenies. There wouldn't be nothing out here but a few smelly trappers and warbling Indians and . . . "

He began to wind down about then, maybe noticing how I looked sort of glum. Finally he stopped talking altogether and took a minute off to gaze up at the sky before muttering to himself, the way he does when our mule won't haul nothing.

"You seem to think the future's a mighty dark place," he concluded. "Why is that, son? Most anybody else you talk to is usually pretty high on her."

"Just a feeling that slides over me," I mumbled.

"Let me remind you of one little thing," Pa went on. "You're going to be living the rest of your life in the future, so you better get on speaking terms with it."

"Yes sir."

"So what troubles you about steamboating?"

"Well," I wheezed, taking the plunge without knowing what was going to pop out of my mouth, "the way this river changes its course so often, who's to say it'll keep going where we need it to?"

That pretty much did it—sealed my fate, so to speak. Pa smoldered for most of a minute, looking like he was about to blow cinders out his top any second. Finally he did, speaking up loud enough for our neighbors a half-mile distant to catch what was on his mind.

"Here's what's happening: You've got a great-uncle, name of Seth, who's down in St. Louis. He used to be a trapper on the Missouri but has turned to tanning in his dotage. Fact is, I hear tell he's the best tanner there is west of the Mississippi. When it comes to treating furs, he knows himself some secrets. Picked 'em up from the Indians, I shouldn't be surprised. We're going to put you on a steamer with a letter of introduction and see if he'll take you on."

Hearing that left me feeling buried alive, with Pa's every word landing like another shovelful of dirt atop me. When it comes right down to it, twelve-year-olds don't have much bargaining power, not with the likes of my pa. So it looked as if I was doomed to learn a trade that didn't have any future at all. What with beaver hats going out of fashion, the fur business was keeling over as we spoke. Beavers themselves were getting trapped out, as was pretty much every other living thing with the misfortune to wear fur and have four legs. Most all the river men said it. What's more, it wasn't just horsehair that made me sneeze—most any kind of fur would do. But when I tried to point out that working with hides might rip my nose apart, Pa claimed that us Crabtrees were made of sterner stuff than I knew. And on top of that, getting from Stavely's Landing to St. Louis would require riding one hundred and sixty-odd miles down the Mississippi on a steamer, which meant I could fall overboard and drown any second. I imagined I'd be turning a hundred and sixty-plus shades of green by the time I got there, *if* I got there. The only good thing about the whole undertaking was a chance to see St. Louis. The bad part of that was this: if St. Louis was only half as amazing as everyone claimed, I'd still probably be knocked blind by the sights.

CHAPTER TWO

Though that conversation snowed down on me in midwinter,
Pa and Ma couldn't ship me straight off to St. Louis on account of spring planting. It wasn't shaping up to be anywhere
near a long enough spring planting from my view.

"You're a goner," Matilda told me. She was my oldest sister, born one year after me, and could generally get away with
such spouting 'cause of her size.

"Not yet, I ain't."

"Heard Ma and Pa talking," she breezed on. "They're
agreed. It's for your own good."

That news struck me like a blow 'cause I'd been angling to
enlist Ma on my side, but if it'd already reached the for-your-
own-good stage, then all was lost.

Everything fell to pieces on me after that. I couldn't seem to talk to no one without provoking some testiness, and scratch as I might, I couldn't uncover so much as a glimmer of hope anywhere. I tried everything, even taking an oath—one hand on the Good Book—that what I really wanted to do was stay home and help run the wood yard, slivers and all.

Didn't wash.

No amount of sass, cow-eyed sulks, filibustering, or flat-out refusals got me anything but trips to the smokehouse. Now some families maybe use their smokehouses for whippings, but being alone with yourself was how ours got put to use. Dark and gloomy as my thoughts were ranging, I almost wished Pa believed in using the strap for misbehaving. But no, I had to sit out there in the dark, with no one to talk to but myself and an old crow who used to come peek at me through a knothole. By the start of April I'd spent so much time out there that whatever that bird was croaking about came so close to making sense that I had to plug my ears. The only good that came of all that was my swallowing hard enough to tolerate fate: I was St. Louis bound.

Pa had even written my Great-Uncle Seth, wanting to make sure he was still alive and would have me.

Yes and yes—for a fee.

Having to cough up money for this apprenticeship of mine nearly saved the day. Pa grumbled about the old skinflint and slammed logs around the wood yard for most of a week before hunkering down and making up his mind: if they was ever going to get rid of me, they'd have to sell off some livestock. In the end he had to unload half our cows and a fine old sow to scrape up seventy dollars, which would buy me six years' training. If I worked out, I'd start earning a dollar a week after three years. That would get bumped up to two dollars after five years. Out of these wages I'd have to buy my own clothes, pay for any doctoring I needed, and set aside enough to repay seventy dollars to Ma and Pa, leaving them fee money for my younger brothers. Food came with the job, though I'd probably have to cook it myself.

Leastways, that's how my contract read. Me, I was wondering what kind of great-uncle charged his own flesh and blood seventy dollars for a chance to work with a bunch of smelly old hides.

Come mid-April the corn and oats was in the ground, and my folks were driving me down to Stavely's Landing on the buckboard. Pa bought me a ticket for the *Rose Melinda*, a big sidewheeler hauling lead from the mines at Galena and picking up passengers on the way downriver. Once to the levee, he tucked the letter of introduction, along with the seventy-dollar fee and directions to my Great-Uncle Seth's place, inside my pants for safekeeping.

"Seth will work you hard but probably not to death," Pa said, giving my hand a shake. "Good luck, son."

My ma gave me a hug along with some advice. "Remember your reputation. It's worth more than gold."

Then she rustled away before coming up a hankie short. Back at the wagon, my brothers, James, Harold, and Lester, were watching mighty close. My sisters, Matilda, Rebecca, and Emily, weren't missing anything either. Up to that very moment, there'd always been seven of us kids who showed up at the dinner table, and that had seemed like the way it'd always be. The only world we'd ever known was our log cabin, which stacked up as a pretty special place, living along the Mississippi as we did. There wasn't nothing but dark woods and tall bluffs all around us, and at night the lights from Quincy, across the river in Illinois, twinkled away like jewels in a crown. The days, they stretched out forever before us, or so we had believed. Given the curious and shocked way my brothers and sisters were watching my departure, other possibilities were dawning on them. Every step I took left me feeling as though I was about to stumble over the edge of a cliff and the whole world seemed to be holding its breath to see how far I'd fall. Hang it all, there was even a dab of wet smearing up my eyes.

But none of that stopped Pa from walking me up the boarding plank and putting my ticket for deck passage in the purser's hand. The ticket cost him two dollar and ten cents above and beyond the seventy-dollar apprentice fee. That done, Pa removed himself from the ship, leaving me all alone for the first time in my life.

Of course, strictly speaking, I wasn't anywhere near alone, not with all the strangers crammed on that steamer, but just then I wasn't paying them any mind. I was too busy watching Pa. He stood on shore while the *Rose Melinda* rang her bells and blew her whistle and backed out into the river. It took only a minute or two, but as minutes go, they were about as jam-packed as any I'd ever find. There were more things swishing around inside me than I could count, and outside of me, deck hands were rushing everywhere with cargo and shouts.

From the wagon, Ma and the others made little, tiny hand waves goodbye, as if their arms were broke. Pa didn't even manage that much.

He stood alone, still as a fence post till he was nothing but a speck on the shore behind us. Then I couldn't see him at all, though I kept looking. Something beneath my ribs told me he hadn't budged yet. What with all them mouths to feed, I'd never seen Pa stand in one place for more than a few seconds, but somehow I knew he'd stay standing on that levee, just to make sure I didn't figure out some way off the boat. My escaping was an unlikely proposition, surrounded as I was by all that water, and I suppose it was awful smallish of me to think that's why Pa stood there watching. Hadn't he been the one to fetch the doc for me in that ice storm? And hadn't he, who swam about as good as a heavy rock, somehow saved me from drowning that time I was fooling around and fell off the ferry? And weren't there a thousand or more other *hadn't*s to boot, every one of them adding to the bulge in my throat? No, something deep inside me said he'd stay planted on that shore till my steamer was long gone and Ma came to get him. But he wouldn't be standing there 'cause he didn't trust me. There were deeper wells than that to the man, or so I told myself.

At the same time, I couldn't help but wonder what kind of folks did such a thing as this to their own son. Weren't they the same Ma and Pa who once let a runaway slave hide in our hayloft for a week? And now hadn't they locked me into an apprenticeship that wasn't but one step removed from slavery? Who could find any sense in that? Up to then I don't think I'd ever hated any people that I loved so much.

CHAPTER THREE

JUST WHEN MY LOWER LIP WAS HANGING all quivery, things took an unexpected turn for the better and I made me a friend. He must have been watching my goodbyes, 'cause without introductions he stepped up and reminisced, "I still recall the day I tried out my own wings."

Looking over, I faced a gentleman dressed like someone who owned ten plantations, and not little ones either. Beneath his black top hat was a head of black hair and a black goatee that was even shinier than his black boots. His voice was low and easy and didn't have no cracker crumbs to it.

"Beg pardon?" I said.

"Son," he answered, "there's no reason to go begging for anything around me. I'm the fellow you've heard of who believes in giving away the best of what he's got. It will only come back a hundredfold. That's my philosophy. What's yours?"

Well, he'd flummoxed me good with such talk, to say nothing of overwhelming me with the fine cut of his clothes and
the lordly line of his nose and the generous gleam of his blue
eyes. His mouth was so full of handsome pearly teeth that it
could have gone neck and neck with a king's. What's more,
smack in the middle of the ruffliest white shirt I ever hope
to see flashed a diamond stud that could have hypnotized a
snake. Without thinking, I answered, "Staying clear of slivers. That's my philosophy."

Such talk tickled him hard. He laughed a bit and then
started stroking his goatee and sizing me up real thoughtful-
like.

"Name's Charles Larpenteur," he said, putting his hand out
for shaking purposes, "though most call me Chilly. What'd
your pa call you?"

"Zebulon Crabtree, sir." I gave him my best manly handshake.

I almost lost my hand in his, oversized as it was. Height-
wise, he may have been smallish, but across the shoulders he
was worth an ax handle and his paws were monsters.

"Most call me Zeb." I pulled my hand to safety. "Do you
mind if we step back from the railing a ways?"

"Not at all, Zeb. Not at all."

He took a leisurely glance up and down the deck, as if on
the lookout for someone, then waved me behind a cord of

firewood stacked for the ship's boilers. We took up residence atop a couple kegs of applejack. One of the barrels was weepy on a seam and the air hung heavy with the sweet, tangy scent of last fall's spitters.

Once settled, Chilly offered me a chaw of tobacco, but I passed, saying I didn't indulge on account of how it knotted up my stomach.

"Sensible," he agreed. "Do you mind if I exercise my powers of deduction on you, Zeb? It's one of the games I like to play on these boat rides. Helps whittle down the time."

"Feel free," I told him, relieved that he hadn't hoo-hawed over my refusing tobacco.

He took a good, long gander at my jacket, which Ma had sewn out of old jeans, my homespun pants, and my resoled boots. If I'd had my way, I wouldn't have been wearing boots at all, warmish as it was, but I figured that without them I'd be so busy watching for slivers that I'd never get anywhere.

"I'll lay you're fourteen or fifteen," he said, "and headed downriver on some important business."

He'd got the downriver part right, though that didn't count for much, seeing as the *Rose Melinda* was pointed that way. I suppose the important business was true enough too, though sort of vague to be worth counting. But the part about my looking fourteen or fifteen was an out-and-out lie. People were generally hard pressed to put me at my rightful twelve.

Most of the time they came up with a guess of nine or ten, sometimes even low as eight, rarely up to eleven. Needless to say, I was considerably charmed.

Skipping over my real age, I said, "I'm headed to St. Louis to learn a trade."

"Don't tell me any more." Chilly Larpenteur held up a hand to stop me. "Let me guess."

So he went over me again, paying special attention to my palms and the profile of my nose, as if they had as much to say as the Old Testament. He counted up the four or five freckles roosting on my cheeks, sneaked a peek in an ear, and pretended to be afraid of my front teeth, which have been compared to a beaver's, though not by anyone I'd call a friend. Satisfied at last, he leaned back and closed his eyes.

"As I see it," he guessed, "there's two possibilities. Both of 'em are likely, but I'm leaning toward the one with more glory. How do you feel about glory, Zeb?"

"All for it." So long as it didn't involve slivers, getting burnt, high places, or swimming. Avoiding the dark was pretty close to being on that list too.

"I thought as much. But before I say my piece, would you hold your hands flat in front of me?"

I did as asked, kind of puzzled and enjoying the game all the more 'cause of it.

"Just hold 'em there," he told me, inspecting them real

close-like, as if they might turn into butterflies or something even more amazing. At length, he chuckled and shook his head.

"Steady as rocks." Chilly clicked his tongue in admiration. "You're not going to make this easy, are you?"

That puffed me up considerable, so I hung my hands out there a spell longer, even though they were already dog-tired.

"Could go either way," Chilly judged. "And that's a fact. Guess I might as well choose and have done with it. I'd say you're headed down to Jefferson Barracks to sign up as a scout for the Army."

He nodded his head sagely, as if he'd nailed my plans dead center. I really had the gent going. Jefferson Barracks was the Army outpost in St. Louis, and they weren't likely to waste their time with an undergrown specimen such as me.

"Nope," I advised him.

Chilly wore a pained expression for a bit, sort of like a man working around a toothache.

"That only leaves one thing." He took a deep breath and plunged ahead. "With hands so steady as yours, a goldsmith or jeweler, I'd say. Are you going to learn to cut diamonds and rubies for some far-off king?"

"Wrong again." Though I mightn't have minded such work at all, so long as there weren't any splinters.

"Well, I'm busted," he muttered. "You'll have to lay 'er out for me, Zeb, 'cause far as I can tell, you're a might too young to be running for president."

"My ma and pa are sending me down to St. Lou to learn to be a tanner."

The instant I said it—why, Chilly's liveliness shriveled up to nothing. All the warmth flew right out of his face, and it felt like a heavy, dark cloud had passed between me and the sun. I guessed he wasn't about to waste any time on some lowly tanner's helper. He looked at me close again, but this time he was checking out my eyes, as if searching for something. There was a worrisome crease to his brows too, which left me feeling as though I'd somehow let him down.

It nearly made me cry. Here I was, all alone on the river, couldn't swim a lick, and about to lose the only friend I had. I may have been only twelve, but I knew that a friend was a rare thing in this world—hard to make, easy to lose. And a man as worldly as Mr. Chilly Larpenteur was a keeper for sure. Trouble was, I didn't know how to make things right again.

After a bit, Chilly hopped down from his barrel and spoke in a tone so polite, it nearly cut me in half.

"I'm sure your ma and pa mean well," he informed me.

Holding out his hand, he gave me as stiff a handshake as you're likely to encounter outside a graveyard and started off as if we'd never met. A feeling of loneliness swamped me, and I couldn't breathe, not a bit. Well, a drowning man's not going down without yelping for help, and I wasn't either.

"Chilly!" I called, hurrying to catch up to him. "What would *you* do?"

He held up, giving me the idea he had something on his mind, but then he shook his handsome head all regretful-like, as if it wasn't his place to say it.

"No," he judged, acting noble, "I wouldn't want to step between a pa and his son."

"If you got some kind of better idea," I babbled, holding on to his coat sleeve, "I'm sure my pa would want me to hear you out. It's not like he had his heart set on my being a tanner."

Which was true—far as it went. The only thing my pa had been really keen on was having me cub on a steamer. I felt a little rumbling below my ribs over the fib but kept on babbling.

"There was a whole bunch of other trades we talked over, but for one reason or another, they didn't pan out. So if you've got some advice to offer, I'd be ever so much grateful."

The way he reached out and patted the top of my head was a comfort. And didn't I need it? You see, I was quaking away, half expecting Pa to come thundering down on me, wanting to know just what in blue blazes I was talking about. But you know what? Pa didn't show up. Ma neither. While I was getting used to that, Chilly was checking up and down the deck as though he didn't want anyone to overhear what he had to say next.

"All right, Zeb," he confided. "Maybe I can offer an idea of how I might help you. But it won't lead to anything easy. I wouldn't want you to have that notion."

"I'm not afraid of hard work," I promised.

"I didn't figure you to be," Chilly assured me. "But can you keep a secret? That's the part weighing on me. This idea I'm going to tell you, it's in need of being kept a secret. You don't, and things can get mighty hot."

"Secrets are my specialty," I said, which was mostly true, except for the time I told on my brother Harold for trying to shoot an apple off Emily's head with a bow and arrow.

"How about loyalty?" Chilly asked.

"Had it for dessert every night to home."

And we did too, seeing as how we rarely had lump sugar or jam lazing about.

"All right then," Chilly said, "but before I can tell you more, you'll have to pass a test."

"A hard one? I ain't had much schooling. Just some reading and ciphering from Ma."

"It's not a school test. More a reading of your character. You game?"

"I'll give 'er my best shot."

"Joan of Arc couldn't ask for more," Chilly declared, back to smiling. That lasted until a dark thought murkied his brow and he lowered his voice again. "Not a-scared of tight places, are you?"

"That part of the test?"

"A qualifier."

"Well, I don't like to brag," I said, "but I been known to take a candle into caves no one else would touch."

If Pa had been around, I'd have got a knuckle up top of my head for such blowing, even if it was true. Scrawny as I was, crawling into tight spaces had saved my hide more than once when dealing with town bullies. Chilly wasn't entirely sold though and asked me to stretch out flat on the deck so's he could do some measuring. Strange though it seemed, I did her, trying not to think of the slivers beneath me or the rushing waters beneath them. Chilly, he kneeled down beside me and pulled out a gold pocket watch that was the prettiest thing I'd ever seen and probably worth an entire farm, live-stock and all. He used the watch's gold chain to measure how far off the deck I came.

"I do believe you'll do." He sounded awfully pleased about it. "Yes, indeed. But now for the test."

CHAPTER FOUR

ONCE AGAIN CHILLY CHECKED UP AND DOWN the deck, casual-like, as if he didn't want anyone noticing him doing it. Satisfied that nobody was paying us any mind, he tugged me behind a stack of chicken crates for some privacy. As a general rule, I keep my distance from chickens, which are about the peckingest bird you can imagine, especially when you're after eggs. To keep from flinching away from their beaks, I concentrated for all I was worth on what my new friend had to tell me.

"Let's say there's an old gentleman planter aboard this steamer," Chilly speculated. "He's here to take in the sights. He's traveled the entire length of the river, or at least the part of it you can reach by steamer, New Orleans to St. Paul, and now he's headed back home. He did it just to see how the river looked and smelled and tasted—especially tasted. He carried a little silver dipper for sampling it each morning. All the way he booked a whole stateroom to himself, ate at the captain's table every meal, and drank bottled wine at the bar. No corn squeezings from a jug for the likes of him. Can you imagine having money enough to do all that, and for no better reason than to say you've done it?"

"Why, no sir, I can't."

"It's hard for me to digest too," he admitted, nodding in agreement. "You might say it makes me uneasy, thinking of a man with that kind of money. Why, he must have whole trunks of it at home."

I caught Chilly squinting sideways at me, so I bore down to show I was keeping up just fine.

"What do you think a man who has that kind of fortune ought to do with it?" Chilly asked.

That sounded kind of like a test question, which threw me on alert. I couldn't for the life of me see what any of this had to do with fitting into tight spaces, but I gave it some major thinking anyhow.

"Oh, maybe build a palace," I guessed. "Paint her white. Lay in some windows and plenty of gold."

When I studied Chilly's face for some hint as to whether I was on the right road, it didn't look good.

"And maybe buy a new suit," I threw in quick-like. "Right from a store, to wear in that palace."

That didn't appear to be any go either, not with Chilly looking ready to wag his head no. Quick as lightning, I tossed out one last guess.

"And 'course I'd order up some furniture and quality stuff all the way from New Orleans. Made in France, they would be, and so pretty that you wouldn't hardly want to sit on 'em. And all the time you'd be after your servants to dust 'em up till they shined enough to show your grin."

"That'd be exactly what most of your basic rich gents would do." Chilly nodded wisely. "And then some. Do you reckon that'd make them great men?"

"Great?" I blinked, not sure if I'd heard him right.

"That's the question before us," Chilly said. "Would all those things you talked up make a rich man stand head and shoulders above everyone else? Would they make him a man that people looked up to? And sang the praises of? And told their grandchildren that they once shook his hand?"

"I don't see why not."

"No, no, no," Chilly moaned, kind of low-like, which made it sound as though I'd muffed 'er pretty bad. "Not by a long shot, they wouldn't. Take your palace—that might work for a king, but just let some ordinary fella try to build one and everyone thinks he's putting on airs."

"That's so," I said, seeing his point.

"And the clothes don't ever make the man."

"True enough," I admitted, thinking that I must have heard

Pa warn me about the exact same thing a hundred times or more.

"And there's nothing ever been made in France that made a man great, unless he was a Frenchman, and this old gent I'm telling you about doesn't have a drop of French blood in him."

"So what would make him a great man?" I asked, figuring the answer was way beyond me.

"*That's* the question," Chilly agreed, sounding mighty pleased with himself for asking it. "What would make such a man great? It's a tough old nut to crack, all right."

Then he commenced to ho-humming and rocking on his feet, which made it seem like he was giving me a second chance at tackling it. I poured on the steam too, giving his question a double heaping of attention, but truth be, I didn't know the first thing about rich folks. Why, the closest I'd ever come to one was waving to passing steamers. Finally I called her quits and blurted, "Well, maybe he just ought to share it."

"That's it!" Chilly slapped me so hard on the back, he nearly knocked me over. "That's exactly the answer, son. He ought to share it. That surely would make him a great man."

He grew real thoughtful then and checked around the chicken crates to make sure no one had sneaked up on us. "But rich men never do," he lamented. "They don't seem able. If you was to ask 'em what they wanted out of life, they'd tell you they hoped to be remembered as great men. I know. I've asked. I see 'em on these steamers, mooning around the railings and looking miserable as fleas, and I've asked. They generally get kind of choked up about it too, 'cause they know it ain't likely to happen, don't matter how many factories or plantations they own.

"But when I tell them how they can pull it off, they blush like schoolboys and say they couldn't ever do it. No sir, not on a dare. It wouldn't be right to share their money, they say. Don't ask me why they cling to it so. I've never heard a satisfactory answer to that one. Why, you'd think it ought to be the easiest thing in the world to dip in their pockets, pull out a bankroll, and pass it around. They can't though. It's a bona fide mystery." Putting a hand on my shoulder, he gazed dead into my eyes and said, "What if I told you that I knew someone whose lifework was helping these rich gents become great?"

"I wouldn't be surprised," I said. "Not a bit."

"What if I told you that this fellow was on the lookout for a helper, an apprentice of sorts?"

I gulped and nodded, too afraid to ask the obvious.

"What if I told you he was a gambler?"

"A gambler?" His answer had sneaked up on me something fierce.

"And not just any kind of penny-ante card shuffler either," Chilly sailed on. "He's a genuine riverboat gambler, top of the breed."

"Riverboat?" I whispered, going weakish in the knees 'cause of course riverboats meant rivers and deep water.

"What if I told you that he was me?" Chilly went on.

My mouth most flopped open like a door in a high wind. You could have hung a lantern on my jaw. In the backwoods where I grew up, you heard about creatures like riverboat gamblers, same as you heard about herds of buffalo flowing like rivers and desert spiders big as your dinner plate. Romantic hogwash, my pa always called it, but for me they was mythical and wonderful as them ancient Greeks.

And here stood one of them before me. I was spellbound, honored, parched, and speechless. Mr. Chilly Larpenteur was saying something, but I didn't catch it and he had to repeat himself.

"You interested?" he said.

The whole world cocked an ear to hear what leaked out of me next, or at least it felt that way. I had encountered my first real decision as an adult, without Ma or Pa yeaing or naying over my shoulder. Not wanting to bungle it, I closed my eyes to concentrate and sort it all out.

And that's when it happened. One of them crated chickens we was standing next to managed to peck the back of my hand a good one. In addition to hurting like the dickens, drawing blood, and proving I was right to be wary of them birds, it also cleared my head considerable. All of a sudden the way my folks had forced me out of my home to become something I didn't want to be—even if it was for my own good, *especially* if it was for my own good—stuck in my craw so bad that I knew I wasn't going through with it. No sir. If I had to pick out something to be for the rest of my life, then the decision ought to be mine. That's what I told myself. Praying that I could somehow or other get over my fear of the rivers that a riverboat gambler would be floating on, I summoned up all the spit I could muster and told Mr. Chilly Larpenteur, "You bet."

He chuckled as though that was a pretty witty thing for a would-be gambler to come out with, then got down to business fast.

"For a hundred dollars I'll take you on."

"I only got seventy," I told him, swallowing hard and holding out the envelope with my money. "Plus a couple of coppers I been saving."

Before my eyes had a chance to go smeary on me, he snatched the envelope and said, "Done. You can pay the balance out of your share of the winnings."

Winnings? Right off I started wondering how much I could send home to Ma and Pa, to show them how well I was doing without Great-Uncle Seth. Chilly tucked the seventy in a vest pocket so fast that I never saw his hands move, and I've no idea where he stowed those coppers. He ripped up the envelope the money had been in, along with the directions to my great-uncle's tannery, and after glancing all around us—even up to the sky—he seemed satisfied that no one was watching and sent the paper scraps fluttering over the brown waters. Why would anyone care about those directions? Don't know, didn't ask, wasn't time. Soon as the last piece of paper touched the river, Chilly declared I was overdue to be introduced to a game of chance. That marked the first thing I learned about my new profession: if you saw an opportunity, you didn't let it spoil.

CHAPTER FIVE

CHILLY LARPENTEUR RAN ME UP some rear stairs to the *Rose Melinda*'s second deck, what's known as the boiler deck. Fast as he moved, you might have thought someone was chasing us. On the way we had to weave in and out of cords of wood higher than my head and stacks of lead rods that rose up to my chin. Pigs of lead, they called those rods. Don't ask me why 'cause I never heard 'em oink.

Before we hit the stairs, I sneezed my way past horses, chickens, mules, goats, pigs—live ones—and a small flock of sheep. I heard three or four languages being jabbered, saw an Indian wrapped up in one of them bright-colored Hudson Bay blankets, and had a mountain man in buckskins wink at me.

We passed a bunch of soldiers lounging around and bragging over who could spew a cheek full of tobacco juice the most accurate. The deck was plenty slippery in spots.

Chilly talked the whole way, though I didn't catch but half of what he had to say 'cause we crossed paths with a side paddle wheel that drowned out all conversation. One step before the boiler deck he stopped to shout in my ear, "Watch close now. We'll double our seventy dollars faster than you can blink."

Then he plunged through the doors leading to the second deck's main cabin, which stretched most of the boat's length. The whole distance was lined up with dinner tables and chandeliers fit for kings and dukes and whatnot. The ladies and gents at those tables—why, every one of them held out their little pinkies as they sipped their midday tea or sarsaparilla. Cigar smoke blued the air real pretty, and somewhere down the line a piano was being plinked at while a woman was singing "The Last Rose of Summer." That main cabin was almost quiet enough to hear every word of her song, and she sang it in tones so honey-sweet, they nearly melted your heart with worry over what would befall that last rose.

We didn't stop for none of it though, just dashed on till we reached some glass doors, first such doors I'd ever spied. As if being made of glass didn't make them special enough, they had a pair of eagles painted in gold on 'em. Chilly held up before those doors but a second, just long enough to make a sign of the cross, kind of secret-like, as if we was entering a church. Then we plowed past those gold eagles to a bar beyond them, where fifteen to twenty fellows were crowded around a single table. The men in back had to stand on chairs to see what was happening.

"Pearl Gulliver's dealing," Chilly said in my ear. "Game's called faro. He's a cheat and a bluffer, but I've about figured out the spots on his deck, so we're set. Watch careful now."

Chilly waded into the crowd, elbowing and whispering his way closer and closer to the table till he disappeared beneath the hatted heads leaning over the game. I heard a low, crackly voice that must have been Pearl Gulliver's. "Back so soon?"

That got a round of guffaws from the crowd, but as soon as it died down, Chilly called out real even-like, "Come back for my money."

"This ain't no house of charity," Pearl Gulliver advised. "It's a game of chance, and I ain't huge on lending losers back their bankroll."

"Nobody's asking you to," Chilly said.

"Not but a half hour ago you was broke and begging these gents to spot you some," Pearl Gulliver pointed out.

"I've come into an inheritance," Chilly answered, which brought on another round of snickers, during which Chilly must have dropped my seventy dollars on the table. That brought on a bout of quiet.

"Mighty puny leavings," Pearl Gulliver observed.

"If you're running an honest game, it ought to be enough."

The drumroll I heard must have been the beating of my heart. Several men tensed up and leaned away from the table, as if about to dive for cover, and Pearl Gulliver didn't settle any nerves by saying, "If you think the table ain't square, don't sit."

That set off a ripple of yeses.

"And leave you with my money?" Chilly laughed. "Deal 'em out."

It took some doing, but eventually I found me a wobbly chair to stand on and tried to forget about how high I was climbing. (Anything much above a footstool gives me second thoughts.) From my perch I had a clear look at Pearl Gulliver, a shrivelly old man with a gray beard full as a brush fence. His eyes skipped around that table so fast, you might have thought someone was trying to sneak up on him. The rough way he handled the cards and chips almost made it seem as if he hated 'em. And wasn't the oilcloth covering that table something? Green as a pasture, it was, and with pictures of cards where the gamblers placed their bets.

As for how the game of faro was played, I never did entirely get the hang of it. Not that day, anyway. Pearl Gulliver slid two cards out of a shiny, silver box that was all decorated up with mother-of-pearl. The cards were face-down and players bet on them by laying money on the pictures of cards that decorated the oilcloth. The face-down card that Pearl Gulliver slid to his right was the losing card, and any money bet on it went to him. The face-down card that ended up to his left was the winner, which meant that Pearl Gulliver had to pay out to anyone who bet on it. Money placed on any cards other than those two rode till the next hand.

To place bets, hands crisscrossed the table worse than summer lightning, shoving money this way and that, collecting winnings, replacing losings. There was more cackling and crowing than the time a raccoon hit our hen house.

Sometimes players won. Mostly, they seemed to lose. All the while Chilly wagered small and studied the cards hard enough to see clear through them.

And I learned that a whole tribe of blacksmiths couldn't have been more superstitious than the men crowded round that table, and I didn't know anyone who spewed out more charms and signs than the ornery smithy back home. Why, nearly every man present was rubbing a rabbit's foot or kissing a clamshell or crossing himself three times—minimum —before every new hand got dealt. I hadn't ever seen such excitement around a table, not in my whole life. Even Thanksgiving or Christmas dinners couldn't hold a candle to it. Those men watched Pearl Gulliver's hands the way a starving man would keep an eye on a loaf of bread that was about to be sliced. The roof might have blown off the boat and I got my doubts they'd have looked up, unless it was to see what cards got sucked away.

The contorting around the table tickled Pearl Gulliver, though he kept his trap shut and never poked fun, not even at the rough fellow who had named his lucky clamshell Sherry-Ann. He just waited for everyone to settle down. The only player who kept his distance from all the good-luck hocus-pocus was Chilly. All the fandango chafed on him some, and he lifted out his gold pocket watch a few times to check on how long all the messing around was taking, but otherwise he bided his time. It left me feeling puffed up as big as all outdoors to be with the one man who took it all in stride.

CHAPTER SIX

ONCE A GAME COMMENCED, EVERYONE WENT SERIOUS as a flock of ministers. Eventually, a couple of gents got up, saying their wells were dry, but Chilly held his own with my seventy dollars, gaining here, losing there. Mostly he was still as a toad waiting for the buzz of a fly. Then all of a sudden Chilly must have seen something on the backs of those cards that he liked, 'cause he bet all we had on a single hand. Everybody around the table took a deep breath and held 'er in, waiting to see.

When Pearl Gulliver flipped the winning card over, he snorted, angry-like. Chilly had won, doubling our pile.

"Luck visits us all from time to time," Pearl Gulliver spouted.

Chilly returned fire by saying, "Some get visited more than others."

He wasn't done, either, not by a long shot. Lump together

everything he'd said about the wonders of being a gambler, and it still wouldn't have impressed me as much as what came next. Soon as Pearl Gulliver slid two new cards out of the box, Chilly shoved all our winnings onto one of the card pictures painted on the oilcloth. Every man round that table went quiet as a deep woods. The only one still moving was Pearl Gulliver, who chuckled softly beneath his beard.

When the next two cards got flipped, I raised my hands above my head and whooped it up with everyone else. Chilly had doubled our money again. We now had upwards of two hundred and eighty dollars looking pretty on our side of the table, and we hadn't been sitting there for more than twenty minutes. It would have taken all six of my years with Great-Uncle Seth to see that much loot. I was beaming like a tree-sized candle, and I ain't talking no sapling either.

And then Chilly did something that had me laughin' for joy, 'cause it appeared he wasn't done working that table yet. Yes sir, when Pearl Gulliver trotted out the next two cards, Chilly toyed with him some by lifting out his gold watch to check the hour, as if it might be time for us to be moving on with our winnings, but then he showed a change of heart and let everything ride on another picture.

A hush fell over the table. Maybe three seconds passed before the dam burst and every player rushed to piggyback on Chilly's run. Holding tight to their rabbits' feet and clamshells and ivory crosses, every man there shoved his money on the same picture as Chilly.

"Out to bust the bank, are you, boys?" Pearl Gulliver's face was pinched up tight as something stitched shut.

"Aiming to see the next cards," Chilly answered, speaking up for the rest of us.

To his credit, Pearl Gulliver flipped the cards over without the slightest tremble.

What happened afterward had best be called an explosion. Everyone rose in the air a foot or so and hats went sailing. There were cries of "Glory be" and "Oh mama" and "We're bucking the tiger, boys. Bucking her good."

Me? The numbers were flying through my head faster than buckshot. We had upward of five hundred and sixty dollars and counting. I would have been a full-grown man before my Great-Uncle Seth forked over that much. It all meant nothing to Chilly though. He sat still at the center of the celebrations, watching Pearl Gulliver's hands for treachery. That's when I knew for sure how Chilly Larpenteur had got his nickname. I'd heard tell of men with ice water in their veins, but that didn't touch how cool Chilly was.

"The game's still on, gents," Pearl Gulliver reminded everyone. There was a terrible fire burning in his eyes that made me look away from him.

The others turned to Chilly, who was just about ready to

shove our winnings onto the picture of a new card when a woman's voice filled the room.

"Gentlemen," she called out. "Please, can you spare something for the poor orphans of St. Louis?"

The whole bunch of us turned as one toward the door, where stood a lady pretty enough to strike you blind if you had sight or give you sight if you were blind. She had honey gold hair and a voice that would have given songbirds the miseries, so sweet did she sound. It was the same lady who'd been singing at the piano in the main cabin. You could hear the heart of every man there take an extra pitter-pat.

The only one who had any wits about him was Chilly, who gathered up our earnings, rose from the table, and made a courtly bow to the lady.

"Those orphans are deserving of some supper too," Chilly agreed.

When I watched him dump half our winnings in a little basket the lady was holding, I couldn't have felt any prouder than if I'd done it myself. Every other man had his eye on Chilly too, and what's more, they all followed him over to do the same.

"St. Jerome blesses you," the lady said.

"And you," she said to the next man.

"You won't be forgotten," she promised a third.

And so on down the line, 'cause dang if every man at the

table didn't make a sizable contribution to the orphans of St. Louis. Every man but me, that is, 'cause I didn't have a cent in my pocket, and Pearl Gulliver, who stayed right at his table, looking devastated by the shower of gold coins raining into that woman's basket. Every dollar that went to them orphans was a dollar he wouldn't be seeing again.

"You've proved to those orphans that the world cares," she told us, dabbing a tear from her eye. "God bless you, one and all."

With that, she swept back out to the main cabin, moving from table to table to ask for more contributions. It looked as though the example set by Chilly and the other gamblers was reaping rewards out there too. All the ladies and gents was dropping money in the basket left and right.

I felt filled full of sparks to think of the good we'd done. Not too long back I'd been wondering if I'd even make it to St. Louis without drowning, and now here I was, helping poor orphans. Wouldn't my brothers and sisters be all atwitter if they could see me now? Even Ma and Pa might have their doubts about the wisdom of packing me off to Great-Uncle Seth's.

As soon as the doors closed behind her, the spell was broken and everyone spun back to Pearl Gulliver, who was waiting for us with a nasty smile wrinkling his face. His hands were resting on the dealer's box and looking none too innocent.

"You do-gooders ready to play?" he asked.

Hearing that, Chilly charged back to the faro table as if a bugle was blowing. Single-minded as he looked, I don't think he'd have noticed a flaming arrow landing square in his chest. I'm ashamed to admit it, but just then a little wave of doubt washed over me and I grabbed at his coat sleeve. I was thinking maybe it was time to scoop up our earnings and call it a day before some calamity hit us. Even after helping out those orphans, we still stood two hundred and eighty dollars up, or thereabouts, which was miracle enough to last me for a stretch. But Chilly brushed me off easily as a leaf, maybe knowing he had one more lesson to learn me that day.

Lowering himself back down to the table, Chilly gazed hard at the two cards that Pearl Gulliver now slid out of the box. Nodding to himself as if everything was in apple-pie order, he checked his pocket watch as though we were on a schedule and proceeded to wager all our money on the picture of one more card. The entire room fell still as something pinned under one of them Egyptian pyramids. Empires could have come and gone while we sat there. Kings could have grown beards long enough to trip over.

Somebody sneezed, ending the stillness. Every other player whipped out his good-luck charm and rushed to catch onto Chilly's coattails.

It didn't look as though Pearl Gulliver had a friend in the

world other than himself, but that turned out to be enough. Flipping over the next two cards without a moment's pause, he knocked the wind right out of us.

Chilly lost.

Everything.

And everyone else went tumbling right down with him.

Pearl Gulliver had broke the entire room in one blow. What with his gloaty, satisfied smirk, the old fraud had to have dealt a crooked hand. While we'd been tending to orphans, he must have been tending to the cards. But losing didn't bother Chilly one bit. He rose up from that faro table without a word of complaint, checked the time as if late for an important appointment, and left without a backwards glance. Such nobility is a rare thing in this world. I may have been only twelve, but I'd seen enough to know that much. Chilly and me had just lost somewhere around two hundred and eighty dollars, but it didn't weigh on him, not a bit. He had faith in his abilities to win it all back soon. You could tell by the lofty way he carried himself out of there.

CHAPTER SEVEN

"LET THAT BE A LESSON TO YOU," Chilly advised once we were back down on the passenger deck. "Every man's got his weakness and mine's faro."

"Know what you mean," I answered, doing my best to sound worldly. "My little sister Emily is mine. She's all the time getting me into trouble without even trying."

"Do tell," Chilly said, without seeming too interested. Something over my left shoulder had caught his eye. At the same time that he was murmuring that, he was also reaching for a piece of kindling off a nearby wood stack. Without warning, he spun and launched the stick, which tumbled toward me end over end like a tomahawk.

I dropped for the deck, not knowing what to think. The wood whirred by overhead and a split second later splashed

into the river, though not before a bird cawed from so close
behind me that I covered up to avoid being pecked.
When nothing happened, I rolled over, cautious-
like, and caught sight of a crow perched on the
railing. The bird tilted its head for a better look
at us, cawed twice, and lifted away from the boat
just as Chilly was grabbing another chunk of kindling. Before Chilly could peg that stick, the
crow dipped below the railing and skimmed
away. Chilly let drive anyway, muttering dag-
gers all the while. "Pesky bird. I can't tolerate a
scavenger."

"Know what you mean," I said, pulling myself up and
dusting off. "My brother Harold is all the time—"

But Chilly had already moved on to something else. "'Pears
we got some unfinished business waiting on us. Try to keep
up, boy." And off he shinned toward the back of the boat.

I jogged alongside him, unable to resist asking one little
thing that was nagging at me. "Shouldn't we have quit while
ahead?"

"'Course we should have," Chilly grumbled, sidestepping
a fella with a wooden leg. "And if I hadn't gotten waylaid by
them poor orphans, we might have, but they broke my con-
centration." He shook his head, disgusted with himself, but
then he sort of chuckled at his own shortcomings too, adding,

"Leastways we gave old Pearl a run that he won't soon forget. That counts for something. The rest of it's all spilt milk, and you know what they say 'bout that. Second-guessing yourself ain't no way for a gambler to carry on. What you got to be thinking of is your next bet. Like right now."

We'd arrived at a knot of deck hands, slaves who'd been rented out to the *Rose Melinda*. They were throwing dice, rolling them against the crates of chickens, who were cackling dangerously. Reaching into a vest pocket, Chilly fished out the two coppers I'd paid him in addition to the seventy dollars of my ma and pa's. I couldn't hardly wait to see what he had to teach me next.

"Might as well find out what I can do with these," he said.

Those deck hands made plenty of room for us when Chilly stepped up to their game. Oh, a couple of 'em might have stared kind of resentful-like, as if we had something of theirs that they wanted back, but for the most part they just beamed and welcomed us right in. The closest I'd ever been to a slave was the runaway who'd holed up in the barn back home, and all I'd seen of him was the empty tin plate I collected every evening after chores. 'Course, every once in a while I got to go with Pa into Stavely's Landing and I'd seen a few slaves there, though always from across the street, never up close, so I took a special interest in this bunch on the *Rose Melinda*. But except for dressing in hand-me-downs about like my own, they didn't sort out a whole lot different from the crowd around the faro table. Naturally, the color of their skin and shape of their faces was different, but they rubbed their good-luck pieces and loved winning same as everyone upstairs. It was kind of a disappointment 'cause I'd been expecting them to be a whole nother tribe.

A tall, sweaty man blew considerable on the dice and talked to them too, like they were old friends, which was what they turned out to be (for him, not us). It took but one throw of the dice for Chilly's next lesson to be over. There wasn't even time to fuss about quitting while ahead. We'd lost before I could get around to it.

"Looks like we'll be enjoying the scenery from here on out," Chilly remarked, sounding almost relieved, as if he could only rest now that he'd done his duty and lost our last cent. "It'll give me a chance to tell you about the telegraph you'll be running."

"Telegraph?" I choked a bit on that one, for it was news to me. 'Course, I'd heard tell of these telegraphs. People claimed you could talk to someone far gone away, clear 'cross the country, if you had a mind to, by using some kind of click code. Such doings didn't hardly seem possible, and I'd surely never thought that I'd be having anything to do with that kind of modern-day wonder. To my everlasting embarrassment, the only thing I could think of saying was, "I didn't know gamblers used telegraphs."

"'Course we do," Chilly said. "But before I tell you about it, I'm going to have to swear you to secrecy."

With that, Chilly led me beneath some stairs, where we could be alone and mostly hear each other, unless someone was clomping up or down above us.

"What I'm about to tell you, Zeb, they're the rules of the Brotherhood of the Gambler, whose motto is 'Secrecy—First and Last.'" He read the deep of my eyes before pulling out a little pocketknife and continuing. "You'll have to take a blood oath to seal this up good and proper. You willing?"

"Honor bright," I told him, shying away from the edge of that knife, which looked sharp enough for shaving.

Grabbing my hand, he nicked the tip of my middle finger a good one before it occurred to me whose blood he'd been talking about. I near swooned, particularly when he squeezed my fingertip to get three drops out. My free hand locked onto a railing and held on for dear life, till he let go of me, saying, "That ought to do the job." His voice sounded far away and drifty, and I half expected to find myself floating up to heaven when I opened my eyes, which had crammed themselves shut. But no such thing. I remained planted on the steerage deck of the *Rose Melinda* with my bleeding finger still attached.

In Chilly's hand was a deck of cards that he'd fished out of somewhere, and decorating their top was three red splots of blood. Even an unrepentant fool would have taken my surviving as a sign that this was meant to be.

"Repeat after me," he pronounced, real solemn-like. "I, Zeb Crabtree, do faithfully swear upon my pa's grave to keep the secrets I am about to hear, from this day forward, in sickness and in health, for richer and poorer, so long as I shall draw a breath."

It was a highflying, noble oath, all right, and just hearing me repeat it came close to drawing a tear to Chilly Larpenteur's eyes. He was probably remembering the day when he had first taken the pledge himself. Seeing that, I knew I was totally honor bound to uphold his oath. If I didn't, some bunch of gamblers would probably hunt me down in the night and cut my heart out and drop it in a jar to sell to some quack doctor as a curiosity for his office.

"But my pa ain't got no grave," I fessed up. "He ain't even dead yet."

"We'll take you on speculation," Chilly said after a moment's considering.

So I swore it all and Chilly said that made me a full-fledged member of the Brotherhood of the Gambler, now and forever.

What Chilly Larpenteur told me next lit up the inside of my head bold as lightning flashes. Turned out that it wasn't only the skills to play a game or two of cards that I'd be learning. Not by a mile or more. Before I was done mastering my new trade, I'd be part banker, judge, lawman, and a touch of preacher, which ought to have shown them back home. There would probably be a few other callings thrown in too, for rainy days, but he didn't bother going into those just yet.

I'd be a banker 'cause before long I'd be floating loans and running accounts in my head as fast as a Cincinnati peddler. I'd be part judge 'cause some who gambled required being penalized for dodging debts or other "crimes of character," as Chilly put it. And since there'd be times when these cutups wouldn't take their medicine happy-like, there'd also be days when I'd have to be part lawman and bring them to justice.

And finally there were going to be occasions when I was acting as a preacher. A gambler had a better look into a man's soul than any other living creature, said Chilly, and it was our *responsibility* to administer to a soul whenever we saw one in need. If Ma and Pa thought about me at all, such news as this ought to have befuddled them no end, a prospect that tickled me more than a touch 'cause I figured it served them right.

After sharing the general headlines on all that, Chilly served up a question. "Tell me, Zeb, what's the first thing a gambling man's got to pay attention to?"

"Where's his good-luck piece?" I was thinking of all the gents at the faro table and how Chilly had crossed himself before joining them. His answer surprised me considerable.

"A thousand times no to that," Chilly chided. "Such superstitions ain't nothing but quicksand. And the same goes for worrying over cracked mirrors or handling snakeskins or roosters crowing at full moons or any other fool sign you been taught. Wipe 'em clear out of your head 'cause the Brotherhood don't allow 'em. You're aiming to be a gambler—a real one—and we make up our own luck as the need arises." He jabbed a finger into my chest to drive that point home. "You'll be learning more about that as we go along. Think of something else."

I stalled a bit before dredging up "How much money's in his pocket?"

"That's the least of your worries." Chilly chuckled, shaking his head as though this was the first mistake every greenhorn made. "Sometimes your pockets are going to be full, sometimes empty. A gambler can't be worrying about the state of his pockets. No, there's something more basic. Give it another go, why don't you."

I danced around it some more, turning everything this way and that in my mind, the way I'd seen Pa do many a time when tackling something stiff. Finally I said, "Playing cards? Making sure you got some?"

"Now that's a sensible answer," Chilly allowed. "A professional man's got to pay attention to the tools of his trade, all right. That's a given, yes indeed. But they can't be his first concern. That'd be putting the cart before the horse. Hit it again."

I sweated whole buckets trying to think of what else there might be, but in the end all I had was a waterfall sound filling my ears. When I fessed up that I couldn't think of something else, Chilly shook his head no and said that wouldn't do. He declared that a gambling man always had to have himself one more answer. I might as well get used to it, he said. A gambler was needing that one more answer for all the tight spots he was bound to find himself in. So I gave it one more shot.

"Wits," I guessed. "He's for sure got to have those."

"You're getting close," Chilly encouraged. "You're headed in the right direction, anyhow, 'cause it's surely true that a gambler's got to have himself more wits than everybody else. He lives by 'em. They're his capital, all right. But it's how he applies those wits that matters. Now listen close, Zeb, 'cause I've taken a liking to you, boy. It's not just anyone I'd be telling this to."

Here he put a hand on my shoulder and stared me in the eye so long that I felt like a looking glass.

"The first thing you've got to mind is who you're gambling

with. You've got to pick your prospects right or you'll come up dry. Or worse."

"You talking about tar and feathering?" I'd heard stories.

"Some. But being railroaded out of a town ain't nothing to be sleepless about. There's always signs, and I'll be teaching 'em to you."

So that's how we passed our trip to St. Louis—Chilly talking, me listening while curled up as far away from the railing as I was worth, 'cause there was a powerful lot of muddy, deep water moving along beneath us.

The *Rose Melinda* shot down the middle of the river, where the current was swiftest. We passed wood yards like my pa's and gristmills and blossoming apple orchards and sprouting tobacco fields—whistling along like a teakettle all the while. Chilly claimed we must have been ripping off a good ten miles an hour when we weren't stopping to pick up letters and passengers and livestock. Anyone strong enough to wave a white hankie from the shore got stopped for.

Night finally eased down over the trees; the river sank into darkness, which made the waters seem all the deeper. Every once in a while you could see a farmhouse lantern twinkling brave as Joshua at Jericho, but mostly what you had was black. Two or three lights meant a village, which was rare. The only lights with us regular belonged to the *Rose Melinda* herself, and they shone on the water like windows to another world, one you could reach only by diving to the bottom of the river and opening a door. Believe you me, I didn't have no plans of going down there.

After a while a half-moon broke through the tree line, turning everything the prettiest ivory. Not that I had the strength to appreciate it any. Right about then Chilly started up with ghost stories concerning floating barrels that were haunted, and hangman trees that dropped all their leaves in July, and sunken steamers whose lights had lured many a pilot to his doom. At least such stories helped keep my mind off all my brothers and sisters, curled up so cozy in the loft back home. But eventually Chilly got tired of talking, which left me alone with the ghosts and the river and thoughts of my family. Finding himself some floor space that wasn't alive with tobacco juice, Chilly rustled up some sleep. But I stayed wide awake the whole night through, taking in the wonder of it all. Not even a feather bed could have put me out.

We were still sailing along under moonlight when we met up with the Missouri River. I couldn't spy its muddy waters, but Chilly woke up enough to claim he could smell 'em, and before long he had me believing my nose was full of stampeding buffalo, blowing grasses, smoky Injuns, and whatever else the Missouri rubbed up against way out west. The adventures sunk in all them smells made me feel pretty bouncy about my decision to bail out of being a tanner.

Not long after that, dawn snuck up on us, making everything fresh and lovely.

Then we rounded the last bend, and . . . well, all of a sudden I couldn't swallow, or spit, or nothing. Stretching out before us was St. Louis, and for a bit I forgot I ever knew how to talk. The town didn't seem to have no beginning or end, just stretched on and on. I'd never seen such a sight before and don't imagine I ever will again—not for the first time, I won't. The place was a hundred times bigger and grander than anything I'd ever come across. Wait, better make that a *thousand* times bigger and grander. You couldn't compare log walls and dirt floors to something like this. I reckon that ancient Rome couldn't have been any more breathtaking to them ancient Romans.

CHAPTER EIGHT

As the *Rose Melinda* chugged along the levee, hunting for an open spot, we cruised past mounds of molasses barrels and ox yokes and rope coils and bales of fur pelts and hogsheads of tobacco and small pyramids made from pigs of lead. Behind all that rose warehouses and church spires and factory chimneys climbing three or four stories high, at least. My eyeballs couldn't jump fast enough to take in everything. Mixed in with all the sights were the tinkling of ships' bells and whistles and the ripeness of horses and mules and oxen that were pulling drays and buckboards and carts all piled high with goods bound for log cabins and soddies in places that hadn't even been named yet, at least not in any language I could get my tongue around. Considering all that left me feeling small as a wheat berry.

When the *Rose Melinda*'s pilot finally found an open berth,

he plugged her quick. With upward of fifty steamers jockey-
ing for position, space was at a premium. And then, just as we
came to a rest, I saw the most amazing sight yet. Right down
the middle of the levee rolled a blue and red wagon that had
torches burning on either side of its front seat. Broad daylight, torches burning! Maybe they helped ward off the smells
floating around that levee. On the near side of the wagon was
a painting of a princess holding a sunburst in her hands. The
painting, it wasn't any slouch and had bold letters running
beneath it that read off this way:

Dr. Buffalo Hilly's Fantastic Indian Medicine Show
AS SEEN BY THE CROWNED HEADS OF EUROPE
ALL OF 'EM

It surely left me with a powerful urge to find out what the
other side of the wagon had to say.

But for right then, one side would have to do me, 'cause
Chilly wasn't in any hurry to get off the *Rose Melinda*. We
stood up on the boiler deck, waiting to see if the coast was
clear, or at least that's why Chilly said we were waiting. What
the coast needed to be clear of remained a mystery, though
Chilly did drag a dinky one-shot pistol out of a vest pocket
when a bird's shadow glided over us. I've a notion he would
have taken a potshot if it'd been a crow, but it turned out to
be one of those long, gangly storklike things that are always

wading around in the shallows. Whilst Chilly packed his shooter away, I shuffled a foot or two sideways, not wanting to get caught in the line of fire should any scavengers come flapping by. I wasn't exactly sure what he had against 'em. All I knew was that I was powerful glad not to be one of them.

Meantime, I kept myself busy watching Dr. Buffalo Hilly up on the painted wagon's seat. He had to be the one driving it. Who else would be dressed up like a cavalry captain? And with a purple plume sticking out of his hat too. He was playing some kind of musical box that I later heard called an accordion.

Did I mention he had a camel pulling that wagon?

I recognized it straight off from a picture in my ma's dictionary, and that dromedary wasn't the end of the amazements either. No sir, what brought up the rear didn't simmer things down one bit, for tagging along behind that painted wagon was an Indian princess. Had to be. She was leading a white-faced pony that was carrying a full-grown Indian chief whose war bonnet was long enough to drag feathers across the ground.

The medicine wagon creaked on past, gathering up the lame and achy and pockmarked as it went, but the Indian princess stopped directly in front of the *Rose Melinda*. Leaving the pony, she worked her way down to the shoreline in front of me. She couldn't have been much beyond fifteen feet distant and had the brownest, swimmingest eyes I'd ever run across. They beat horse eyes and cow eyes all flat. In fact, most every other pair of eyes I've seen before or since weren't nothing but washable buttons compared to 'em.

And then she blinked!

I flinched.

That made her smile a flicker, if that long, before turning and warbling something in Indian lingo to the chief.

Up to then the chief had been staring straight ahead, but now he turned toward the *Rose Melinda* and gazed at me. You could tell in a flash he was blind, as both his eyes were snowier than a blizzard, not that it mattered. I sure enough felt as though he was seeing parts of me never before seen under the sun, parts I didn't even know I had.

After a bit, he raised his right hand, kind of stern-like, to show me his palm. I'd heard that's how Indian folks say hello, so I raised my hand back.

The instant I done it, the chief smiled possum-wide and dropped his arm! Now how'd he know to do that? The princess sure had never said a word to tip him off. What's wilder, my hand flopped down in the same breath, without any marching orders from me. Why, I didn't feel much different from some puppet on a string, which spooked me considerable. To get a good deep breath in me, I had to step back from the railing.

"Looks like old Chief Standing Tenbears has cards on his mind," Chilly said, satisfied-like.

"Y-you know him?" I stuttered.

"More than I care to admit," Chilly mumbled.

"He lives here?" St. Louis appeared to have everything.

"So long as I still got his medicine bundle, he does. I don't imagine he can go home without it. That thing means more to him than life itself."

"How'd you get ahold of such a thing as that?"

"The chief likes to imagine himself a poker player. Matter of fact, he's got a solid gold crown you're going to help me win."

"I am?" I edged back to the railing for a peek, but the princess had already returned to the chief and moved on.

"Oh yes," Chilly predicted. "You and that telegraph I told you of."

We stood there quite some while longer as Chilly explained that a little ways back the chief had wagered the most valuable thing he owned against a sizable pot of cash. Chilly took the bet, assuming that the chief's prize possession was a gold crown he was supposed to tote around.

"Wasn't the case though," Chilly muttered. "When that scamp lost, he trotted out a moth-eaten old medicine bundle, claiming it was what he owed me. There was tears pouring down his cheeks—that's how shook up he was 'bout parting with it."

Seeing how much that ratty bundle meant to the old man,

Chilly had offered to take the chief's gold crown instead, but that wouldn't do. The princess declared that above everything else her father was a man of his word. He'd wagered his most valuable possession and that meant his medicine bundle, which was worth a half-dozen gold crowns so far as he was concerned.

"Couldn't budge him on it either," Chilly complained. "But it ain't no matter. I'm still going to get that gold crown or my name's not Charles Ambrosius Larpenteur—the Third."

Hearing his whole name roll off his tongue like quicksilver gave me goose flesh. I, for one, wouldn't have bet against him. The freight wagons and Conestogas rolling by on the levee didn't stop to call him on it either. Even a policeman strolling past bit his tongue, though he did seem to keep a wary eye on us.

Not till the policeman was good and gone did Chilly give the sky one last peek and decide that the coast looked about as clear as it was likely to get. We headed ashore, jumping aboard a coach that was leaving the corner of Locust and Second streets for the south part of St. Louis. That suited me about perfect, since my Uncle Seth's tanning yard lay to the north end of town.

For a few blocks the coach clacked over cobblestones, which took some getting used to after the muddy, rutted lanes back home. The storefronts along the way were mostly stone or brick and right smart looking. Off to one side I saw a hotel so fancy, it flew its own flags up top. Down another street rose up a domed courthouse, though I didn't know what a dome was till I asked. Chilly explained that to me as if I was some kind of chucklehead, which didn't rub me too wrong, not busy as I was taking in the sights. There were tobacco warehouses and stove works and a church with a spire so tall that its clapboards must have got their white from rubbing against the moon. I saw a game of ten pin and noticed that most everyone who could afford the luxury was puffing cigars. The smoke must have scared off some of the odors ranging around.

Any kind of critter capable of pulling something was on duty. I even saw a dog harnessed to a toy wagon full of coal chunks. The ragamuff guiding that dog was a lippy little thing, sticking his tongue out at me as we rolled by. The brat's ma caught him at it and right there in public took a broom to his bottom. He commenced to weeping and wailing, but I didn't feel too sorry for him. Unlike some of us, didn't he still have a ma standing beside him?

The boy's coal must have tumbled off one of the full-sized wagons hauling it up and down the street. And the drivers of those bigger outfits certainly had a la-di-da way of cracking their whips. Then too, there were gents and ladies riding in fancy rigs and riffraff just woke up from their beds of straw.

Most every block had one or more grog shops or beer houses or saloons or coffeehouses that appeared to sell drinks strong enough to rattle your teeth, if you had any.

Pretty soon the pavement piddled out and dirt took over. There were holes and ruts that must have seemed as deep as small canyons to the coach's horses, easy as they spooked. The streets narrowed up and went all crooked as everything got older, and storefronts gave way to houses that appeared thrown together out of wood and spit. Old ladies on caved front steps sang out, *"Bonjour."* Chilly told me that was French for "Mind your own business." I figured maybe he was funning me, friendly as those ladies seemed.

Finally the coach creaked to a halt and the driver called out, "End of the line," which meant we had to hoof it from there, with me lugging Chilly's carpetbag along with my poke and boots. There wasn't even any discussion about my being a pack mule. Chilly just dropped his bag on my toes and headed off without checking to see how I was keeping up. Not that I minded. Eager as I was to see where we were headed, I'd have tried to carry Chilly too, if he'd asked me. We kept moving away from the river till we nearly ran out of town, picking our way from one patch of shade to the next as if hiding from something, though surprising us would have been a task, what with the way Chilly kept a weather eye on everything, including the sky. The only man I ever saw watch the heavens any closer was my pa, who foretold rain, sleet, and hail regular as clockwork.

At last we pulled up to a rambling, old two-story house that was knocked out of dark timbers. There was a sign hanging over its front door that had a red, spouting whale painted on it. I wished I could have shown off that sign to my littlest brother, Lester, who was all the time wild about whales. Being but three, he couldn't hold chalk proper yet so was forever pestering me to copy the whale picture from Ma's dictionary for him. Thinking of that gave me a pang. Anyway, somebody had peppered the whale on that sign pretty lively with shot, but it kept right on swimming along, which I figured I better do too.

To one side of the house was a tipsy balcony where a man sat on a split-bottom chair playing something weepy and mournful on a violin. He didn't hold it like some country fiddler but had it tucked under his clean-shaven chin. Dignified as he sat there, you didn't hardly notice the pair of Shanghai chickens pecking around his boots. More what caught your eye was the way he pursed his lips, as if tasting the music, and how what few wisps of hair he had left fell across his smudged eyeglasses whenever he leaned forward to tease out a high note.

"That fool's the Professor," Chilly informed me. "Don't get any notions about those hens of his. They follow him everywhere, worse than family."

Without any further to-do, Chilly pushed on up the front steps and into the house, which had itself quite a stock of glass in its windows and real fetching calico stretched over the panes that had gone missing. There were several dogs howling out back who seemed to be objecting to the piano playing going on inside the place. I couldn't see how the Professor's violin would have set 'em off, but that piano playing was another breed of music entirely. Whoever was pounding on those keys knew no mercy.

"This here's Goose Nedeau's place," Chilly said, "or at least half of it is. The other half come into my hands a while back over a matter of some deuces. It's where we'll be holing up. There's only but two things you got to remember if you're going to get along with Goose."

"What's those, sir?" I had to speak up loud to be heard above the dogs and piano and violin.

"Don't talk harsh of his piano playing and keep your hands off that whale sign. It was handed down from Goose's father, all the way from the isle of Nantucket."

I vowed I'd do my best.

CHAPTER NINE

THE NEXT FEW DAYS FLASHED BY quicker than a jenny wren. Chilly and me shared a room on the second floor of the house, which turned out was really an inn. He got the bed, leaving me any spot I wanted on the floor. I didn't get so much as a corn-shuck tick to curl up on, just an old patched-up throw like the one the hounds bedded down on back home. At night, when I rolled up in that ripped old blanket, the back of my ears went all lonesome on me, 'cause of course that's where Pa used to scratch his dogs if they nuzzled his leg.

One corner of the room had a wardrobe, where Chilly piled all his truck, including everything from vests with hand-painted tigers on 'em to an alligator hide. Winnings, he called 'em. Over in another corner stood a wood stump with a fancy silver box resting atop it. When late afternoon sun hit that hammered silver, it hurt just to glance that way. And that was only the beginning of what I could tell you about that little treasure chest. It was where he stashed good-luck pieces won off other gamblers. That thing was jam-packed with the most unlikely collection of stuff imaginable: a blue-jay feather, a brass ring, a tear-soaked letter. One misguided fella had contributed a walrus tusk, or at least that's what Chilly called it. He let me heft it in my hand while advising, "Let that be a lesson to you. There wasn't a thing under the sun going to help that fool fill an inside straight. Not while I was dealing."

I'd have to say that nothing pleased Chilly more than dropping some poor gambler's last hope inside that box and closing the lid.

The room also had a washbasin, and it fell to me to keep fresh water in it. Hanging above the basin was a gold-framed mirror that Chilly used for shaving. If you glanced in the mirror just right, from the side, you could see that atop the wardrobe sat a deerskin wrapped around something bulgy. That was the Indian chief's medicine bundle, I guessed. I kept at least as far away from it as I did from the gator hide.

The window in the room had several pieces of glass left in it, though there was one pane less after the second morning we pulled in. That day started out sunny, but I woke to a clap of thunder and a crash of glass. Chilly had spotted a crow at the window and taken aim. He sent me outside to hunt for a bird carcass and wasn't pleased when I couldn't find so much as a feather. 'Course, Chilly's shot turned out all the hounds that was tied up in back, but as I was to learn, it generally took considerable less than gunfire to roust those dogs. They harmonized with Goose's piano playing, barked at roosting passenger pigeons, and snarled up a storm at any raccoons crossing by upwind. Once they got going, sleep was all uphill.

The meals served down in the kitchen weren't regular, but they weren't skimpy either. The fellow doing the cooking was a largish, roundish slave, name of Ho-John, whose skin was dark as good, rich earth and who three times had been caught clinging to a log while trying to swim to Illinois, which didn't tolerate slavery. Goose made him wear chains around his feet 'cause of his swimming habits, and Ho-John made sure everyone could hear those chains jangle and clink with every step he took. He also had himself a real stubborn way of burning most everything on the edges and leaving it runny toward the middle. Even the porridge had singe marks. No amount of thundering could shake him of the habit either. He claimed he was a carpenter slave by trade—no cook—and that till he figured out some way to use a hammer and nails and saw to fix up meals, he reckoned we could expect more of the same to land on our plates. Since there weren't any ladies allowed at the inn, he did all the seamstressing too and could sew a tolerably straight line, though he didn't think any more kindly of that duty than any of his others.

I gave Ho-John a careful looking over but couldn't spot nothing out of the ordinary 'bout him, 'less you counted the lodestone he kept on a piece of rawhide around his neck. He claimed that stone always pointed north, which was the general direction of the Free States and his hopes. I'd known others with hopes, of course, but none what had a north, south, east, or west attached to 'em. Other than that lodestone, the only thing that Ho-John cared for at all was the hounds living out back. He considered those dogs family and pampered 'em worse than royalty.

There were six guest rooms at the inn, all upstairs. One room was Goose's, one belonged to the Professor, and one went to Chilly and me. The rest were on hand for any gambler too liquored up to make it home without falling flat. The first floor had a couple of gaming parlors out front, the kitchen to the rear. Large affairs, the parlors were. They had tables built from scratch by Ho-John, right handsome ones too, with plenty of split-bottom chairs around 'em. Lanterns hung everywhere, as nighttime was when all the gambling got done.

Paintings fancied up some of the walls, with President Washington being a favorite. Goose Nedeau liked to claim he was related to the old French families around town and so gave Lafayette equal billing. Napoleon and a couple of French kings named Louis got footage too. The guests were pretty rough on the paintings—sassed 'em regular. Their words were considerably shocking, but their tongues never did fall out, the way Ma had always claimed mine would if I'd dared speak thataway. It was just one revelation after another around that inn, and grown up as most of these discoveries made me feel, I wouldn't have had it any other way.

'Course, the reason all these paintings got talked to so much was the bar, which took up the side wall in the main parlor and served everything from bust-head whiskey to some special punch dipped from a kettle. The Professor, who presided over the bar, wore a mostly white apron and tied black garters around his sleeves. He had a slow, friendly way of pouring a drink that made everyone feel welcome. All the gamblers said so.

It didn't sit too good with Chilly, but me and the Professor and Ho-John fast became friends. The reason for that was the respectful way I kept my distance from the Professor's hens and the fact that I didn't complain none about Ho-John's cooking. I ran errands for one or the other of them whenever I had the time, but mostly I was kept hopping with my apprenticing. My days didn't have much room for being homesick, though such feelings did rear their heads at the darnedest times, say when passing the whale sign, or when listening to the hounds howl, or when a steamboat whistled away over on the river in the middle of the night when everything was lonesomest. But such bouts lasted only as long as it took me to remember who'd bundled me off to St. Louis in the first place.

Since Goose Nedeau was in league with Chilly, he now became my teacher too. He appeared to be thrown together out of gristle and ruin, a hard-luck gambler who made little honking squawks in his throat all the time, like some sick goose. Most days he spent a good deal of time complaining that he hadn't had a good solid breath since Andy Jackson first muddied up the White House twenty years back. He shaved regular and missed various patches of stubble regular too. Bad as his hands shook from swilling whiskey, he rolled a loose cigarette that dropped enough ash to set himself on fire once or twice a night. His prize paisley vest was pitted with burn holes, and smoke seemed to rise like early morning fog off his silver mane of hair. He said he'd been forced into innkeeping 'cause of his health, though he didn't seem to take much interest in his new profession. Mostly he sat around dredging up days of yore, when he claimed to have single-handedly captured Black Hawk and made the entire Mississippi River safe for settlers. He had a go at the piano regular too, though he was banned from playing music, as he called it, whenever a card game was in progress.

On the day after we pulled in, Chilly sat me down in the main parlor. It was early yet, which around there meant any time before noon, so there weren't any customers about. Goose was already slouched at the table Chilly steered me to. The Professor had tied on his apron and was wiping out glasses over behind the bar. His chickens—Aphrodite and Venus— were up on top of the bar, inspecting each glass when he was done cleaning it.

"How you liking your new digs?" Chilly asked me.

"It's awful grand," I answered.

There wasn't any early-to-bed, early-to-rise philosophies, and the burnt edges on the vittles hadn't started to churn my innards yet. What's more, being around a pair of birds named after the Greek and Roman gods of love seemed powerful civilized. And 'course I was looking forward to doing more for the orphans of St. Louis, and showing Pa and Ma by sending winnings home to 'em, and maybe even buying myself a first-class pocketknife.

"Are you sure he's small enough?" Goose piped up while casting his eyes in my general direction. At the moment he was studying the empty chair beside me.

"Measurements have been taken," Chilly boomed, speaking twice as loud as normal 'cause he'd been contradicted.

"How's his eyesight?" Goose asked, resorting to his nose to find me. He had himself eyeglasses but rarely trotted them out, claiming they were about as helpful as a pair of stove lids.

"Keen enough," Chilly reported. "Did you want to check his teeth?"

"He got any extras?" Goose asked, sounding ready to claim 'em. Those of his teeth that hadn't gone missing had a mossy shine to 'em.

"The main thing you need to know about Zeb," Chilly said, "is that we can trust him. He's been sworn into the Brotherhood."

"Which brotherhood's that?" Goose wanted to know, turning suspicious.

"Why, the Brotherhood of the Gambler," Chilly answered, considerably put out over having to explain something so secret. "What'd you have for breakfast, anyway?"

It might have seemed a queer question if but a half hour before I hadn't seen Goose tell the Professor to pour him a good stiff breakfast of his best medicine. The Professor's restorative smelled the same as a small bottle of rye whiskey my ma kept on hand for toothaches and other ailments too terrible to think on.

"Zeb," Chilly said, appearing tired of shouting at Goose, "come out to the kitchen. There's something I want you to try on for size."

So we trooped out to the kitchen with Goose bringing up

the rear 'cause he needed a couple of sit-down breathers on the way. Ho-John sat over by the stove, whittling a toy out of a block of wood and paying us no mind as we all squeezed into a pantry.

"Climb onto that middle shelf there." Chilly pointed. "Take a look through that hole in back."

I did it without no trouble, though I wasn't thrilled by its height, and if I'd bulged an inch or two bigger in any direction, it would have been a pinching tight fit. There was a crowd of crockery on the shelf above me, all full of pickles and relishes and such, while a troop of bottles and jars were spread across the shelf below me. The middle shelf had been cleared of everything but some grains of spilt salt, which was about as worrisome a sign as could be. Knowing how stern the Brotherhood felt about charms and portents and what have you, I waited till Chilly wasn't watching before sneaking a pinch of salt to throw over my left shoulder. I didn't skimp on crossing myself either. There wasn't any telling how long those grains had been laying there churning up bad luck, and I didn't plan on taking any chances.

"What do you see?" Chilly asked.

Rolling on my side, I squinted through a hole in the back wall.

"The main parlor," I said.

"All of it?"

"Well"—I pressed an eye against the hole and searched around some—"pretty close to all of it. But mostly I got a view of the big table in front of me."

"Perfect. And are you comfortable?"

"Tolerably." I skipped over mentioning the salt or the height or how cramped it was.

"If a pillow and blanket will square things, we'll get 'em for you. And anything else that'll make that shelf feel homey. You just name 'er and it's yours."

"Oka-ay," I drawled, puzzled-like. "But why would you want me to feel at home on a pantry shelf?"

"Oh that's not a pantry shelf," Chilly corrected.

"It's not?" I squirmed around to see if I might have missed something. But no matter how hard I scouted her over, it still stacked up as a plain old wooden shelf.

"No sir," Chilly boasted. "That there's our new telegraph office."

CHAPTER TEN

LINED UP AGAINST THE OTHER WONDERS of St. Louis, that new telegraph office was a considerable letdown. I put a brave face on my misgivings, not wanting Chilly to think me some ungrateful little carp, but my disappointment must have showed through, 'cause Chilly laid down the law.

"Now see here, Zeb, can't everyone go expecting to start at the top. That ain't the way things work in this here world."

"Expect not," I mumbled.

"Come along now," Chilly ordered.

And he jerked me off that shelf and marched me out of the kitchen, and back around to the parlor, where he stood me right before the wall shared with the pantry. As walls go, it weren't anything more special than some rough-cut old lumber that was pegged together. A long time back somebody had splashed Spanish brown wash over it. There were two pictures hanging on it, one of George Washington, all noble, the other of King Louis something or other, doing a bang-up job looking important too, though I wasn't in any mood for admiring them, not as sore as my arm felt after Chilly's roughhousing. If I'd been back home, my brother James would have been making crimpy baby faces at me, the way he did whenever I was about to cry. Just thinking of that made me want to blubber all the more, so I bit my lip and did my best not to snivel.

"Now where do you reckon you were looking through this wall?" With a sweep of his hand, Chilly invited me to check things over.

Well, the whereabouts of that peephole was a champion mystery. I couldn't find it anywhere, not in George Washington's or King Louis' eyes, nor any of the knotholes to be found here and there, which were all plugged solid.

"Check that lower corner there." Chilly pointed me toward the frame around President Washington.

Painted all gold and green and blue-purple, that frame was crawling with curlicues and carved vines and clustered grapes that looked more artful than the picture itself. After a minute or two of snooping, I found the hole I'd been peering through. The bottommost grape in a ripe-colored cluster had been punched clean out, not that you'd have ever noticed without putting your nose right up to it. The pantry on the other side was shadowy as Pa's smokehouse, so there wasn't any light leaking out.

"You see?" Chilly said. "Won't anyone know you're there at all."

If that's what Chilly thought was souring me, he was way past wrong. What had me so puckered up was that I'd just caught a whiff of something, maybe a rat.

"I'm kind of wondering," I said, picking my words with care, "what I'll be doing back there?"

"Why, helping rich men share their bounty," Chilly explained. "Here, let me show you something."

He set Goose Nedeau down in the chair nearest the portrait of President Washington. Pulling out a deck of playing cards, he fanned five of 'em out in Goose's hand. "Sit still," he ordered Goose before parading me back to the pantry and waving me onto the shelf again. When I put my eye to the hole, I found myself looking over Goose Nedeau's right shoulder. He was holding two nines, a king, a ten, and a six.

"That's the news you'll be spreading over the telegraph," Chilly said.

"Ain't there supposed to be a wire or something for me to work with?"

"Zeb says we need a wire," Chilly yelled out to Goose. I could tell by his uppity tone that he was poking fun at me. He knew full well that a telegraph needed wire.

"He's a sharp one, all right," Goose heckled.

"Even if I had a wire," I went on, "wouldn't somebody have to teach me how to talk over it with clicks and clacks? That's the way it's done, ain't it?"

"He says we got to learn him clicks and clacks too," Chilly shouted to Goose.

"Sounds like a job for the Professor," Goose yelled back.

"Best leave me out of it," the Professor warned from behind the bar.

Chilly jabbed my shoulder hard and asked in a mean voice, "Anything else bothering you?"

"No," I sulked, though I did have one mighty big question circling around in my head.

Try as I might, I couldn't quite figure why anyone on the other end of a long telegraph line would give a hoot about what cards Goose Nedeau was holding in his hand. Wouldn't they want to be hearing about something more important? Wouldn't floods or elections or steamboat races be on their minds? Wasn't that the kind of news fit for telegraphs? I couldn't get a hook on any answers to that question at all, though it turned out I didn't have to worry over it. Right about then, Chilly called out, "Ho-John, come in here. Got a job for you."

Clinking chains all the way, Ho-John shuffled into the pantry, took one look at me, and announced, "I don't think he'll cook up none too good."

"This ain't a cooking job," Chilly explained. "It's a carpentering job."

Ho-John straightened up some upon hearing that and said, "You tell old Ho-John what you're needing. Leave the rest to him."

"I want you to run a good stout wire up to this shelf that Zeb's on. I want you to run it down through the floor, under the house, and attach it to the bottom side of a floorboard in the main parlor."

It didn't amount to much of a telegraph line. The total length would have run maybe ten to fifteen foot worth, give or take.

"That mean you done found some new way to cheat the poor gents what come in here?" Ho-John wanted to know.

I recoiled some at the sound of that. Back in Stavely's Landing, hauling out a word like *cheat* often as not ended in fisticuffs.

"Well I like that!" Chilly cried, his cheeks taking on color fast. "Where do you think these gents get their money if not by cheating somebody else? Answer me that."

"I wouldn't be knowing 'bout that," Ho-John said. "Imagine each of 'em gots their ways."

"And if you add all those different ways up," Chilly came right back, "what do you think we'd have us?"

"I've done heard your preachering before, Mr. Chilly," Ho-John said. "There anything else you want fixed?"

Ho-John could have done a better job on sounding respectful, but he could have done worse too. Mostly, he sounded kind of lukewarm. But answering Chilly's questions with a question, that wasn't anywhere near a good idea. It got Chilly's back up even more.

"Only your manners," Chilly bristled.

"Are we going to be cheating then?" I asked kind of peaked-and worried-like in the silence that followed.

"*Cheating*'s a mighty harsh word," Chilly commented, still glaring at Ho-John. "It ain't one the Brotherhood much favors."

"What word does the Brotherhood go for?" I asked.

"*Shortening*'s the way we put it." Turning toward me, he simmered down enough to say, "Let me ask you this, Zeb. If one man's got a thousand dollars to make a thousand bets with, and another man's only got one dollar to make one bet with, who do you think's going to win?"

"Why, the man with the thousand."

"And does that seem fair?" Chilly asked.

"If you're going to put 'er that way . . . " I backed off.

"That's the only way to put it. 'Cause the fellows that come in here with their pockets bulging, in the long run they're going to win every time. Unless we do something to *shorten* 'em up some."

"Still sound like cheating to me," Ho-John said, "and the Sunday preachers say there ain't nothing going to make that right."

"Far as I can tell," Chilly reasoned, biting back some bile, "there ain't enough right to go around in this world, and a man in your shoes, Mr. Ho-John, ought to be the first to know it." To me, he added, "What you got to ask yourself, Zeb, is whether you want to lend a hand in spreading that right around. 'Cause what do you think the Brotherhood has me do with the money we earn from all this?"

"Help out orphans?" I guessed.

"That's exactly right," Chilly agreed, "along with other poor and needy. Old widows and one-legged Indian scouts and what have you. You remember why we share our winnings?"

"'Cause sharing is what makes a man great," I quoted, double relieved to have remembered that lesson.

"That's right, Zeb. It does. Now isn't that something you think worth doing? And before you answer that question," Chilly piled on, "you better answer this one: how do you think those rich folks got rich in the first place?"

He had me there.

When I said hard work, he pounced, asking if I'd ever seen any calluses on a rich man's hands.

Well, I'd never seen a rich man's hands, not close up, but I didn't imagine they had any slivers sticking out. So I asked if they couldn't have maybe inherited their riches. Chilly allowed I might have a point but said if inheriting was all there was to it, we'd still be ruled over by some king or other back in England. That seemed an even sprucier point.

When I guessed maybe they had found their riches, say in a gold mine or something, Chilly came right back with the news that whoever found a fortune still had to keep it, and how did I reckon they'd manage that, what with every chicken rustler and snake charmer between here and kingdom come after it.

By then I was pretty much played out for answers and finally just came out and told him so. Chilly filled me in on the right answer pronto.

"Zeb, my boy, nine times out of ten a rich gent got his fortune by cheating somebody else out of theirs. If they run a plantation, they got wealthy off the sweat of someone like Ho-John over there. If they own a store, they got it by charging everyone a nickel too much for whatever they're buying. So if you're bound and determined to think in terms of cheating, you better first give some thought as to who you'll be cheating. Hereabouts, you'll only be cheating the cheaters and taking their money and putting it in the hands of the less fortunate."

I hadn't ever thought of all that before, and I must say it was an approach that took some getting used to. I'd got caught cheating once back home, when I'd bribed my sister Becky into copying some definitions from Ma's dictionary for me. Such lessons was how Ma taught us penmanship, and she spotted the difference in our handwriting without a blink. Even now I don't care to dwell on what happened next, 'cause I spent an awful sorrowful string of afternoons writing out triple the number of definitions I'd started with. Ma had been a schoolmarm before hooking up with Pa, and not one you ever wanted to cross.

"What about that one rich man out of ten who earned his fortune without cheating?" I come back with, kind of weak.

"You don't have to worry any about him," Chilly promised. "He ain't never going to be showing up around here trying to double his fortune. He's going to be plenty satisfied with what he's got and won't begrudge us what we're getting."

Answers such as Chilly's deserved to put my mind to rest, and maybe they would have, if Ho-John hadn't been clucking his tongue real soft—the same exact way my pa was known to—and shaking his head as though Chilly's calculations beat all. When Chilly slapped a dime in my hand and told me to run down to First Street to get some telegraph wire, I jumped at the chance, more than happy to get shut of all the bothersome, naggy questions swarming around me.

"Just don't let any crows follow you back," Chilly warned out of the blue, right before pushing me outside.

"Do they do that?" I stalled in the doorway.

"They've been known to, on occasion, and I won't tolerate 'em around. Hear? No scavengers. The Brotherhood won't allow it. Either you pull your own weight or you're out. That's the rule."

Prickly as he sounded about it, I promised that I'd heard him just fine, though I was wishing hard that I hadn't. On top of everything else, now I had to worry about being followed by crows, who didn't fool around when it came to having beaks and claws.

CHAPTER ELEVEN

I SLUNK DOWN TO FIRST STREET to hunt up a general store that carried wire, but what should have been high adventure ended up with considerable droops. For one thing, I couldn't let loose of the way that Chilly's explanation had made Ho-John wag his head no till he looked weary as Moses telling everyone one more time where he'd found those commandments. On top of that, I was supposed to be keeping an eye out for crows? And before long it occurred to me that I might even bump into my Great-Uncle Seth, though neither of us had the foggiest what the other looked like. Still and all, I steered clear of anyone with the slightest hint of a tanner about him, say a buckskin vest or coonskin cap or moccasins 'stead of boots.

The first store I stepped into wanted a nickel for twenty foot of wire. The second store asked for a dime. Same for the third, so I headed back to number one. The starchy clerk behind the high counter there might have bumped up to a dime too, if he'd known how much Chilly'd given me, but at least I knew better than to go flashing money around before it was time to pay. Back home I would have heard plenty about shelling out such a sum for wire, and I headed toward Goose Nedeau's in spirits low as a swamp full of sorrowing frogs. But pretty soon I heard something that nailed my boots square to the road.

"Ladies and gentlemen," a voice palavered, squawky as a jay, "friends and neighbors, countrymen and visiting nobility, cardsharps and low-down polecats, I'm here to tell you how to save you and your loved ones, if you tolerate any, from pains too demoralizing to mention. There's vapors and symptoms loose on the land. Don't make the mistake of thinking it's clear sailing just 'cause you and yours breezed through this past winter with nothing but the sniffles. You're not in the sunshine yet. There's ill winds blowing from far gone away. Mountain fever, rheumatic pains, the poxes—they're all but small potatoes if lined up with the troubles headed our way."

Yes sir, it was Dr. Buffalo Hilly, all right, breathing hope and fear into a crowd of gawkers and especially into me. Why, I'd never before got around to considering half the hazards he was hanging out to dry. All of a sudden slivers and pecking hens paled. Buffalo Hilly's admonitions pushed 'em right out of my head.

Still in his calvary suit, he'd climbed up top his wagon and was giving his accordion a solid pump every now and then to liven up his spiel. About the only one unimpressed by what he was spewing was the camel hitched up front. Everyone else was looking at one another out of the corners of their eyes, wondering if anyone had heard of some new calamity brewing nearby. I know I was. Here and there wise heads were nodding yes, that they'd been expecting just such troubles any day now, which left me feeling in powerfully good company. And all the while everyone was creeping forward so they wouldn't miss a lick of what Buffalo Hilly had to say. Naturally, I was inching ahead right along with 'em, keeping an eye out for the Indian chief and princess as I went.

"I've found the one treatment that casts out everything from consumption to tapeworms, female distresses to catarrh," Dr. Buffalo Hilly proclaimed. "It's a brain tonic of the first degree! Disordered stomachs, beware! We're talking herbs of joy! You can call me a yarb and root doctor if you've a mind to. All I can say is that this elixir works wonders and I'm the living proof."

To get his point across, he threw back his head and clear out of the blue crowed like a rooster. "Cock-a-doodle-doo!"

I couldn't help but laugh with everyone else.

Right on cue a cross-eyed man in a mud-splattered, ragged shirt lunged forward, shoving money at Buffalo Hilly, though where he'd come up with the price of the elixir was an open question and drew some snickers from the crowd. Still, the doctor treated him as if he was the genuine article—a sick man in need of healing. Flinging back his cape, Buffalo Hilly climbed down off his wagon to oblige his tipsy customer as if they were old friends, which somebody in the crowd accused them of being.

"Friends in good health," Buffalo Hilly shot right back, taking such ragging right in stride, which primed the pump good. People surged forward.

You might have thought he was the captain of a sinking ship stepping into the last lifeboat, the dignified, high-minded way he came down off that wagon. Along with a couple of real friendly assistants, he started passing out tonic bottles and reeling in dollars fast as his hands could jig. And all the while he done it, people couldn't resist reaching out to touch him, to reassure themselves he wasn't river mist, I guess. He let 'em do it too. He patted and hugged 'em for free, just 'cause they needed it, and told 'em, "There, there, everything's going to be all right now."

That elixir of his sold for a dollar and ten cents a bottle, with refills promised at half price. What with all the dangers roaming this world, it sounded pure bargain.

"What about boils?" a doubter called out.

"Wallops 'em without mercy!" answered Dr. Buffalo Hilly.

"Pinworms?"

"Mortifies 'em with a slug."

"What if you're healthy?"

"Makes you healthier."

By then I'd crept close enough to add my own question. "How about cheaters? What would it do for them?"

"Son," Dr. Buffalo Hilly said, sweeping off his plumed hat and covering his heart with it, "I'm sorry to report it can cure most everything but dishonesty. Why, it's even been known to work on Mormons."

That earned a round of catcalls, seeing how unpopular Mormons had lately become in the state of Missouri, but even if that elixir could have cured the pope of being Catholic, as my pa was known to say of something first-rate, I didn't have a dollar ten to spare. All I had me was a nickel left over from buying Chilly's telegraph wire, and Dr. Buffalo Hilly didn't look the breed to hand out discounts, no matter how desperate the need, not with bottles fairly flying out of his mitts at full price. So I hung around, mostly fretting about poxes and fevers and every once in a while remembering to check up above for crows.

After Buffalo Hilly and his assistants had wrung out every sale they could manage from the crowd, the doctor spread his arms wide and started yapping again. "Some of you've got ailments and infirmities that can't be cured by anything that comes in a bottle. I know that and so do you. A bottle can only hold so much. But don't think I've forsaken you, 'cause now comes the time to introduce you to the most amazing oracle this side of ancient Thebes. I'm talking 'bout a man who can look so deep into your very soul, it'll make your heart flutter. He can separate the wheat from the chaff and advise you with the mystical, otherworldly seeing powers of his people. I've seen him listening to owls and conversing with catfish. I'm talking about none other than the noblest of savages, Chief Standing Tenbears, who's visiting your fair city for a short spell only."

Right then that Indian princess, the one with the swim-mingest eyes, came leading Chief Standing Tenbears around the medicine wagon. Good thing she hadn't picked me out of the crowd yet, 'cause I was blushing like a spring rose just to see her. Don't ask me why. What with all my sisters, girls weren't anything new, but this one sure was different. Maybe it was the way she carried herself so proud-like, without look-ing to either side. Or it could have been the way her hair was black and shiny as the river at night. And then there was

them eyes of hers, which didn't seem to have no beginning nor end.

The chief rode with his arms crossed over his chest. His war bonnet was still dragging its bottom feathers in the dust, and this time I was close enough to notice a few other details of his outfit. His leggings had fancy bead and quill work up and down the sides. His moccasins had more of the same on the top. A staghorn knife was tucked under a red sash wound around his waist, and a fur bag, bulging with tobacco, was riding on his hip. He dressed up real handsome, but all the regalia paled before the power of his eyes, which were whiter than cream and quivered as though searching everywhere and nowhere at once.

The sights he'd seen with those eyes had turned the rest of his face to stone. There wasn't any more expression to his mug than to a clock, and the similarities to a tick-tocker didn't stop there either. Something about looking at the chief's blank face set you to thinking of vast stretches of time. As many years as was packed in the Bible seemed buried beneath his cheeks. Nobody standing in that crowd doubted that old chief had himself some powers, especially when a crow swooped down out of nowhere and landed right on his shoulder! Everybody gasped and ducked, but the chief stayed still as a tree limb.

That crow looked us over pretty good and croaked some too. Everybody had the idea it was talking to them. I know that's what it felt like to me, and I could see others stepping out of sight behind the handiest tall person. I began to understand why a gambler as pernickety as Chilly might object to having such a pert bird around. There wasn't any telling what such a creature might do.

'Course, all the while everybody was eyeballing the crow, Dr. Buffalo Hilly never shut up. Not once. If that man hadn't been born talking, he must have taken to it soon thereafter. He carried on about the powerful medicine the chief had inherited from his tribe and how he was willing to part with some of it at the bargain-counter price of two dollars a consultation. (Naturally the doctor took a lot more words to say it than that.) He went at it so long that the crow decided he had business elsewhere and took his leave.

"In case you're thinking two dollars is a steep price to fork over, let me tell you about the missing child who got returned to the bosom of her family thanks to the chief's visions," Buffalo Hilly said. "Happened just last week, off west a ways."

And he was off and running, talking up what a precious young thing that missing child was, taking after her loving mother in every possible way. I caught every word of it as I watched the crow flapping across the river.

"One morning, shortly after chores," Buffalo Hilly was saying, "that sweet young thing went missing. She wouldn't come for calling or nothing. Days went by and her folks had about given up hope when they heard of the chief's powers and come to see him. To make a long story short, which all of you know how much I hate doing, the chief sent them poking around a mossy old cabin deep in the woods. And there the child was, being tended by an old granny who'd lost her senses and mistaken the child for her own."

Don't think that news didn't turn some heads.

And according to Buffalo Hilly that was just the beginning of the chief's powers. Broken hearts, misplaced heirlooms, lost relatives, next season's weather, general all-purpose sage advice, horns of a dilemma, buried treasure, unexplained griefs—the chief was willing to take a crack at all of them and more for as long as he was in St. Louis, which wasn't going to be forever, only until he'd wrapped up some personal business. How much time that would take, Buffalo Hilly couldn't say. A day or two, maybe longer if they were lucky, but nothing was guaranteed, not in this life. Pretty soon the chief would be pushing on, headed out West for his own people with a message from the king of France, which was where he'd just come from.

"What I'm trying to tell you," Buffalo Hilly pledged, "is that this golden opportunity won't last forever. I don't think I can say it any plainer."

People were getting ready to be convinced. You could see it in the way they was whispering to one another and tilting their heads this way and that for a better look-see of the chief. A glint of wonder swirled in their eyes, as if they wanted nothing more than to believe the chief could predict where to dig for gold. I caught some of their excitement and found myself leaning forward. But still the crowd hung back. Seeing that we needed one last little nudge, Dr. Buffalo Hilly took a gamble.

"To show you what can be done," he called out, "we'll take a volunteer from the audience. Free of charge. Then you be the judge if the chief's powers don't confound and amaze."

That brought one fellow to life, but when he stepped forward, everyone could see it was the same cross-eyed plant who'd earlier bought the first bottle of tonic. Having him pop up again set off enough jeers for Buffalo Hilly to wave the man away with a secret little shake of his head. There things stalled, as nobody else was brave enough to step forward. Otherworldly as the chief sounded, everybody shrank back the tiniest bit, which left me standing closest to the chief and princess 'cause I'd weaseled my way up front during all the fast talking. When I saw that nobody was going to do 'er, I seen my chance and grabbed it.

"I got me a question," I said.

CHAPTER TWELVE

Dr. Buffalo Hilly pretended he couldn't see who'd spoke up, though I was standing right before him. The Indian princess ignored me likewise. The two of them peered all up and down the crowd, skimming over the top of my head every time. Standing on tiptoe didn't buy me anything. Same for clearing my throat. Little as that made me feel, I could barely manage to raise my hand above my ear to get their attention, but in the end they couldn't ignore me forever, not with everyone else shying away. When the doctor finally got a bead on me, he acted surprised. "You're not still fussing over cheating, are you, son? That kind of question might not be worth troubling the chief about."

But right then the chief spit out something in Indian, and the princess, who'd been keeping him current on everything that was happening, now translated for us. "He's the one my father wants to talk to."

"I stand corrected." Buffalo Hilly made a lordly bow that the crowd ate up. "What's on your mind, son?"

"Can he tell me," I asked, feeling my way, "is it all right to cheat?"

"First off," Buffalo Hilly protested, "you wanted to know if I could cure cheating, and now you're asking if it's all right to cheat?"

"That's about the size of it, sir."

"Figure if you can't lick 'em, join 'em?" he guessed, playing to the crowd.

"Something like that."

"Why, I'm ashamed of you, son. Any fool can tell you it ain't seemly to cheat. We don't need to be bothering the chief with nonsense so simple as that, do we?"

"It don't stack up so simple to me."

"I'm thinking we can all see that," the doctor agreed, earning a hearty chuckle from most everyone. "Maybe what you need is some of my tonic after all. It's been known to smarten men up quicker than universities."

"Guess I ain't asking it right," I sort of mumbled.

"Speak up," Buffalo Hilly urged. "So we can all hear and profit from your miseries."

"Maybe I should ask the chief *this*," I rallied, feeling inspired. "Is it all right to cheat a rich cheater? Maybe that's what I'm driving at."

"Now you're only fixing on cheating someone with money?" Buffalo Hilly shook his head kind of groggy-like, as if he was trying his darnedest to keep my questions straight.

I told him that was the case.

"It still don't seem like much to bother the chief with," Buffalo Hilly cautioned, joshing me along and drawing the crowd closer at the same time.

"Seems like plenty to me," I said. "I've got some big decisions to be making. Decisions that could change my whole life."

Soon as I said that, I saw it was true as an oak tree. I'd reached a kind of crossroads, and a rutted, muddy one at that. All this talk about cheating had got me wondering if maybe I didn't still have time to hunt up my Great-Uncle Seth. Even big as St. Louis was, there couldn't be that many tanning yards around its north side. If I was honest with him and handed over whatever money Chilly would refund me, maybe he'd still take me on. If he needed more convincing, I could grovel up a storm and promise to work an extra year's worth of apprenticing for free. That ought to show him I meant business.

If being a tanner was the way I wanted to go . . .

But wouldn't you know, I still wasn't won over to it. Even

after seeing how small my telegraph office was and hearing about the cheating, I couldn't quite let go of the idea of being a gambler and living by my wits and being so dashing whilst I rained good deeds down on the needy and shipped gold bullion back home. I clung to the simple-minded hope that I could somehow or other become a riverboat gambler without drowning or becoming a rapscallion along the way.

"Well-l-l . . . " Dr. Buffalo Hilly dragged the word out while casting one last glance over the crowd in hopes of bigger fish. "All right, let's see what you got. Guess there ain't no law saying the young can't have terrible afflictions too." Then, gruff-like, he added, "Stand in front of the chief, boy, where he can see you proper."

"Thought he was blind," some joker called out.

"To the natural world he is," Dr. Buffalo Hilly answered without missing a beat. "But the natural world ain't where he does his seeing."

With that, the doctor lined me up before the chief's pony and none too gently either. Above and beyond the pony floated the chief's milky whites, and if that wasn't enough, off to the side the princess was watching me with them perfectly brown peepers of hers. With all those eyes peering into me, there wasn't anywhere to hide. I could feel emotions and stray thoughts and such swirling around inside me faster than I could name 'em.

"Speak up," Dr. Buffalo Hilly said, giving me a rough nudge.

"Is it okay to cheat a cheater?" I asked. "One who's rich."

After the princess switched that into Indian for the chief, me and him faced each other for a couple of years' worth without a stir, reminding me of how long Pa used to say grace over Sunday victuals. It went on so long that latecomers kept asking what was happening. People up front whispered back that there didn't seem to be much of anything going on, while those in the middle were shhhing the others for all they were worth. Finally even Dr. Buffalo Hilly got impatient and raised his voice to say, "Wants to know if he can sleep nights after cheating a cheater."

Once the princess had shared the doctor's words with her father, the chief answered something back that the princess translated. "This boy needs a lot of looking."

Another couple of years hung fire, solemn as a courthouse.

Finally the chief seemed content that he'd looked over everything there was to see inside me, and he lifted his eyes away and cocked his head a touch, as if listening to a voice from clear across the river. He even cupped a hand around an ear to help hear. But I couldn't catch nothing, even though Ma and Pa always claimed my ears were too keen for my own good.

Satisfied at last, the chief lowered his hand and proceeded

to rattle off a flood of Indian talk. The princess took it all in, asked a question or two, and got another long answer from the chief. When convinced she'd got all her father's meaning, she turned to me and said, "That's not your real question, is it?"

"I sure thought it was," I answered, blinking fast.

The princess relayed that to the chief, who snorted, then asked her something back. Leaning toward me so that no one else could hear, she whispered briefly. Her voice swished around and around in my ear, tickling like moonbeams. But slowly, one by one, her words drained into my head, and I realized she was quizzing me hopeful-like, saying, "Did Birdman send you?"

"Sorry," I whispered back, and I was. "Don't know any Birdman."

"So what *did* you come for?"

"To, ah, find out about cheaters?" I answered lamely.

That made her puff out her cheeks as if I was a lost cause. By then the crowd behind us was growing restless about our huddle, so the princess quieted them by raising her voice to ask, "You're far from your folks?"

"I reckon so," I admitted, still racking my brains over this Birdman, though nothing come of it. With such a name as that, I figured him for an Indian, but I hadn't met up with any other Injuns, except on the *Rose Melinda*, and I hadn't talked to a one of them.

"Missing them?" the princess asked, still talking about my folks.

"Guess so," I said, my voice getting squeaky without my permission, especially with the chief gazing over the crowd and kind of upriver, in the general direction of my home. After a bit, he spoke some more.

"Don't worry about your family," the princess translated, all serious. "They're fine. But they worry about one thing."

"What's that?"

"Are you getting enough to eat?"

That sounded so much like Ma that I couldn't speak for a bit.

"Especially hot, buttered biscuits," the princess added.

I found me enough voice to answer like a week-old kitten. "That's my favorite."

Those words came out so low and soft that most everyone in the crowd was buzzing, "What'd he say?"

Regaining my footing, I said loud enough for all to hear, "I ain't losing any weight."

"Good," the princess said. "The chief will tell your ma."

And somehow or other I trusted he would find a way to do it too. He hadn't done anything but name what could have been said 'bout anyone freshly cut loose from home, but I gobbled it all up, especially when he stared upstream a bit more and again cupped a hand around his ear as if catching some far, distant message. I guess it's fair to say that I wanted what he said to be true.

When he spoke again, the princess relayed, "He also wants to know if your mother will sell her picture of the two-humped horse."

"Beg pardon?"

"He'd like to buy it. To show his father."

Huh? At least this answered what a blind man wanted with a picture, though it was a stretch to believe the chief's father was still among the living. Rather than ask about that, I said, "She don't have a picture of a two-humped horse, not so far as I know."

"He's seen her looking at it," she insisted.

"Okay," I answered, figuring it might be best to jolly them along. "If she's got one, I'd guess she might part with it."

When the princess relayed that, the chief looked real pleased.

"As for your father," the princess said, moving right along, "he thinks you're worth every dollar he gave you and's prouder of you than his mule."

I almost asked if Pa had come down with a fever, 'cause that mule of his had won every pulling contest he'd ever been in. Pa had been offered good money for that critter and had people show up from clear over in Illinois just to take a look at him. But in the end, I couldn't get a word past my lips on account of a new suspicion that overtook me. Pa hadn't acted so bright and sunny when he'd had to sell off half his livestock on account of my apprenticeship. Why so cheery now? The only answer I could dredge was that he was happy to be rid of me. That'd explain his change of heart, all right. What spared me from hitting myself over the head about it? A new notion that reared up and bit me on the toe, right through my boot. How could the chief have known about Pa's prize mule? Or the money my folks had given me? They both could have been lucky guesses, I supposed, but what if he really did have visions? That was a possibility filling every head around me. A gent in back called out cautious-like, "Your pa got a mule?"

"Sure enough," I said.

"That he's proud of?"

"Busts his buttons," I answered, which started everyone to buzzing so loud that Buffalo Hilly had to whistle for quiet, which gave me a chance to ask the chief, "Should I give up on this new trade I picked?"

"Not yet," the princess answered after conferring with her father.

Such an answer as that landed me on an awful muddy bank. I'd been hoping for a *yes* or *no*. Those were answers with some teeth. But *not yet*? What use was that? There wasn't time to ask for more details either, not the way Buffalo Hilly was turning me around by the shoulders and pushing me out of the way to make room for paying customers, who were shoving closer now that the chief had gone on about Pa and Ma.

But how was I supposed to know when *yet* would arrive? Could be tomorrow, could be forty years up ahead. I had a bothersome hunch this was turning into one of those questions that I was supposed to answer for myself. I hated those worse than slivers, deep water, heights, and blazing camp-fires all combined.

CHAPTER THIRTEEN

By the time I wriggled free of the crowd, they were peppering Chief Standing Tenbears with mysteries enough to knot up a dozen sphinxes, and all the while I was slinking off, Dr. Buffalo Hilly was promising people there wasn't any need to push or shove. The chief had vision enough to go around. After what I'd heard, I didn't doubt it either, which made me wish he'd at least gotten around to sharing his thoughts on cheating a cheater.

But I didn't have time to dilly-dally, not with Chilly waiting on me, and pointed my nose toward Goose Nedeau's place, except that it didn't seem a day for going anywhere in a straight line. I hadn't trotted but two or three blocks before spying someone else I had run across before. It come close to striking me dumb to think that I knew anyone in a place so overgrown as St. Louis, but right across the street—lovely and fresh as ever—stood the lady from the *Rose Melinda,* the one who'd collected money for orphans. I mightn't have noticed her, busy as I was dodging wagons and mules and jug-bitten loafers, but she was singing the same song as before, "The Last Rose of Summer." She still sounded every bit the nightingale too. I wasn't the only one who had pulled up helpless at the sound of her voice, though I was the only one near run over by a wagonload of bricks. Dusting myself off, I headed across the street as if lassoed. Soon as she was done warbling, I asked how the orphans were doing without even introducing myself.

"Ever so well," she said, smiling down on me warmer than spring sunshine.

Being looked at so gracious and kind wiped away all my worries in a flash. And to think that I wouldn't have been beamed down on at all if I hadn't hooked up with Chilly. It put a whole new shine on gambling and cheating the cheaters, just the way Chilly said it ought to. Didn't I feel small and wormy for daring to question all the good that Chilly and the Brotherhood were doing for those less fortunate than themselves? Why, quitting my new trade just *yet* was out of the question. To make amends for even thinking such a thing, I up and asked, "Are you still collecting for 'em, ma'am?"

"Alas, I am," she sighed. "Poor things are in greater need than ever. This cold, cruel world knows no bounds."

I didn't need any more convincing than that. Now that I'd been forced to fend for myself, I was more than primed to help those orphans any way I could. Digging into my pocket, I come up with the nickel left over from buying telegraph wire. When I held it out for her to take, she didn't reach for it a bit. Not that lady. She was too genteel and refined to do such a thing as that. No, she turned to the side and lifted the top of the basket she was carrying. Inside sat a china bowl with several coins already in it.

"St. Jerome blesses you," she said as I dropped the coin into the bowl.

I stood there speechless, gazing up into her eyes like some kind of thick-skulled ape. She must have been used to spreading stupefaction wherever she went, 'cause she took my admiration serious as could be. Bending over, she planted a little peck on my cheek to prove it. I felt like never, ever dabbing water on that cheek again but making a kind of shrine out of it. Those poor orphans couldn't hardly have been better cared for if the clouds had parted and two hands the size of Goliath's, or bigger, reached down from the heavens to tuck 'em in every night. A toasty feeling warmed me up just thinking of it.

"Your ma and pa must be awfully proud of you," she said before leaving.

I'd have given anything to believe those words as I watched that orphanage lady chat up gents all the way to the end of the block. I was just about to drift after her, to bask in her glow a little longer, when something latched onto the top of my ear. Looking up, I found Chilly glaring down.

CHAPTER FOURTEEN

My pa had never grabbed hold of me thisaway, and when I
tried squirming free, Chilly only twisted my ear all the harder.
I flopped around like a snagged fish till he pinched the meaty
part of my shoulder, locking me up on the spot. He knew right
where to squeeze to stop my thrashing.

"Didn't I send you after wire a good two hours back?" he
asked, and none too friendly about it either.

"Could have been longer," I fessed up, standing on tiptoe
to ease the ripping on my ear.

Such honesty seemed to throw him off track, though not
for long.

"So what have you been doing all that while?" he thun-
dered. Spittle flew off his lips, which were raging sort of pur-
plish.

"I seen a medicine show," I squeaked.

"And?" He was pretty near lifting me off the ground.

"I watched it. Never seen one before."

Chilly let up on my ear, though he wasn't done with my shoulder yet. Leaning over, he got close enough for counting eyelashes and growled, "So why were you talking to Rebecca?"

"Wh-who?"

"Don't go playing deaf and dumb with me. Won't wash."

"But I don't know any Rebeccas," I babbled. "Not 'less you count my sister way back home, though she usually goes by Becky, 'lessing it's Sunday and the—"

"I'm talking 'bout the lady you was only just hobnobbing with," he said. "And don't go pretending you weren't."

"You m-mean the orphanage lady?" I sputtered. "I was just asking her how them orphans was doing."

He pulled back from me, eyes jigging, and gave me a rough warning. "You wet-nosed pup. If you know what's good for you, steer clear of her. And never you mind why." He went for my ear again, yanking it extra hard. "Just come on along now 'fore I blow a boiler."

And he led me to the nearest coach he could find, chucking me inside like a head of cabbage and following behind himself, after a quick check of the sky. Shook up as I was, I didn't know what to think.

The reception I got back at the inn was almost as rainy, though Goose didn't start out by grabbing any ears. He went for a more schoolteachery approach.

"Now listen here, Zeb—your monkeyshine's come close to costing us a night's use of the telegraph."

"And he was talking to Rebecca," Chilly fumed.

Goose ditched the schoolteacher then and there. Whirling on me, he blasted, "You what?"

"I just asked her about them orphans."

"Never you mind 'bout them orphans," Chilly barked.

"'Less you care to join 'em," Goose added, raising his hand as if to slap me. "Anybody see you?"

"Only Chilly." I was doing my level best not to quake or teeth chatter or sniffle. At least my answer got Goose to drop his hand, but what I'd said wound Chilly up even tighter.

"Hogwash," Chilly said. "He was talking to her right on Market Street. The whole town seen 'em."

Chilly set to pacing. Muttering too. He appeared to be pulling a storm cloud right behind him and every once in a while he let a question rip, sharp as a crack of thunder. Mostly he asked what did I think I was doing? And didn't I have any sense? And how could he trust me after such business? He didn't slow down any for my answers either, which was good, since mostly all I had to say was a bunch of mumbled yeses and noes and I-don't-knows.

Then he hit a stretch of pacing where he didn't ask nothing, which was worse than all the questions. Even the Professor didn't speak up on my behalf, as he sometimes did, but kept his head down, straightening up things behind the bar. I winced every time Chilly changed directions and went all crumbly when he spun on me to ask, "So that's what took you so long? Talking to Rebecca?"

"No sir," I volunteered. "Finding the wire ate up some time, and then I seen that medicine show and took a look."

"Buffalo Hilly, I suppose."

"The very," I admitted. "And Chief Standing Tenbears. He knew so much about me, it was scarier than I don't know what."

Upon hearing that, Chilly threw back his head and horse-laughed, which made me cringe and wonder what I'd done now, but after Chilly had himself a good, long laugh, he cooled off a bit, seeming more like the man I'd been eager to sign on with, which was a welcome relief.

"Goose," he said, flashing all friendly again, "I'd say we owe this boy an apology."

"We do?" Goose sounded as surprised about it as me.

"Yes sir, we do. We keep forgetting he's green to all these matters and that we're supposed to be smartening him up as we go along." Talking to me, he added, "Now looky here, Zeb—St. Louis ain't so big a town as it likes to think, and if people see Miss Rebecca mingling with a gambler's apprentice, why, all that fine work she does for them orphans will go up in smoke. We wouldn't want that, would we?"

"No sir."

"Good." Chilly sized me up carefully. "Now I want you to be honest with me, Zeb, 'cause that's the way it is in the Brotherhood. Do you think you can manage that?"

"I do."

"Was there anything else that happened on your errand?"

I started to say there wasn't, which was an outright lie, 'course, so I pulled back on my reins, hung my head, and come out with it. "I seen a crow."

"Where?" In a flash, Chilly had ahold of my ear again.

"On the chief's shoulder," I squawked.

"Tell more," Chilly ordered, giving my ear just an outstanding twist.

So quick as I could I filled them in on how the crow had landed on the chief's shoulder and all. Any second I expected to lose an ear, but the more I laid out, the looser Chilly's grip went, till at the end he let go of me entirely and exchanged the queerest kind of twinkle with Goose, as if the two of them couldn't have wished for anything better than having a crow visit the chief. Why that struck their fancy so, I couldn't say, and I wasn't about to go upsetting the apple cart by asking. But they surely were pleased, which was something I stored away for future pondering. Then Chilly noticed me watching him kind of strange and said, "There anything else you're holding back?"

'Course there was, and I didn't reckon Chilly was going to take to it kindly. Hadn't I given the orphanage lady a nickel? I didn't guess that it mattered if I'd seen him give her over two hundred dollars back on the *Rose Melinda*. Something warned me that he might not feel so generous about *my* being free and easy with our money. The thought of setting him off again egged me toward fibbing, which naturally I knew better than doing. What kept me from taking that plunge was hearing my ma's voice pop up in my head and warn me off it by saying *Zeb* in that all-knowing way she had that made me want to wilt, so I changed course and trotted out the truth, confessing, "There was one other thing. I gave the change from your dime to that Miss Rebecca. For the orphans."

Chilly pulled back and gave me a double-hard look.

"Don't that beat all?" he pronounced at last.

"He's a country unto himself, all right," agreed Goose.

"Do you think we can ever learn him anything?"

"It seems doubtful," Goose answered.

"You're a regular saint," Chilly said to me. "Now here's what I want you to do next. . . . "

He never did say a mean-spirited or stingy thing about my giving that nickel to the orphans, which goes to show you the high standards he had. Just thinking about such nobility nearly lifted me right up out of my boots and floated me away, though not so far away that I lost track of how close I was to Chilly. After all this, I made sure to keep an extra foot or two between us, in case he went for my ear again.

What he had in mind for me to do next was help Ho-John put the telegraph wire under the inn. 'Course, I couldn't tell him I was afraid to go rooting around beneath the house, not when everything was so light and airy and back to friendly between us. All I could do was hope there wouldn't be any slivers involved in stringing that wire.

CHAPTER FIFTEEN

GOOSE NEDEAU'S INN WAS STACKED UP on wood stumps on account of a nearby creek that was prone to flooding. The crawl-space under the house measured maybe a foot and a half tall and wasn't no trouble at all for me to handle on my stomach. Squeezing Ho-John under there was another matter. He had to go on his back, which he claimed left him feeling trapped, but the fit was too tight for him to flip over later on, so he didn't have much choice.

Dark as it was down there, I couldn't see what might have holed up beneath the inn over the years. Mummies and head-less riders, I shouldn't have been surprised. Rough old cobs who wouldn't care a bit about picking up any slivers. And camping below that house must have been just the ticket for any varmint needing a roof over its head. The way the hounds tied up out back set to baying sometimes, you just knew

something had to have scampered under there—escaped
monkeys or roving night vipers or who knew what all. Ho-
John wouldn't let me light the candle either. It was the only
one we were getting for the job, and he didn't want it burned
up before we got the real work done. (At least I didn't have to
worry about singeing myself till later.)

So we shimmied along, heading for a dim square of light toward the middle of the house, where Ho-John had cut a board
out of the pantry floor. The rattle of the chains holding his
feet together gave everything fair warning that we was coming
through. 'Course, we slid under the house from the rear side
'cause Chilly didn't want anybody seeing us and wondering
where we were going with a candle, hammer, and nails. Might
raise suspicions, which was the last thing a gambler wanted.

Ever so often I felt a shiver working up my spine and would
say, "You hear something?"

And Ho-John would mostly answer, "Not yet."

That didn't settle me down any, since it left me thinking he
was expecting to hear something anytime now. It also fizzed
me up some because it was the exact same answer that Chief
Standing Tenbears had given me. I was fussing over how
strange it was to get the same answer twice in one day, when
Ho-John tried to calm me down by pointing out that I was
probably hearing Goose shuffling around the kitchen above
us, hunting for eats.

"You believe in ghosts and witches and suchlike?" I asked.

"'Course I do."

Which didn't comfort me much, particularly when my hands kept running into stray bits of this and that, which didn't seem to have any business being under the inn. My fingers tugged a ribbon out of the dirt. Attached to that ribbon was a baby's Sunday bonnet. Then my belly met up with a marble, a good-sized one too, and somehow or other, a broken-handled hammer and chisel had found their way under there. When I asked Ho-John how he could explain such trappings, he said he didn't have no trouble explaining them at all.

"Some children probably lost 'em over the years," he said.

"But what would they be doing with a hammer and chisel?"

"Oh, that probably belonged to their pa. This here house wasn't always a gamblers' den, you know. Once upon a time there was families lived here."

"What happened to 'em?"

"Probably something terrible and wicked," Ho-John answered, real casual-like. "So maybe we best leave their things alone."

I was agreeable with that.

"Do people really think of this place as a gamblers' den?"

"Mostly. And if you're bound and determined to become

some kind of gambler yourself," Ho-John added, "just don't go thinking you're something important. That's all I'm asking."

I didn't know how to handle such a request as that, so I didn't say much of anything to it. It was the kind of undermining talk that nags at a person though. After a bit, I said kind of sassy-like, "So what exactly is it *would* make a person important?"

"That's a question every man's got to answer for himself," Ho-John said, ignoring my tone, "but owning my own tools would do 'er for me."

There wasn't much I could say to that, coming as it did from a slave, who had never owned anything his whole life and didn't have no hopes of ever owning anything either, not unless he ran away again. 'Course, I knew what Chilly would say. He'd say that sharing with the poor and needy was what made him feel important, and that was an answer I sure couldn't fault.

We snaked along under there for most of forever, till we reached the square of light and Ho-John took hold of the wire he'd dropped through the hole in the pantry floor. After that, we got down to work, pulling the wire toward the main parlor. Whenever we reached a wood beam, I handed Ho-John a tenpenny nail and he pounded it in halfway, then rapped the nail sideways, bending it over till it made an eyelet. Through

the eyelet, we threaded the telegraph wire. For a few feet, the
hole in the pantry floor gave us light enough to work by, but
before long Ho-John had to light up the candle so we could
see to do the job. He said he wasn't big on trying to cheat
folks, but if it had to be done, then he wanted his part in it
done proper. Hearing that reminded me of how my own pa
had always wanted things done right too, though I was too
busy keeping my distance from Ho-John's candle to remark
on it.

We lined the wire up for nine or ten feet, all in a straight
line. Up above, Chilly thumped his heel on a floorboard they'd
loosened in the main parlor. Ho-John knotted the wire's end
to an eyelet he'd made in that loose board and shouted out for
Chilly to put his foot down on it.

"It's there," Chilly said.

Ho-John gave three tugs on the wire and called out, "Feel
that?"

"Not a bit," Chilly answered. "Try it harder."

Ho-John gave three hard yanks.

"How 'bout that?"

"A tickle," Chilly said. "Hold on. Let me try it with my
boot off."

Footsteps crossed the floor to a chair. There was a grunt
as he pried off a boot, which landed heavy as a cannonball
above us, making me flinch. Then came his footsteps again,

but this time it was one loud clunk followed by a soft, squishy one, so you knew one of his feet was only stocking covered.

"Now try 'er," Chilly called out.

Ho-John did.

"We're in business," Chilly announced. "Feel it just fine now."

And that was the telegraph I was going to be operating. It was also what you might call the official start of my career as a gambler, though it wasn't anywhere near as high-flown a starting point as I'd have ordered up on my own. As soon as Ho-John and I wormed out from under the house, Chilly led us to the pantry shelf I'd be working from. Ever the carpenter, Ho-John ran the loose end of the telegraph wire up to my perch by threading it through some holes he drilled in the shelves. He wrapped the end of the wire around a small block of wood and hung that on two nails that he pounded in about level with my shelf. I could fit the block in my hand, slivers and all. If I gave it a tug, Chilly's foot would feel a silent vibration in the floorboard the wire led to.

They had me crawl onto the shelf for some practice runs. Through the peephole in the wall I could see over the shoulder of whoever sat in the nearest chair. For the time being, that was Goose. In his stockings, Chilly sat across the table from Goose, dealing a hand of poker. When Goose didn't get anything to speak of, I kept the telegraph quiet. If all he got was a queen or higher, I gave it one tug. If he was dealt a pair, I yanked the wire twice. Two pair needed three pulls on the wire. Three of a kind got four tugs. A straight needed five. A flush, six. And so on up the ladder to a royal flush.

It worked pretty slick, I must say. Chilly knew what Goose had almost as soon as Goose knew himself, which allowed him to call bluffs and lay off betting against strong hands and slip a card into his mitt whenever the time was right. What's more, he didn't need to deal himself seconds nearly so often nor resort to marked decks at all. About the only thing he had to do was cut a hole in the bottom of his boot so that his stockinged foot was always pressed directly on the loose floorboard, feeling for vibrations.

We were all set up to help rich gents be a bit more charitable and Christian-like with their pocketbooks. Understand now—every once in a while I had me an uneasy twinge or two over what I was about to do and could hear my ma tsking from far away, but such notions are pretty easy lost when an Indian chief with eyes white as snow has told you it isn't time to quit your new trade—not yet, anyway.

CHAPTER SIXTEEN

THAT VERY NIGHT WE STARTED WORKING the telegraph. Chilly sat straight across from the peephole while Goose filled the chair to his right. To the left of Chilly went some small-time player, such as the one from the *Rose Melinda* who wandered in with his lucky clam named Sherry-Ann. Chilly didn't need any help from me to clean out someone like that and then offer him one last wager—everything he'd already lost against his good-luck charm. (Stripping some poor soul of his lucky piece put the highest kind of gloss on Chilly's night.) But it was the chair right in front of me that was always left open for the "guest of honor," as Goose called whatever high roller we were fixing to educate. With the lantern next to President Washington's portrait turned up, we were all set to make things better for the orphans of St. Louis.

On that first night, we trimmed a braggy cotton buyer and shortened up an Army paymaster who lifted out his false teeth and set 'em onto the table beside his money, saying they always guarded his wampum. Crafted together out of silver and ivory, those chompers were a sight to behold, but they didn't bring him any more winning cards than a bent doornail would have, not with the telegraph working against him. Chilly, he just pulled out his pocket watch to check the time, as if this particular hand of five-card was already taking too long. Those teeth and the shell named Sherry-Ann were dropped in the silver box upstairs with all the other good-luck pieces well before the whippoorwill nesting down the creek got started on her *good morning*s.

Given excitement such as that, I didn't fuss too long about how Chilly had tried to remove my ear. I was too busy feeling smug about how easy and smooth the telegraph worked. Back home everyone would have taken a dim view of my putting on such airs, but here at the inn such strutting seemed to be expected. Everyone paraded out a smirk soon as they got a chance.

Night two saw a horse trader who was all talk about the best ways to pawn off whistlers and biters and rackabones. He claimed to have outfitted just that afternoon a boatload of German farmers with the worst herd of crowbait he'd ever seen. He bragged about getting top dollar too. After we did all we could to teach him it was better to give than receive, that horse trader called Chilly a low-down, straw-stuffed cheater.

The whole table flashed quiet. There wasn't much being said at the two other tables in the parlor either, especially not when Chilly pushed his chair back and stood up.

"Sounds like you know a book's worth about fleecing folks," Chilly declared loud and clear, "so I guess I ought to be complimented to have the likes of you calling me a cheater. Excepting I ain't. 'Low-down' and 'straw-stuffed' kind of burns my hide, so here's what I'm aiming to do. I'm going to take my coat off. That way you can see I don't have a single card up my sleeves."

"Not anymore you don't," the horse trader came right back.

"And I'm planning to let you peek in all my pockets," Chilly said, ignoring the trader's salt with confidence, seeing as how he had me backing him up. "So you can see they're empty. If you want, you can count the deck we're playing with and hold 'em up to the light. Feel free to look under the table if it'll clear your nostrils any. In short, I want you to do whatever you need to. Yes indeedy, I'll strip down to my silk undergarments if it will help convince you that the reason you lost here tonight doesn't have nothing to do with me. The reason you lost is all between you and your Maker."

Well, Chilly stood there glaring at the horse trader, and the horse trader, who was standing by then too, returned the favor. Or at least I guessed that's what he was doing. From where I was peeking through the wall, I couldn't see nothing but the back of his coat, which had a split down its middle seam. Heavy as he was breathing in and out, that split seemed to be spreading.

The air in the main parlor didn't have a single wiggle-waggle to it—everything was so still. I know *I* wasn't breathing. After a bit, the horse trader said real gloaty-like, "When's your coat coming off?"

"Soon as you promise me one little thing," Chilly replied, cool as a spring day. "And I want you to call it out loud enough for all these gents to hear."

The horse trader just hunched his shoulders with a grunt.

"Once you're satisfied this here game is on the up and up," Chilly said, "I want you to tell us where those German farmers are headed with the nags you peddled to 'em. I aim to take the money you've dropped here tonight and send it their way."

It was the kind of gesture that would have left a Sunday-school teacher glowing with admiration, though the horse trader wouldn't divulge those Germans' whereabouts. He flat out said that Chilly wasn't nothing but a fool and stomped out of Goose Nedeau's inn with a slam of the front door. Everybody in the main parlor gave Chilly a big round of applause for showing such mettle. The clapping got even louder when the horse trader shot a new hole or two in the red-whale sign out front of the inn. Taking himself a bow, Chilly shouted over to the bar, "Professor, a round of your finest for the house. None of that Arkansas bust-head, if you please."

That pretty much marked the high point of the week, and an awful high point it was, but after that, there was enough sitting around, waiting for the next excitement, to make me wish for a cast-iron bottom. The majority of players who passed through Goose Nedeau's weren't nothing but smarty-pants clerks and skunky river men who were hardly worth bothering to educate about the benefits of being charitable. And most of the time we didn't. All total, there probably wasn't but one or two poker players out of five when Chilly parked his whiskey glass at his left elbow, which was the signal to work the telegraph. The rest of the time Chilly shifted the whiskey back to his right elbow, meaning I could take a rest. "If we go winning every hand," he explained, "even the fools that come around here are going to get suspicious."

So mostly I lay cramped on my narrow, wood shelf in the dark, peeking out my little hole and fussing over slivers. It all got fearful wearisome. Waiting and waiting and waiting to tug on my wire didn't show anywhere near the dash I'd been expecting as Chilly's apprentice. Truth be told, it sort of brought to mind sitting in the smokehouse back home.

Most nights it was all I could do to stay awake, though I knew better than to raise such complaints around Chilly. I liked my ears right where they were.

The poker playing usually ran down by two or three in the morning. As the last guest either left for home or got carted upstairs to a room, they unlatched the pantry door and let me out. At the same time, they put Ho-John in, for he spent the rest of the night locked up. After I swamped out the parlors, I was free to turn in too.

Cleaning up used to be Ho-John's lookout, but that had meant somebody had to stay awake to make sure he didn't go running off soon as everyone was sawing wood. They passed the job on to me so's everyone could get some rest. Happy as I was to be rid of my shelf for the night, I didn't put up any squawk over inheriting Ho-John's chores, especially since it only took me maybe a half hour to draw a bucket from the creek out back, splash the water over the floor, and swash it around some. Stacking unbroken glasses on the bar added a few minutes more. What coins I found went in my nest egg, long as it didn't amount to more than a dollar. Over that amount was the inn's property, so belonged to Goose and his silent partner, Chilly.

Those gamblers may have sloshed their whiskey and dropped their cigar ashes, but they kept powerful good track of their every last penny. The first week I pocketed a grand total of four coppers and an old Spanish bit from beneath the tables. My second and third weeks didn't bring in even half that much, though I had to work just as hard.

By the time I made it upstairs at night, it didn't matter much that I was sleeping on the floor; I could have winked out atop a thistle patch.

CHAPTER SEVENTEEN

In the mornings, everyone but the Professor slept in, rolling out somewhere around noon. The Professor wasn't much on sleep and got up not long after sunup, letting Ho-John out of the pantry to start his morning chores. When the rest of us woke up later to the smell of something burning in the kitchen, I always sprang downstairs to make sure the place wasn't on fire.

Once I knew we weren't going up in flames, I fetched water for Chilly's washbowl, then hung on to watch him shave around his goatee and trim his sideburns. The way he spruced up was too grand a show to miss. He went after his teeth with wood picks and gargled up good from a black bottle of forty-rod. And all the while he was cleaving whiskers and plastering down his hair, he had me rubbing soda on any soiled spots his suit had picked up. He never talked much during all this, except maybe to say something like, "You see that pair of queens I dealt out last night?"

Sometimes he felt a powerful urge to improve his hand after I'd signaled what his opponent was holding. Folding just wasn't his style at all.

"Why no, sir," I admitted. "I didn't."

"That's 'cause you weren't supposed to," he said with a grin.

On occasion I got brave and asked a question. "Was it your pa who taught you 'bout gambling?"

"Not likely," Chilly answered, on the gruff side. "He run off with some duchess when I was a tyke."

"Where'd they go?" I asked, stupefied to hear of such goings-on.

"Now where do you think?" Chilly sniped.

I was about to guess they'd headed off for a castle, but right about then Chilly nicked himself with his razor. Though it was the only time I ever saw his hand slip that way, it pretty much marred me for life when it came to shaving, and I never did get back to asking about his pa and that duchess.

Once satisfied with how he presented, Chilly made me stand on a chair to hold his coat open so's he could step into it. If I was going to learn to be a gentleman, he said, the best way was to serve one. There was even some idle talk about getting me outfitted with store-bought clothes.

"So you'll look more like a squire," Chilly said.

Nothing much come of it though, or leastways, not any new clothes. He said I could pay for 'em out of my share of the winnings—only trouble was, he kept forgetting to pass on my share. Any time I asked when I might be seeing some of those winnings, he flat out told me not to worry, they was coming soon as I paid him the thirty dollars I still owed for my apprenticeship. "You didn't expect me to forget that, did you?" Chilly asked. I told him that I surely didn't, though I couldn't resist asking—without luck—exactly how much my winnings had amounted to so far. You see, paying back Ma and Pa's seventy dollars had begun to weigh on my mind pretty regular, so I was itching to ship some money home to prove how well I was doing without 'em. Chilly didn't appreciate such an uppity attitude at all and, to remind me of my place, took to calling me Squire Zeb every chance he got. It was *Squire Zeb, could you fetch me my coat?* Or *Squire Zeb, I've a hankering for a cigar.* Or *Any squire worth his salt would keep these boots of mine better polished.*

Anyways, after I held Chilly's coat open, he had me sprinkle rose water on his shoulders. Closing his eyes, he'd tell me to let a few dabs fly at his face too. Then it was downstairs to tackle whatever Ho-John had scorched for breakfast, though late as it was by then, most folks would have called it lunch.

Ho-John's keeping all the vittles too close to the fire didn't slow down anybody's appetite. We tucked away seconds, sometimes thirds, complaining about the biscuits and gravy and bacon all the while. Once everyone let out a notch on their belts and eased up shouting for more fried ham and fixings, they leaned back and worked some on my education. Moving out to the parlor, Chilly dealt cards to everyone and we got down to rehearsing ways to help rich gents share their wealth with the less fortunate of this world.

Since there were sure to be times when we took our gambling elsewhere and couldn't cart the telegraph along, we practiced fake shuffles and false cuts and dealing seconds. Every once in a while Chilly or Goose or the Professor would say something like, "Now here's how Feathers McGraw used to stack decks down on the Red River." And everybody studied real careful how he done it. We'd ask him to do it again, slower, so we could get the hang of it. We all wanted a turn at trying our hand at it too. 'Course, I usually botched her pretty bad, small as my hands were, but every day my fingers limbered up a little more, allowing me hope that I was making progress, particularly when Chilly saw fit to present me with one of his old vests. It was a shiny thing and I wouldn't have taken it off for money, though it hung on me like a blanket and was fraying at the bottom and losing thread along its seams. Three secret pockets had been stitched into it, two in back, one on the side, and they were exactly the right size for holding cards.

I practiced slipping kings and aces in and out of that vest's pockets everywhere I went, all in the name of helping orphans. Day and night I was at it, clumsy at first but gaining confidence and improving my handiwork till I could switch cards under Goose's nose without his catching on. Given his eyesight, that may not have meant all that much, but it was a start.

"Zeb," Chilly told me one day, "you got smooth hands and that's a fact. You'll be going places with them."

Such flattery kept me plugging away harder than ever. 'Course, I was learning from the best. Anytime he wanted, Chilly could deal himself, or anyone else bellied up to the table, as many deuces or treys or jacks as need be. Swapping one whole deck for another didn't even make him break a sweat. His fingers struck like snakes. At first I couldn't spot none of it, not unless he wanted me to. Even old Goose, blind as a mole, could fling those cards around easy as pie, though he couldn't always tell which cards he was tossing.

Most every day they got out a satchel full of playing cards that the Professor kept tucked away behind the bar. There must have been thirty to forty decks in there, each marked up so their backs could be read good as their fronts. It was done by lifting a spot of glaze off here, or putting a dab of ink there, or trimming the edges of some cards so the dealer's fingertips could feel what they were when he flung them. They practiced handling those cards until playing poker began to seem more like reading a book than any game of chance. It was so handy that I couldn't help but ask why they even needed to bother with me running the telegraph.

"Oh, there's never enough ways to skin a cat," Chilly reckoned.

"Or get caught skinning one," the Professor added.

"What's that mean?" I asked.

"Just that nothing works every time," the Professor said. "There's always someone around who might have already seen what you're doing."

"Even the telegraph?" I didn't like the sound of this.

"There's nothing new under the sun, Squire Zeb," Chilly cautioned. "Telegraph's been run before."

"Didn't Ruby Ed run one on the *Still Kicking*?" Goose asked, naming a steamboat they liked to gas on about.

"Among other things," Chilly agreed.

"But what happens," I broke in, "if someone comes along who's seen a telegraph?"

"Why"—the Professor acted surprised to hear me ask it—"you get caught."

"Shoo, fly." Chilly waved the Professor off. "There's no need to go putting fool ideas in the boy's head."

The way he said it so throaty and low warned the Professor not to say another peep, though he looked sorely tempted. The Professor had been tending bar at the inn long before Chilly had horned in, and the two of them didn't often see eye to eye.

Up to then I'd had no idea that gambling took so much hard work, but I began to see that doing it proper took years and years of practice. Understanding why some gamblers leaned so hard on a lucky piece? That wasn't any strain at all. I told Chilly and Goose so too, maybe secretly hoping they might change their ways and settle for whatever they could win fair and square, which would help me out of the fix I was in over cheating. I pointed out that if we applied half so much sweat and toil to anything else, we could probably invent some way or other to fly.

"Son," Chilly told me, "playing cards beats flying any day of the week. Ain't nowhere else that you can get such satisfaction from helping your fellow man."

I do believe he meant every word of it too. He was rock solid on what he did for a living. You could tell by the way his voice got so swelled up and important sounding whenever he talked of it. Just hearing him carry on that way brought me scurrying back to the fold, filling my head with such thoughts as *Everything'll be fine . . . Just got to give it some time,* which soothed me, though sometimes I had to repeat it to myself often as a clock ticks.

So we honed our card skills till late afternoon, me whipping cards in and out of my vest, everybody else brushing up on what suited them. Eventually we retired to gather strength for the night's work.

Around six or so, it was time for some more of Ho-John's crunchery. Come seven or eight in the evening, when most folks were snuffing out candles and fluffing their straw ticks for a good night's shuteye, Chilly would drift out of the inn for a promenade around town to take care of the charitable work the Brotherhood required of him. He dropped off packages of food and clothes for orphans and poor old widows and the like. The reason he waited till dusk? So he could do these deeds without anybody knowing who he was.

"We in the Brotherhood don't want no one feeling beholding to us," Chilly explained.

When he told me that, didn't I feel small for ever doubting him? If all the good we were doing required a little cheating, well, maybe that was the way of the world, says I to myself.

Depending on how much rich-man's money Chilly had to parcel out, some nights his do-gooding walk took longer than others, but eventually, say around ten or eleven, he drifted back to the inn, where he acted as though he hadn't seen Goose or the Professor for days and didn't live right upstairs and wasn't sure if he had any time to sit in on a hand of five-card. Though it always turned out that Goose could talk him into staying.

There weren't any promenades around town for me though. Right after supper, before any gamblers showed up, I was latched into the pantry, with a molasses barrel rolled in front of the door in case any of the inn's guests got to wandering. I had to crawl in so early to keep everybody from knowing my whereabouts. And there I stayed the whole night long, learning my trade and peeing as quiet as I could into a chamber pot if the need arose. Some nights it got so dag-blasted cramped and shrinking tight in there that I must have died a hundred times. I figured they'd find me in the morning, blue and ripe as country cheese. Thank goodness Ho-John sometimes slipped up to the pantry door and whispered a word or two.

"You in there?" he'd always start out.

It struck me as a strange question, considering there was but one door and he was stationed outside it. But glad as I was for some company, I never asked where he thought I might have gotten to. I'd just slip off my shelf and whisper that I was still there.

"Good," Ho-John would huff, sounding relieved, as if something might have happened to me that was too terrible to ponder. Then he'd sigh and say something like, "What would your ma and pa think 'bout you wearing that kind of vest you do?"

"Wouldn't matter to them," I'd answer, all stiff upper lip.

"Don't think that I'm believing such an answer as that. They the ones that raised ya, ain't they?"

Having said his piece, he'd shuffle and clink and mutter all the way back to the stove as if put out with me, though later on he always cracked the pantry door to slip me a drumstick or biscuit that wasn't burned too bad. I appreciated his concern but could have done without the ma-and-pa questions, which always left me feeling kind of low and moldy, even if my folks were the ones who'd shipped me to St. Louis.

That takes care of my first month or so on the job. It wasn't till my second month that I run into some real, honest-to-goodness troubles.

CHAPTER EIGHTEEN

———◆◆◆———

We were getting into the middle of May by then and the days
had a low fire under 'em. Goose kept the windows of the inn
propped open most always; I kept my vest unbuttoned.

By then I could pretty much tell ahead of time which guests
I'd be running the telegraph on. Lying there in the dark, trying to hold my breath as I pressed an eye to the peephole, I
began to feel more than a little sorry about it. We might be
helping these fellows to learn about sharing, but they were
mighty poor students. The way a few came back night after
night for another lesson—that was heartbreaking.

Then Chief Standing Tenbears dropped by to try his luck.

The first I knew of the chief's arrival was a commotion that
broke out in the front parlor, which was mostly used for drink-
ing and eating the inn's burnt fare. There was some rough

shouting, followed by a gunshot, which put a lid on all the hullabaloo.

"Let him through," I heard Goose yell into the silence. "The chief saved my hide once, over San Carlos way."

The next thing I knew, Chief Standing Tenbears came trailing the princess into the main parlor, head held high. He was wearing his buckskins and war bonnet, with his right hand resting on the princess's shoulder.

"Chilly Larpenteur," the princess announced, "my father wants to win his medicine bundle back. He thinks you've had it long enough now."

There wasn't any back-down to that girl, and you couldn't help but admire her for it.

"He does?" Chilly acted powerfully surprised and lamb-like all at once, which was one of his talents.

As the princess led her father forward, Chilly sprang to their side, chock-full of warm smiles and Sunday greetings while guiding them to the chair dead in front of me. There hadn't been anyone sitting there for a half hour or so, ever since Chilly and me had wrung the last dollar out of a traveling portrait painter from Louisville.

Something told me I wasn't headed for one of my proudest moments. All the other poker games folded quick, with the players bunching around Chilly's table as he fanned the cards, rippled them back together, and slapped them on the table so the chief could cut 'em. For gathering attention, there ain't nothing beats an Indian chief and princess dressed for show. It was lucky for telegraph operations that the gawkers couldn't squeeze between me and the chief, whose chair was tight against the wall. Chilly had seen to that.

"Did the Chief have one of his famous dreams?" Chilly asked solicitously.

When the princess translated that question, the chief pulled out a fur-lined pouch and dumped a good thirty to forty gold eagles on the table. The princess stacked the coins in four piles, each worth a hundred dollars. Trying to figure how many visions the chief had needed to earn all that knocked my cipherer clean out of kilter.

"I wish my dreams were so profitable," Chilly chuckled, which earned a general round of agreement from the crowd.

The chief spoke up before Chilly could start dealing.

"My father asks," the princess relayed, "if that boy helper of yours is still around."

Well, I nearly fell off my shelf when she up and said that.

"Oh, I expect he's hereabouts somewhere or other," Chilly answered, vague as could be. "Want me to scrounge him up?"

"My father just asks you to give him a message from his mother."

Hearing that poked me like a stick in the eye. From out of

nowhere, a stick-bur rasped in my throat, 'cause I figured that by now they'd have forgot all about me back home.

"I'll see that it gets to him," Chilly said.

"Tell that boy," the princess went on, "that his mother asks him to write home. She's worrying about what's become of him."

I had to bite a knuckle to hold a whimper back. Maybe Pa and Ma were having second thoughts about packing me off the way they had.

"Any particular reason she's needing to hear from the young scamp?" Chilly asked.

"She didn't say."

"Well, I'll be sure to let him know," Chilly promised. "You ready to win that medicine bundle back now?"

But the princess had one last request to make for the chief. "My father wants to sniff the cards."

"Why, I wish he would!" Chilly cried out with a laugh. "There ain't nothing in this world smells better."

The chief didn't agree though, not for the first deck of cards, anyway, nor for the two decks that the Professor brought over next. Not until he whiffed the fourth deck did he agree to let the game begin, if Chilly would hunt up the medicine bundle he hoped to win back.

"Not so fast," Chilly cautioned. "If I'm remembering right, the last time we sat down together, I had to put up a thousand dollars against that most valuable possession of yours. When you manage to run your grubstake up to a thousand, then I'll haul out that bundle. Not before."

The chief grunted an answer when the princess told him what Chilly had said. "My father doesn't think it should take long to win that much. The spirits are with him."

"Maybe not all of them," Chilly warned, with a big wink for everyone else in the room.

Then the cards started flying, with the chief scooping his up for the princess to see and Chilly, after sneaking a quick look at his watch so's he could remember the exact minute the game started, going for his. Once the chief fanned the cards open in his hand, I got my look and gritting my teeth, sent the news flying over the telegraph. *"Sapua sapua,"* the princess would sing out, reading the cards for her father.

I could see that meant the chief had a pair of sevens.

Or she would say, *"A te dami."*

That meant the chief held three kings. By the time the princess was done filling the chief in on what cards he held, Chilly already knew, so the coins rolled pretty steady to his side of the table. Chilly did manage to work in a feel-good hand now and then, letting the Chief win back a gold eagle or two, but in general the gold flowed only one way.

Every hand that Chilly won made me feel smaller and smaller, especially after the chief had gone to the trouble of bringing me a message from home. Fast as I was shrinking, I could almost have gone swimming in a teacup if I'd known how to swim. The chief took it all right in stride though, and when his last gold coin went missing on him, he rose and announced through the princess, "Maybe you can keep my father's medicine bundle for a while longer."

"Guess the spirits got their days mixed up," Chilly commiserated, genuine as some teary-eyed old humbug.

"Keep it in a dry place," the princess warned him.

"Won't a drop of water touch it," Chilly vowed. "And if he wants to take another crack at winning it back, why, tell him I'm always open for business, 'specially if he's got something valuable to put up against it."

"I will tell him," the princess promised, and without another word, she led her father out of the main parlor. When Chilly bought a drink of prime stuff for everyone, a huzzah went up. None of it put me in any mood for celebrating though. We were only kidding ourselves if we thought we'd taught Chief Standing Tenbears anything about sharing. Near as I could tell, the chief already knew a sight more about it than we could ever hope to pass along.

CHAPTER NINETEEN

THE NEXT DAY I MOPED AROUND worse than mumps on your birthday. I kept my hands stuffed in my vest's pockets and my head down. Not only was I tortured 'bout cheating the Chief, but getting up steam enough to write home was a good ten miles beyond me, and every inch of it upriver. Not till midafternoon did I finally find the gumption to at least try to get my hands on some paper and quill.

The first fellow I ran into was Goose, who was serving himself breakfast from behind the bar. When I asked if he had any writing supplies, he scratched behind his ear so long that I started thinking fleas. Finally he come out with what was on his mind, saying, "You're not considering that old redskin's nonsense, are you? Writing letters home and all? That won't lead you nowhere but into a nest of trouble."

"Really?"

"Boy, how do you think I ever made it out West, became a famous Injun fighter, and took possession of so fine a gaming parlor as this? It didn't happen 'cause I was all the time dashing off letters back to Nantucket, I can promise you that. Not at all. If I'd been doing that, there'd have been letters come flying the other way too, wouldn't there? Letters from my pa second-guessing everything I'd ever done and ordering me home to captain one of his leaky old ships to some watery corner of the world, some place where the ocean's deeper than the sky and the wind howls your name till you jump overboard just to find some peace. Mark my words: letters from home won't lead to nothing but an early grave. I've burned every one that ever came my way."

'Course, by then I'd been around the inn long enough to pass over most of Goose's blowings, especially when it came to Nantucket or Indian fighting, but maybe I'd been a little hasty. The way he talked about his pa didn't sound like no flimflam, which left me wondering if the two of us didn't have more in common than I cared to admit. Hadn't my pa shipped me off on a leaky old ship too? But as Goose had pointed out, there was a whole side of this letter-writing business that I hadn't considered—namely, letters *from* home. That possibility gave my heart an unexpected ache. What if Ma and Pa had reconsidered and wanted me back? That's why the

instant Goose slumped back on his chair, I shoved off to keep on searching for writing supplies.

The weeping of the Professor's violin pulled me upstairs. Knocking on his door and getting no answer, I invited myself in and right away knew I was trespassing on a man of learning. A little desk in a corner had four leather-bound books lined up on it, gold lettered and thick as some lawyer's. And hanging on a wall was a heart-shaped silver locket that made you think of fancy, rhyming poetry just looking at it. Everything else was laid out neat as a general store that ain't yet open for business.

The Professor himself, he was playing his violin out on the balcony, with Venus and Aphrodite fluffed up contentedly at his feet. Soon as he saw me, he lowered his bow and waved for me to join him. I made it as far as the window leading to the balcony before my toes knotted up on me. Heights, you know.

"I was wondering," I said through the window, "if you had any writing supplies I might borrow?"

"Zeb," the Professor answered, resting his violin on his lap, "I had to quit writing down my thoughts years ago. It got so's I was spending so much time doing it that I never got anything else done. Did the chief put a bee in your bonnet?"

"'Fraid so," I confessed. "Do you think he really could see my ma?"

"Goes without saying," the Professor answered, rocking back on his chair. "He seen mine once, you know. When the chief and Buffalo Hilly first landed in town, he had that daughter of his pass on that my ma was sending me her heart. I laughed that off and told him that so far as I knew, she still needed it. But then two or three weeks later I got news from my sister that Ma had passed on, and then came a package holding her favorite keepsake, which she'd always wanted me to have. It's that heart-shaped locket hanging on the wall behind you. I keep it there to remind me of what's good in this world."

Right then he played a snatch of the sweetest, saddest song imaginable. Stopping, he brushed back a wisp of hair and gave me a kindly look.

"I don't care if you don't believe anything else I ever tell you," the Professor went on, earnest as could be. "Just so you trust me when I say that the chief had known I'd be getting that heart. So if someone asks if I think the chief really can see things, I always tell 'em that his eyesight's way better than yours or mine. The question is, Zeb, are you ready for what he's seen? That's the thing. If you are, then I'd say check with Ho-John about writing materials. He's the one keeps track of such odds and ends around here."

Not sure what I was ready for, I traipsed out back of the inn, where Ho-John was plucking some fresh-wrung chickens while conversing with the hounds. Considering what the Professor had just shared, I'd gone and lost the urge for a letter from home. Who knew what I might hear? I may have been gone only a little more than a month, but wasn't that long enough for something terrible to have happened? Rolling up a log for a chair, I sat me down to give a hand with a pullet.

"You're looking considerable stretched out," Ho-John observed.

I thought about telling him my woes, but they seemed too big and never ending to even get started on, so I settled for saying, "Oh, I been all over this place trying to find me some writing paper and quill and things."

"Ain't likely to find none of that in these parts," he declared, without giving it any thought at all.

"Why's that?" I asked, surprised at how quick he answered.

"'Cause there ain't nobody can write 'round here."

That news struck me midpluck, befuddling me worse than two black cats walking side by side. My ma had taught me the three R's, and though I knew there were plenty who never got such an advantage, I surely never figured Chilly nor Goose nor the Professor—especially him—to be among them, not the way they dressed and carried on so high toned.

"You got to get over thinking of these gamblers as gentlemen," Ho-John advised. "They may dress like 'em, and lounge around like 'em, and now and then even try to use a knife and fork like 'em, but that's all for show. If you ever stacked 'em up next to a real gentleman, you'd see they weren't nothing but bad-made chalk copies."

"But what about the Professor?" I asked, kind of desperate-like, I suppose. "You ain't meaning to tell me that he can't write."

"Makes an X for his name, same as the rest. Maybe a little fancier is all."

"But he's got those thick books in his room."

"Could be, but owning a book and reading a book is two different things."

"That's a fat wad to swallow," I mumbled.

"First time down, maybe so," Ho-John agreed. "But you ain't the only one to choke on it. The thing you got to understand 'bout these gamblers is that they're all show. Why, they don't gamble to win money. If they did, don't you think they'd keep more of it? Sure enough they would. But whatever they win, they plows right back into the next game that comes along. No, they gamble so's they can rub elbows with gentlemen and feel like gentlemen and maybe have a few bumpkins like me or you mistake 'em for gentlemen, 'cause that's what they want to be. Worse than horses want to run, that's what they're wanting, but they ain't never going to make it, not even if they had a good-luck piece dug up at the end of a rainbow."

"Chilly don't believe in good luck," I came back.

"Now who told you such nonsense as that?" Ho-John clucked his tongue. "Why, he's so superstitious that he won't even admit he's superstitious. He's afraid it'll bring him bad luck."

"Then how come I ain't ever seen him pulling out rabbits' feet or saints cards or drilled coins or . . . " I started losing my way by then 'cause of the way Ho-John was shaking his head at me, pitiful-like.

"Why do you think he's all the time checking that gold watch of his?" Ho-John asked. "It ain't 'cause he's worrying about the time, I can tell you that much. It's 'cause he won that watch off some gent who carried a cane and claimed to be a duke. Why, I heard Chilly tell Goose that watch has protected him from shed snakeskins and evil eyes and stepping in front of a parson on a Saturday night. And I seen him almost plug Goose for even daring to touch it. He don't go nowhere without it, not even to bed, I'll bet. You check under his pillow sometime. No—you ask me, Mr. Chilly Larpenteur's got more superstition bottled up in his little pinky than the rest of us uncork in a year or more, and the only reason he pretends different is 'cause that's what he thinks a gentleman would do."

Hearing all that wrapped my head in fog and cottonwood fluff. Worse storm of it I'd ever seen. The way Chilly checked his watch whenever playing cards came rolling back to me, proving Ho-John's point.

"If you're wanting paper and such," Ho-John went on, setting down one clean-plucked chicken and starting right in on another, "try one of them general stores. They be happy to sell what you need."

That was an answer I'd probably known all along but hadn't wanted to go into. I just didn't have the strength to go trailing all the way down to the levee again. What if I ran into Chief Standing Tenbears? What if he'd run across more news from home? Then what? It'd peck my bones clean to hear it, that's what. 'Sides, I didn't have any idea what I could put into a letter to home that wouldn't leave me feeling airy and blue as some ghost doomed to haunt the Mississippi till it ran dry.

Leaving my half-plucked chicken with Ho-John, I went out toward the front of the inn, where I stood gaping at the road as if the answer to all my woes had gone trotting past just before I had got there. I was still standing there all woolly headed when Chilly caught up with me.

"What's this I hear 'bout you wanting paper and things?" he demanded, pinching my upper arm hard.

"It's just a thought I had." I tried squirming free without luck.

"Well, put a torch to it. You ain't got no time for such truck, no matter what that fool chief heard from your ma. I bet I've heard him tell twenty others their ma wants a letter. It's one of his favorite fallbacks."

"But down to the levee," I said, "he knew all about me."

"That's 'cause I had a talk with him and his daughter right after we hit town and maybe let slip more about my new assistant than was smart. I can see that now. He's a curious old cuss and wanted to know all about you."

"He did?"

"Only 'cause the princess spotted you standing beside me."

"She did?" That perked up my ears.

"She don't miss much. Now listen up, boy: that chief ain't got any more visions than a wood stump could have."

Don't think that I swallowed much of that, not after hearing the chief name Ma's biscuits and Pa's mule. And what about the Professor's heart-shaped locket? None of that sounded like something a stump could rattle off. But I didn't have the steam to tell Chilly so, not the way he was crowding me. And while he went on, I couldn't take my eyes off the gold watch chain dangling out of his vest pocket, not after hearing what Ho-John had to say about it. Wanting to believe at least one thing Chilly'd told me, I asked, "But the chief does have a crown, doesn't he?"

"Never you mind about that crown," Chilly growled. "I don't even want to hear another breath out of you 'bout it. And being as how you're a member of the Brotherhood, there won't be any letter writing home either. We don't allow that till you been with us ten year or more, and then only on good behavior. Hear?"

"Yes sir." I swallowed hard, 'cause there was another fair-sized chunk of me that was vengeful and hoped Ma and Pa couldn't do nothing but wring their hands and feel terrible about shipping me off to some distant, star-crossed land. But if ten years had to pass before I had a chance to write and remind 'em what they'd done, well, they'd have forgotten all about me, which didn't seem right at all.

"And I better not have to tell you again," Chilly rumbled on. "Now get back inside and practice hiding cards or something."

Then he gave me a shove toward the inn, where I found myself being pulled toward the pantry. More and more regular my shelf had been calling out to me. With as much time as I'd been spending there, it'd begun to feel comfortable when nowhere else did. I'd made it up neat as home, with a ten-pound sack of oats for a pillow, a scrap of quilt for a blanket, and a crockery or two of pickles and crackers to snack on.

Curling up on the shelf, I promised myself that if Mr. Chilly Larpenteur ever laid a hand on me again, I was going to settle his hash. How I'd manage that wasn't too clear at the moment, but I vowed that he'd be thinking twice about ever roughing up a Crabtree again. Gradually, my mutterings lessened and the next thing I knew, I was asleep and dreaming. I'd rather not go into what I was dreaming, except to say it was full up with Ma and Pa and my brothers and sisters and every other little thing in life that was guaranteed to wet up my eyes real good. They were calling to me from across the river, clear over to Illinois, trying to warn me off something or other. All their shouting and arm waving and hollering was what woke me.

Or at least I thought that was the case. At first. After a bit though, I came to see that it was talking in the parlor that must have roused me. 'Course, the real voices weren't calling my name or shouting. Just the opposite. They was whispering and carrying on as secret as a gang of grave robbers.

Wanting to see who was sneaking around the main parlor in the middle of the afternoon, I rolled over and squinted through the peephole. Sitting at the table before me was Chilly, in his usual chair over the loose floorboard. To his right, pulled up close, was a woman wearing a hooded cloak.

CHAPTER TWENTY

—◆—

I BLINKED AND SHOOK MY HEAD SOME, but none of it changed the
cloaked figure into a man. For a tremble or two I thought it
was my ma come to rescue me, but that was my fuzzy-headed
dream talking. This woman's voice didn't have Ma's snap to
it at all. The trouble was, I couldn't get a clean look at her
face. If it had been night, the lanterns would have been lit
and I wouldn't have had any trouble seeing her, even with
her hooded cloak, but during the day the parlor was splotchy
with shadows.

"I told you never to come down here," Chilly scolded in a
whisper.

"Oh now don't you worry," she teased sweetly. "Nobody
saw me."

"Still and all . . . " Chilly complained.

"And even if some old busybody did see me," the lady whispered, "they wouldn't have recognized me, all dressed in gray like this."

"Well, that's true enough," Chilly allowed. "I hardly knew you myself. But why take the risk at all?"

"Now you know how these orphans are," the lady said with an easy laugh that made you glad to hear it. "They take a lot of looking after."

Cloak or no cloak, I figured right then and there who she was—the orphanage lady named Rebecca! It appeared that somehow or other she and Chilly knew each other pretty well, close together as their heads were pressed, though not a month before they'd acted like perfect strangers on the *Rose Melinda*. Now they were thick as thieves, which I had a low-slung feeling was exactly what they were, especially after Chilly had got so overheated 'bout my talking to her.

"What if I told you," Rebecca went on, "that Captain Horacio has an excursion of high hats leaving for St. Paul tomorrow? Then would you know why I'm here?"

"Horacio?" Chilly moaned, sounding sick to hear it. "Why, he looks the other way for next to nothing."

"So what do you say?" Rebecca asked.

Chilly didn't cave though. He seemed to have some other pickings weighing on his mind.

"That I hope they make it back from St. Paul with some money left in their pockets."

"Now Charles," she pouted, using Chilly's proper name, "I've never known you to be so shortsighted. There's a world of bad things that could happen to them between here and St. Paul. And not a one of them has anything to do with lining your pockets."

"True enough," Chilly agreed, acting terribly put out to hear himself say it.

"And Charles," Rebecca went on, sounding as though reasoning with a stubborn child, "you know how rich people get to feeling all generous and lordly if you up and mention orphans. It's a proven fact. And once you've got 'em leaning that way, it's only a matter of time before they're wanting to shell out a little something for a child who might not have had the same luck as them in this cold, cruel world. It makes them feel ever so much better about themselves. I'm guessing we could double or triple what we took off the *Rose Melinda*, and same as always, it'd be half for you, half for me."

"Don't forget them orphans," Chilly quipped.

"They can have the half that's left."

To which they both cackled as though she'd said something powerfully witty, though the only thing that adding up all those halves gave me was a terrible longing to be dead and gone.

"Oh, it's tempting," Chilly admitted. "But I've got my own gold mine right here and it ain't no humble pie either."

"You mean your little telegraph?" Rebecca teased.

"Have you been smiling at Goose again?" Chilly asked, turning cross at the thought of her pumping his partner.

"Oh now Charles," she coaxed, resting a hand on his arm, "won't that telegraph and the silly boy you've got running it be here when we get back?"

Silly boy!

"I expect so," Chilly said. "Least I believe the boy would be. His head's got more sap than a swamp pine. Why, do you know that I got him believing I pass out my winnings to the poor every night?"

"Now when do you find the time to do that?" she tittered.

"On my way to the faro tables."

They had themselves a good, long snicker over that. I sort of blacked out to hear it. Not that I really went under, 'cause I could see Chilly's lips moving and all, but I couldn't hear a word of what he was saying. If you dragged me behind a stagecoach clear across Missouri and out into the territories, you might be approaching how busted up I was feeling on the inside, 'cause right about then I was poleaxed by what had been slowly creeping up on me all along: we weren't cheating just rich gents who needed help in learning how to be generous. As the nights wore on, it turned out there weren't enough of them to keep us busy. So we'd started working the telegraph on as many store clerks and liverymen and stage drivers as we could without raising suspicions. And now it turned out we were even cheating the orphans too?

Finally, I forced myself to hear more.

"But you see," Chilly was saying, "I just about got my hands on the chief's crown."

"You and that crown," Rebecca scoffed. "How do you even know he has one?"

"Buffalo Hilly vouches. Says he was sitting right there when King Wilhelm of Prussia or Italy or someplace dropped it on the chief's head, a gift from one monarch to another. Buffalo says that seeing that thing in bright sunlight nearly knocks your eyeballs out, it's so stuffed full of diamonds and rubies and emeralds and what have you."

"And how long have you been after it now?" she reminded him.

"Too long."

"So won't it keep a week or two longer?"

"Maybe that's a yes," Chilly grumbled, "and maybe that's a no. I skinned the chief good last night, and something tells me he's going to come roaring in here real soon to win back his medicine bundle. I'm betting he'll finally have to put up his crown to do it, which is something I don't plan on missing. Ain't every day you get a chance to win what belonged to royalty."

So Ho-John had read Chilly's secret desire to be a gentleman exactly right, and he appeared to have been talking straight about Chilly's feelings concerning good-luck charms too. The whole while Chilly sat there, he couldn't keep his hands off that gold watch of his.

Just hearing how Chilly was lying in wait for the chief boiled my blood so fast, I could hear it bubbling in my ears. At the same time, I'd have to say I was getting a taste of what it felt like to be cheated, 'cause what else could you say Chilly had done to me, right along with everyone else? At last I understood in my gut that cheating was cheating, no matter how fancy you dressed it up, and that was what made up my mind for me: I was going to ask for my seventy dollars back. Oh, if Chilly made a fuss, I'd tell him to keep five dollars of it, though I thought he owed me way more than that piddling amount for my share of our winnings.

What's more, I planned on telling that Rebecca to hand over the nickel I'd given her on good faith. And once I'd straightened them out on all that, I'd march myself right down to the levee to hunt up the chief and warn him that Chilly was after his emperor's crown. (I wondered how the princess would think of me after that.) Then I'd search up that excursion boat of rich folks and make them take a pledge not to go donating money to any orphanage ladies who might show up, no matter how good it might make them feel.

Oh, the chickens were all coming home to roost, and what a pecky, mad lot they were too.

With all that out of the way, I supposed rather reluctantly that it would be time to humble myself in front of my Great-Uncle Seth and see if I couldn't wrangle my way into his services yet. Being a tanner might not be glory wrapped, but at least it was honest. I was beginning to see there might be something to be said for that, though I couldn't help but wonder if working with hides wouldn't leave me sneezing my way to an early grave.

The only trouble was, before I could do anything about these revelations, the pantry door creaked open and in tiptoed Ho-John, his arms full up with a tin box, a rolled-up blanket, and a medium-sized poke that looked awful stuffed. He left the door open a crack for some light, and it was a shock to see him move so catlike, what with his chains and all. Quiet as he was creeping, he must have known that Chilly and Rebecca were out in the parlor, but it didn't appear he had any idea I was holed up on my shelf. I didn't say nothing either, figuring that if I did, it would make him jump and give away the both of us.

Kneeling down on the floor, he pried up the board we'd

loosened for stringing the telegraph and set it aside. Then he picked up two other boards, one on either side of the first, and set them aside too. Not a one of them was nailed down at all! With the hole triple wide, he lowered himself through the floor, moving slow and careful-like so as not to rattle his chains. When he ducked out of sight, something told me he was stashing his things right next to that broken hammer and chisel we'd run into down there.

Done with that, he pulled himself back into the pantry, replaced the boards, and crept away without clinking his chains but twice. Both times he stopped dead, his shoulders all hunched, but there wasn't any need for him to fret. Out in the parlor, Chilly and Rebecca were plotting away so thick that they never heard a thing.

There didn't seem much doubt that one of these nights, after he was locked away in the pantry, Ho-John was planning on taking himself another dip in the Mississippi, headed for Illinois. It didn't take me but a blink to decide I wasn't going to tattle on him, not after all I'd finally figured out about the workings of Mr. Chilly Larpenteur. But seeing Ho-John planning his escape so careful-like did slow me down consider-able and make me think that maybe I shouldn't go rushing into anything without some planning of my own.

So I lay there in the dark, listening to Chilly and Rebecca carrying on worse than South Sea pirates. They eventually judged they'd just have to coax the chief back that night with his crown. That way they wouldn't have to let Captain Horacio's excursion boat leave without them in the morning. Chilly guessed that maybe if he paid his respects to the chief that evening, while on his way home from helping the poor and needy, it ought to goad him back to the inn.

"He's a proud old peacock," Chilly confided.

"Don't lay it on too thick," Rebecca warned. "You might scare him off."

"Leave it to me." Chilly patted his watch pocket. "I've been baiting hooks for many a year."

Not this year, I thought to myself. *Not if I got anything to say about it.*

CHAPTER TWENTY-ONE

I STAYED HOLED UP IN THE PANTRY till the orphanage lady cleared out and Chilly went hunting for me, wanting to make double darn sure I was on hand to work the telegraph. He wasn't going to tolerate any slip-ups on such a night as this. First off he popped into the kitchen, asking Ho-John if he'd seen my worthless hide anywhere abouts.

"Why don' you leave that poor boy alone?" Ho-John wanted to know.

"Don't you start talking like a fool," Chilly warned, "or you might find yourself sold off to some cotton field, hear?"

"I hears ya," Ho-John muttered.

"So let me try again," Chilly said. "Have you see that no-good squire of mine?"

"Last time I seen him," Ho-John answered, "was when I

was plucking chickens. He was headed back into the house. That's all I know."

"All right then," Chilly growled.

Next I heard him calling out my name as he clomped upstairs, where I'd been known to sneak a nap, but I still couldn't bail out of the pantry, not with Ho-John chopping taters in the kitchen. If I popped out now, he'd see that I knew all about his getaway plans, which might force him to do something desperate, or at the very least leave him sick with worry that I might go blabbing about what he'd been up to. Kind as he'd been to me, I didn't want to put him through those miseries, so I started considering whether I ought to risk lifting up the pantry's loose floorboards to crawl out that way, slivers and all. Seemed like I should be able to pull the boards into place from below, so no one'd be the wiser. But that'd leave me in the dark, under the inn. What saved me from having to chance that terrible fate? Ho-John clanked into the parlor to call after Chilly. "Will that lady you was whispering with be staying for supper?"

"Never you mind about her," Chilly said from halfway upstairs. "If you know what's good for you, you'll forget she was ever here."

Seeing my chance, I squeezed out of the pantry and rabbited through the back door. Quick as you can dot an *i*, I buried myself in the pack of hounds tied up behind the inn.

They may have been rough on raccoons, but they didn't have no issues with friends of Ho-John's and washed me with their tongues to prove it. That was exactly the kind of welcome I was in desperate need of. I stretched out there, soaking up their attentions, trying to conjure up what to do next, and—I'm sorry to say—asking all sorts of why-me questions till Chilly tracked me down.

"Get out from under them dogs," he ordered, yanking me to my feet. "It do beat all the places you find to get to."

Here was my golden opportunity to teach him a lesson for shoving me around, but fast as he was hustling me along by the scruff, I couldn't do nothing but kick air as he herded me back toward the inn, where he could keep an eye on me.

"Squire Zeb," he railed after planting me on a kitchen chair, "tonight you're going to learn a thing or two." When I didn't act grateful enough about that prospect, he added roughly, "If you know what's good for you."

Supper was sootier than usual, but Chilly didn't notice, busy as he was bragging about how he was going to do the chief out of his crown. Then, when everyone finally had his fill of scorched chicken and undercooked beans, Chilly announced all casual-like, "I guess maybe I'll go pass on some winnings to the poor and needy."

Hearing such a bold-faced lie riled me up bad, which at least proved that I had some pride left. What I didn't have was a lot of sense, 'cause I up and blurted, "I been meaning to ask if I could get me a refund."

"A refund?" Chilly snorted, not understanding what I was getting at. "On what?"

"My apprenticeship."

"What's this about?" Chilly froze halfway out of his chair.

"Well, sir," I jabbered despite myself, "I've been working it over in my head and it's got me thinking that maybe gambling ain't exactly the life for me. I ain't sure my hands is fast enough."

"Didn't you slip a king in your hand just yesterday afternoon without my seeing?" he came back.

Well, I thought I had but apparently not.

"And the late hours," I mewed. "They seem to be giving me a rash. Under my arm."

I held up my arm, where I had me a handy rash from a spider bite, but Chilly wasn't interested, so I kept on gibbering away, fast as I could muster.

"And my eyesight's going down on me too. Some nights I can hardly tell the difference between a king and a queen. So it's all got me to thinking that you might be better off finding another boy. One who's better suited for your needs."

Chilly sat still as a rattlesnake while listening to all that. One of his hands went to jingling some coins in his pocket, adding to his rattler qualities. When he started in on a smile that even an undertaker wouldn't have called warm, my insides turned all to mush.

"'Course, I wouldn't expect the whole seventy dollars back," I stumbled on. "Not with you having educated me for going on a month now. But if you could see your way clear to giving back sixty-five of it, I'd say we could call 'er square and I'd be on my way. You could even keep my share of our winnings."

Right about then old Goose couldn't hold it in no more and threw back his head to bray like a donkey. It was so unexpected and loud that I jerked backwards in surprise. I didn't tumble off my chair though, not with Chilly's big hand nabbing my upper arm.

"After all I've done for you?" Chilly snarled. "Why, I'm so disappointed, I could cry."

"Oh, please don't cry," Goose begged, once he managed to quit hee-hawing. "I can't stand to see a full-grown gambler cry."

"I say you should indulge yourself," the Professor advised. "I generally feel better for days after I've had me a good weep."

"Say," Goose said, sounding inspired, "ain't we forgetting

something here? Ain't this boy sworn into some brotherhood or other? You know the one I mean. That outfit that never lets anybody quit except to go to the cemetery."

The Professor just looked at me kind of pitiful-like for believing such truck, but Chilly and Goose had themselves a good hoot over my predicament. My blood ran icy to hear 'em, 'cause you could tell by their jeers that the Brotherhood wasn't nothing but another lie they'd served up to trick and hogtie me. But what really stung was how well it'd worked.

"You fellas don't fool me," I sputtered, brave as I could muster, which wasn't much puffier than a church mouse. "There ain't no Brotherhood."

"Oh yes there is," Chilly came back. "And you're looking at 'em."

With that, Chilly dragged me over to the pantry, flung me inside, slammed shut the door, and rolled a barrel before it. I dug in my heels some, for all the good it done me.

"What's got into that boy?" Chilly yelled.

"Maybe a conscience," suggested the Professor.

"Where'd he all of a sudden get such a thing as that?" Chilly demanded.

"Some claim we're born with 'em," said the Professor.

"More likely you've been talking to him," Chilly shot back. "You just keep this in mind, Mr. Professor: I'll put the boot to any conscience that sticks its nose in my business, and I'll do it good and proper too."

By then my jaw was too locked up for my teeth to be chattering, and my heart was thumping against my chest like a trapped bumblebee. I punched out in the dark as hard as I could, aiming at Chilly for all the good it did me. My fist smacked a timber and my arm bone rang clear up to my ear. "Pa!" I shouted, maybe blaming him for my fix. That might not have made a whole lot of sense, but it's the way I felt about it. If he'd let me stay to home, none of this mess would have ever happened to me. And besides, didn't blaming him beat blaming me? Better yet, it helped me skip over all those promises I'd been peddling myself about stopping Chilly from treating me worse than mud.

Outside the pantry, the gamblers were commiserating over what an ungrateful little twig I was, and how a good tanning would likely do wonders for my attitude, and how it never rained but it poured. Even the Professor allowed I wasn't to be trusted, though the way he said it, he almost sounded proud of me. None of that mattered though. By then I was so full of wretchedness and general all-around despair that I just crumpled up and fell to the floor and lay there like some June bug caught on its back.

By and by it got quieter out in the kitchen, and after a bit

I heard Ho-John creep to the pantry door and whisper, "You all right in there?"

I didn't have the heart to answer, so he gave up and left me alone to wallow. But after a while I felt something hardening inside me that I hadn't known was there. It must have been backbone I was feeling, 'cause pretty soon I was telling myself that I shouldn't take being treated such a way and that I ought to do something about it. That sure enough sounded like some free advice of my pa's, which surprised me, all right, mad as I was with him. But it wasn't long till such thoughts left me feeling a touch braver too. About then I seized up hard, struck by an idea on how to help the chief and myself. The only problem was getting word to him of my plan. In the end, it was hearing Ho-John rummaging around the kitchen that gave me a notion of how to proceed.

I could still hear Chilly going on about all the generous turns he'd done me and how these days everyone spun right around and bit the hand that fed 'em and wasn't it a crying shame how parents didn't bother to teach their offspring any better. Somewhere in there the Professor struck up his violin and Goose retaliated at the piano, which started the dogs off. Chilly announced at the top of his lungs that he was going to tidy up before heading downtown on business. "And that fool boy better be in that pantry when I get back!" Hard as Chilly then stomped upstairs and loud as the Professor and Goose were having at their instruments, I figured it was now or never if I was going to do something. What with all the noise, nobody was going to hear me lifting up Ho-John's floorboards, no matter how trembly and clumsy I was about it.

Dropping beneath the house, I started to lower the floorboards down after me but stopped with only one in place. Fast as I'd be moving when I came back, I didn't guess there'd be much time for hunting up the pantry's loose boards, so I left the hole wide open and struck out for the street, praying that no one would dare pay the pantry a visit, not after the way Chilly had carried on. Luck was with me, and I didn't run into any rampaging mummies or half-buried coffins while crawling out of there.

Once out from under the inn, I headed for the levee and Chief Standing Tenbears, running all the way 'cause I knew that Chilly was somewhere behind me. By the time I made it to the river, Dr. Buffalo Hilly and the chief were done hawking elixir and visions for the day, but I did have a dab more luck and spotted the cross-eyed loafer who'd been so keen on sampling Buffalo Hilly's tonic. He was weaving sideways down the street in between nips on one of the doctor's bottles and told me straight off where the medicine show could be found.

"This time of night?" He hiccupped. "They'll be camped up to Chouteau's Pond. Direct across from the mill."

CHAPTER TWENTY-TWO

I FOUND MY WAY BY ASKING FOR DIRECTIONS and following the accordion music. Dr. Buffalo Hilly had set up camp between a couple of low-hanging trees, on the edge of a half-moon-shaped pond that in the gathering darkness looked too wide for swimming and just right for drowning.

As I squirmed in closer, I seen that the doctor was serenading his camel, which stood there chewing thoughtfully on a shrub and gazing off into the night. Since Buffalo Hilly appeared to be on speaking terms with Chilly, I didn't barge right in and ask where I might find the chief. Instead, I crept around the edges of the campfire till stumbling across a deer-hide tepee on the far side of the medicine wagon. It was smallish, not much taller than a man, and hung on three or four poles that crisscrossed up top. A kitcheny kind of perfume curled out its smoke hole. There was some singing too—low and solid and hard-driving—an Indian song, all right, and hearing it give me a chill, creeping around under a dark cloudy sky as I was.

When the song pulled up lame for a bit, I cleared my throat real polite-like, not sure how you were supposed to come calling at a tepee. After the third time I ahemmed, the princess lifted her voice to say, "My father wonders if that is the west wind talking to him."

"'Fraid not." I apologized in a hurry-up whisper 'cause I was expecting Chilly to show any second. "It's only me, Zebulon Crabtree, come to warn you off something."

The princess's head popped out the door flap right quick after that. One look at me and back inside she went. There followed a flurry of Indian words, and then out she came again.

"Did the Birdman send you this time?"

"Not that I know of." I winced, hoping she wouldn't send me packing, but then she surprised me.

"Doesn't matter," she said, holding the tent flap open. "My father's been expecting you."

I had a rough breath or two soon as I heard that, but I moved ahead anyway, ducking through the door flap and past the princess in a flash, not wanting anyone else to see me. Inside, a leathery, smoky smell covered me like a nice, homey blanket. Lit up by a fire, the tepee was surprisingly bright. A pot was simmering away over the coals. Grass had been piled up around the bottom of the walls so there weren't any distracting drafts. Logs had been laid around the fire to hold in sparks.

Old Chief Standing Tenbears was sitting with a buffalo robe slung over his shoulders and a long pipe stuck to his lips. The pipe couldn't have been doing him much good, for every once in a while he had to leave off sucking on it so that he could have himself a low, racky cough. In the glow of the fire, he didn't look too much older than stone. He'd taken off his war bonnet, which must have been a heavy load to cart around, and replaced it with a top hat that had two black feathers sticking out its back. His eyes were white and ghostly as ever.

"What's this big warning?" The princess sounded snippy, like she didn't believe I had any such thing.

"Only that Chilly Larpenteur's been cheating you."

There. It was out. I sure wish I could report that saying it aloud lifted a weight off my chest and shoulders and every other part of me too, but it wasn't anywhere close to so. Soon as I quit worrying about the chief I started feeling powerfully low and itchy about Chilly. He wasn't anything but a scoundrel and a blackleg who'd locked me in a pantry and scuffed me up regular, but then again, hadn't he been willing to take me under his wing and say a kind word when I'd needed it most?

To top it off, I didn't exactly get the idea that Chilly's cheating habits were a whirlwind of news to the chief.

No, when the princess told the chief what I'd said, he threw back his head and laughed real bold, plenty long and hard too, which started him to coughing. I got me a pretty good look at his tongue and the few yellowed teeth that floated around it. After settling down, he speechified a long spell to the princess, who summed up what she heard this way: "He knew that."

"Did he need all them words to tell you?" I crabbed, still fretting about Chilly.

"He asked if you brought something for the cooking pot."

"Was I supposed to?"

"Only if you'd been raised right. And he wanted to know if you'd written your ma yet."

"I'm working on it," I grumbled, not taking kindly to being reminded.

"Don't forget to ask about the picture of the horse with two humps."

"I thought I told you—"

"It's in her book," the princess insisted. "The one with all the words in it."

"Her dictionary?" I said, dumbstruck.

Without having a vision, how could the chief have known Ma had one of those left over from her teaching days? Chilly couldn't have told him 'cause I never brought that book up around the inn, not even during the night when I sometimes whimpered in my sleep. How did I know that? Simple. I'd never in my life dreamed about that dictionary, thank goodness. The thought of copying out the definitions to all them words never failed to give me the fantods.

"The only horse pictured in Ma's dictionary is a unicorn, and it's got a horn, not humps."

"The horse like Buffalo Hilly's," the princess told me. "Buffalo Hilly won't sell his, so my father wants a picture instead."

"Are you talking about that camel?" I asked, sitting up straighter with a jerk.

"Some call it that, yes."

Soon as I heard her answer, something big crashed inside my head. Ma's dictionary did have a picture of a camel in it. I could see it plain as day and could even remember getting hand cramps writing out its definition. His knowing about that picture sealed it for me. Far as I was concerned, the chief really did have powers enough to confound a minister. Ma's dictionary sat closed on a shelf a hundred and sixty-some miles upriver. But even if that book had been sitting in the tepee with us, would his seeing inside it have been any less a miracle? He was blind as some anchor but could see far as the ends of Missouri, if not beyond.

And if that was the case, then I was honor bound to believe that he'd seen my ma and pa wringing their hands and wanting a letter so they could know how I was doing. I nearly shouted *Hallelujah!* Right there I understood that I'd been holding back on something that scared me worse than slivers, deep water, heights, fires—the whole kit and caboodle. The way my folks had bundled me off to St. Louis had pretty near convinced me that they didn't care one whit what happened to me. Hadn't I pleaded with 'em to keep me? Hadn't I reasoned? Begged? Sassed? Stormed? But far as I knew, they hadn't listened to a smidgen of it. So what was I supposed to think?

'Course, in the back of my heart I'd always sort of secretly hoped that I was wrong about their not caring, but now I had certifiable *proof* that I was wrong. And when it comes to questions big as how your folks feel about you, proof is the difference between lightning bugs and lightning. There wasn't time to celebrate though 'cause right about then someone called to the chief from outside the tepee. Even though it was a voice I'd been expecting all along, hearing it still gave me January shivers. Chilly Larpenteur had arrived and was sounding mighty full of himself.

"You to home, Chief?"

CHAPTER TWENTY-THREE

I MUST HAVE LOOKED DESPERATE as a trapped possum, 'cause the princess had to jerk on my arm to get my attention. Pointing out a pile of buffalo robes, she gave me a shove. I scrambled around the chief and burrowed into those robes without any thoughts of tomorrow.

"Who's asking?" the princess said, buying me some time.

"Why, your old friend Chilly Larpenteur. I was just heading home and thought to stop off and offer my condolences."

"We didn't know we needed any of those," the princess answered, opening the door flap.

Then came the jingle of coins in Chilly's pockets, followed by the rustling of his feet. Pretending to be brave, I straightened a finger to push up on the robe covering my head. I couldn't see much of anything though, only the chief's back and, on the far wall, the shadow of Chilly's top hat.

"After you lost all them gold eagles?" Chilly gushed, smooth and friendly as ever. "I believe that a kind word is the least I can offer."

"We've been thinking you did us a favor," the princess countered. "Now we don't have to carry that heavy sack around."

"Well, I'm glad to lend a hand with such a problem whenever I can," Chilly answered, serious as a sermon. "But I've still got my regrets about it."

The princess translated, the chief answered, and the princess reported back to Chilly, "My father says you don't sound like a man with regrets."

"Oh, I've got 'em," Chilly lamented, sincere as a weasel. "I've suffered many a sleepless night worrying that someone's lost money they couldn't afford to. That's why I stopped by. To let you know that if you've a mind to try your luck again, I'm game. And if you're strapped for funds, well, don't let that hold you back. Rest assured that I'll consider taking something of value in trade."

The princess and chief went back and forth after that little hint till the princess informed Chilly, "My father says he'll keep all this in mind."

"I figured he would," Chilly said. "But I best warn you, I'm only going to be in town for tonight. I'm afeard that tomorrow I'm being called away on business . . . "

Monkey business, thinks I to myself.

" . . . and who knows when I'll be back."

That pretty much wrapped up Chilly's visit. He said his goodbyes and vowed he wouldn't let anybody touch the chief's sacred medicine bundle, which up to then no one had mentioned a word about. He did feel obliged to point out, though, that he was traveling light on this trip so wouldn't be able to take the bundle along nor protect it while he was gone. But he promised that he'd hide it somewhere perfectly safe, if there was such a place in this world. (The way the orphanage lady had warned him not to lay it on too thick must have slipped his mind.) He also couldn't resist reminding them one last time that he was more than willing to take something in trade for the bundle, particularly if it was something gold and shiny. And then he left, though I'm pretty sure I heard him clicking open his pocket watch before ducking out the flap. Me, I hung tight under the robes till the princess said Chilly was good and gone.

"Are you ready to hear exactly how he's been cheating you?" I asked, popping up.

They were and so I told 'em, holding up every so often to allow the princess to pass along all I was saying. I filled 'em in on the telegraph and the peephole in the wall and how I had my shelf in the pantry all fixed up like home. I might have talked up my shelf too much, but only to impress the princess, which didn't go down well at all. She was glaring so fierce that I could feel my edges starting to smoke. When I wrapped everything up, the princess told the chief the last of it, and there was a long pause before the chief answered back.

"My father wants to know why you're telling us all these things."

"'Cause I'm hoping to mend my ways," I reported. "And maybe teach Chilly a lesson."

"What kind of lesson?"

That's when I filled 'em in on how Chilly was hoping to cheat 'em out of the crown that the king of Prussia or wherever had given the chief. And I explained how my cheating days were behind me too. Aside from the low and dusty way it left me feeling, there didn't seem to be any future in it, not if a person hoped to live with himself and tuck into a decent night's sleep now and then. I told them that if they'd give me a chance, I just might be able to help 'em get the better of Chilly—all fair and square—and get back that sacred medicine bundle they were missing. As plans went, it wasn't any slouch, and I spelled out every little detail of it too.

"When you look over your cards," I explained, talking fast 'cause I still had to beat Chilly back to the inn, "I'm supposed to signal what you've got by tugging on the telegraph wire. One tug means you ain't got nothing but a high card, queen or up. Two tugs, you got a pair, and so on. And if you got nothing, why, then I don't tug at all, which is exactly what I aim to do—no matter what you're dealt."

"You plan on doing nothing?" The princess made it sound as though a dung beetle could have come up with a better notion.

"Don't you see?" I persisted. "That's the perfect way. If I don't touch that telegraph, Chilly will think your hand's a bust and won't bother dealing himself much of anything to beat you. Maybe an ace or something, but that's about all. Gamblers don't ever want to raise any more suspicions than they have to. So you ought to have a pretty good chance to win."

"What if our hand *is* a bust?"

"Well, there ain't no guarantees," I mumbled.

"Why don't you come up with some way to let us know what's in *his* hand? Now that'd be a plan."

"But that'd be cheating, and I'm aiming to turn over a new leaf."

"So it was all right to help him cheat us," she scolded, "but not to help us do the same?"

I almost said, *Well, that was then and this is now,* but something else sneaked up on me. "Are you saying it's all right to cheat a cheater?"

She reached out and rapped a knuckle on my forehead,

which I'm sorry to say sounded kind of hollow. "'Course I am, if you're the one being cheated."

"What about 'do unto others'?" I asked, quoting the golden rule.

"If you're being cheated, cheaters are the others."

Fast as her answers were flying, she left me feeling slow as a slug, and though I wasn't entirely satisfied with what she'd said, I wasn't totally out of sorts with it either. After all, Chilly had brought all this down on himself with his crooked ways. But the princess didn't worry herself much over how I might be twisting about in the wind. She'd already moved on to flinging words at her father.

The chief, he peacefully sucked on his pipe the whole while she had at him, which lasted long enough for him to have a couple of hacky spells. When she was done, the chief had his turn, which didn't last anywhere near so long but didn't have any back-down to it either. Then around they went again, though this time the chief's answer was even shorter and flintier than before.

The princess didn't like what she was hearing at all and grumbled with a long face, "He wants to know if you can caw like a crow."

"Guess so," I answered, caught so unawares that I didn't even ask what that had to do with anything.

"He wants to hear you do it."

"I'll try." I tilted my head back a touch and situated my tongue, but all I managed was a measly little "Aw-aw."

The chief shuddered as if it was the most pitiful half-starved crow he'd ever heard.

"Crow," the princess scoffed, "not sparrow. Try again."

"There a reason I should?"

"My father says your plan's not enough, but maybe we can strengthen it, if you can crow."

"How's that going to help?"

"By spooking Chilly. He thinks crows are the worst kind of bad luck."

Soon as she said it, I knew it was right, 'cause Ho-John hadn't minced any words about Chilly being more superstitious than a one-armed fisherman. It explained why Chilly had shot out our bedroom window, and paid more attention to the sky than a farmer caught up in a seven-year drought, and acted so tickled when he'd heard that a crow had visited the chief instead of him. Still and all, I couldn't resist asking how they knew something so private. 'Course, they had an iron-clad answer—a crow had told them. Now how could I argue with such reasoning as that? So I buckled down and put my mind to work on thinking *crow* with all my might.

"Aw-AW."

The chief wrinkled his nose at my efforts. To prove his

point, he laid down his pipe, cupped his hands around his mouth, and cawed so pretty that I almost checked the tent flap to see if one hadn't hopped inside.

It took at least a good dozen tries, along with some stiff coaching, before I got off a good enough caw to satisfy him.

"All right," I said. "Now what?"

"When Chilly's dealing out the cards," the princess instructed, "you caw three times."

"That's all?"

Apparently not. Just then the chief cupped a hand around his ear in that way he had when getting news from far off. His face took on a startled look, as if someone who never lied had just told him the moon was on fire. He shook his head in disbelief and said something to the smoke lifting out of the tepee, or at least that's what he seemed to be talking to. The princess rolled her eyes disgusted-like, particularly when her father cocked his head to hear more. After that, he answered softer, as though apologizing to someone.

Turning to the princess, he spewed out some blistering-hot instructions. Her eyes flashed and she answered back all shrill, but he held his ground and real gently, with both hands, pulled off his top hat, revealing a small leather pouch riding on his head. He lifted the little bag up and held it out to the princess, who snatched it from him and thrust it toward me. "My father wants you to have this."

"What's in there?" I asked, leaning back 'cause I thought I heard something rustling about inside the pouch.

"My father's eyes."

I didn't swallow that one, at least not all the way down. Far as I could tell, his eyes were still sitting in his head. But he was able to see someway or other, wasn't he? Cautious, I asked, "What do you mean?"

"The spirit in this bag sees for him," she said. "That's why he carries it on his head, so he can always hear what the spirit has to say."

"You mean he doesn't see all them things himself?"

"Only a spirit could manage all that, and right now it's taken pity and offered to help you. Don't ask me why."

She sounded middling jealous, as though maybe she'd been passed over, which bucked me up enough to ask, "Where'd he ever meet up with such a thing as that?"

"Atop a mountain, when he was young and brave."

"And what on earth am I supposed to do with it?"

"Listen to its advice. It's strong medicine."

Well, if the chief was offering me strong medicine, I wasn't going to turn him down. *Stronger the better*, I say to myself, 'cause I knew Chilly was a haystack waiting for a spark. When I put my hand out for the pouch, the princess couldn't resist warning, "Don't lose it."

"Guard it with my life," I promised.

She scowled but dropped the little bag on my palm just the same. Picking up its leather drawstring, I agreed to bring it back after tonight. Then I cleared out of there lickety-split, knowing I had to beat Chilly back to the inn if any of this was going to happen. I needn't have worried though. He was partaking of a chaw and nip with Dr. Buffalo Hilly on the other side of the medicine wagon. They were having themselves a back-slapping laugh about all the cawing coming from the chief's tepee. Buffalo Hilly was going on about how if it wasn't one thing, it was another flying down the chief's smoke hole. "Everything from fireflies to crows."

"Just so long as they stay away from my chimney," Chilly declared.

I hustled onward, thinking we'd see who got the last laugh 'bout all this.

Halfway to the inn something started whirring around inside the bag, and I could almost make out a few words too. They echoed a bit, seeming to come from at least ten different directions, the way voices skip about in a cave. It took a minute or two before I found the spit to take a peek at what was stirring in there.

What I saw nearly gave me the faints. There was a bird's foot in the pouch. A crow's, if I was any judge. Now how was that going to see anything for the chief? Or talk to me, for that matter? But when I fussed about it longer, I recalled the princess saying it was a spirit that did the seeing and talking. The leg must have been all that was left of that poor creature's earthly remains. Thank goodness it'd lost its beak.

Thinking I'd put all this to the test, I closed up the bag and plopped it on my head same as the chief did, to find out what it might have to say for itself. But it'd turned silent for the moment; all I could hear was the clip-clop of a horse prancing down the lane. Lucky for me I'd felt kind of foolish about wearing a leather pouch for a hat and had slipped behind a wall. The horse coming my way carried the Professor, who appeared to be headed down to the levee on important business, fast as he was moving. He'd have spotted me for sure if I hadn't been hiding.

CHAPTER TWENTY-FOUR

I TOOK THE POUCH OFF MY HEAD and held it the same way I would have handled a snapping turtle—by the tail (or drawstring) and at arm's length. Whatever was inside stayed still as I raced the rest of the way back to the inn. By the time I reached Goose's whale sign, I was in such a pant that I just dove under the house. Tearing along beneath the floorboards wasn't any bother at all, not with Chilly somewhere behind me. The footsteps and gruff voices up above my head moved me along too. Here and there shoots of light cut through cracks in the flooring, guiding me, and I was glad of it. Getting tangled up with Ho-John's hidden poke and blanket was the last thing I needed.

Back in the pantry, everything was exactly where I'd left it. So far, so good. I replaced the floorboards and climbed onto my shelf, where I did my level best to catch my breath and pretend I didn't have a pouch with a crow's leg in my hand. It took me a good while to calm down, and then, just when I'd started to get a grip on myself, Ho-John came shuffling into the pantry for a cup of flour, which stirred me up all over again.

"Suppose you're helping skin the chief tonight," Ho-John grumble-whispered.

"Hope not," I answered.

"Going to take considerable more than hope to put a stop to that. Right here's the time for taking a hard look at yourself. Ain't going to be none better. You needs to remember that we all gots to carry our mistakes with us, wherever we go, for the rest of our lives, and toting 'em around can get to be blistering hard work."

Hearing all that made me want to blurt out my plans in the worst kind of way, but before I could, Chilly came barging in. Chasing Ho-John out of the pantry, he grabbed hold of my ankle with one hand and aimed considerably higher with his other. Tight as his fingers were clamped around my throat, I couldn't stutter nor swallow nor breathe as he dragged me partway off my shelf. He never even noticed the pouch I was still holding 'cause he stuck his face right up next to mine. His goatee bristled my cheek and his breath, all minty and fiery with Dr. Buffalo Hilly's tonic, made my right eye moist and fluttery.

"You handle the telegraph right tonight," he rasped so nobody out in the main parlor could hear him, "or I'll flay you like a rabbit."

With that, he latched onto the back of my neck as if to show me how such a thing could be done. Hard as he was squeezing me, I couldn't hardly think straight and bucked against his hand without shaking anything loose but a low, cruel cackle from Chilly. Spots danced before my eyes as he bent my neck till it almost snapped.

Lantern light from the kitchen glinted off the gold stem of Chilly's pocket watch, which was nearly poking me in the nose. While he was growling threats in my ear, I found myself doing the most foolish thing imaginable, but I just didn't care. I wanted to teach that man a thing or two about mistreating people, especially if their name was Crabtree, and I didn't mind about the risks. You see, my fingers were reaching for his watch.

Maybe he was too busy tormenting me to catch on to what I was up to. Or possibly all my practicing sleight of hand with cards was paying off. I wasn't about to ask which 'cause right about then I was unhooking the watch's gold chain from Chilly's vest pocket. When he shoved me back onto my shelf, threatening me with a hiss that burned hot as a branding iron, I'd already dropped his watch into my own vest pocket.

"S-s-s-s-s-s-s-s-s!"

Being threatened that way cleared up any doubts I had about if I was doing the smart thing. My business wasn't smart at all. Pure dumb, you might call it, crazed as Chilly was acting. But it sure felt right, and when it came to measuring things, I was praying that counted for more.

CHAPTER TWENTY-FIVE

CHILLY HEADED STRAIGHT OUT TO THE PARLOR, where he told the Professor, who was fresh back from his errands, to set him up a drink, a good stiff one. "And now." He chased that one with another. "To keep the first one company." But the third drink that the Professor served up? Chilly didn't touch it at all. He just stood there gazing down into it as if peering into the eye of some creature from the depths of the ocean.

My breathing kept speeding up on me till I pried the chief's pouch out of my hand, which was cramping bad, and set it on the shelf. When I scrunched against the peephole just right, I could see enough of Chilly to know that the drinks hadn't improved his mood any. I even saw him aim a boot at one of the Professor's chickens when it strayed too close. For a second or two, the Professor acted like he was going to stand up for his hens, but one look at Chilly must have warned him off it.

So there Chilly stood, brooding so deep over the chief's crown that he still hadn't noticed that his pocket watch was gone.

That was the way things hung together for a while, long enough for two or three fellas already at the poker tables to fold their hands and say they were cleaned out. Two or three others drifted along to take their places. There didn't ever seem to be any shortage of men willing to fill an empty chair at one of the tables.

Then, without warning, Chilly up and laughed, booming out, "I was betting you'd join us tonight."

With a start, I saw the princess lead her father into the parlor. The chief held up in the door for a long, roving, general all-purpose sniff of the room. He'd changed back into his war bonnet and had tucked his clay pipe under his red belt. One of his hands rested on the princess's shoulder, while the other held a beaver pelt tight against his chest. Whatever was wrapped up in that shiny brown fur was about the size of a man's head and poked everyone in the curiosity real good. Tight as the chief was squeezing his bundle, you could see he didn't have any plans of dropping it. After giving every corner of the parlor a good, solid sniff, the chief talked to his daughter.

"My father wants to play one hand of five-card," the princess announced. "For his medicine bundle."

"Then he's come to the right place," Chilly promised.

He led the chief and princess over to his special table. Acting as if waiting on royalty, he pulled out a chair for the chief in order to plop him down square in front of me. He surely didn't want any mistakes made with the seating, and just this once, we were in complete agreement. What was coming next I wanted to be done with in the worse possible way.

Chilly wasn't done fussing either but made sure the lantern in that corner of the parlor was burning bright—so the princess could see the chief's cards, he said. Seeing his hand brush so close to my peephole nearly put me on the run, but I held on. From there, he crossed over to his chair and lowered himself down without once looking away from the chief's bundle.

By then the two other games had broken up and the players stampeded over to catch the show. The Professor even came out from behind the bar, followed by Venus and Aphrodite. In nothing flat everyone was crowded around Chilly's table, all winking and elbowing one another, probably figuring the chief didn't stand no more chance than a grasshopper in a snowstorm. Not with Chilly Larpenteur. What they couldn't figure out, and what they all had a hankering to find out, was what was inside the pelt that the chief had set on the table.

On that point, I guessed I was one step ahead of things, but that didn't make me want to see it any less.

"I told you I'd take something in trade," Chilly said, nodding at the beaver fur, "but if you're after your medicine bundle, I best warn you I ain't taking no trinkets."

"*Du ska,*" the princess told the chief.

She must have said it was time to open the bundle, 'cause the chief laid his wrinkled old hands on it. His fingers were knobby and bent, and it took him upward of a year and a day to unwrap the thing. Nobody blinked the whole time. When he got the job done, a puff no stronger than a baby's breath could have knocked over every man and chicken in the place.

Lying atop the glossy fur pelt was a solid gold crown. Looking at it pretty near started angels to singing in my head—that's what a something it was. It had spikes like a castle's turrets, and right smack dab in the middle of the tallest spike was a red stone the size of a sparrow egg. I figured that for a ruby. The way it gleamed in the lantern light didn't hardly seem possible. There weren't any diamonds or emeralds stuck in the crown, but there didn't hardly need to be, not the way that ruby set off all the gold around it. The whole thing blazed away bright as a Christmas tree lit by a hundred or more candles. You could tell right off it had been custommade to sit on some grand nabob's head.

The chief pushed it to the center of the table. For a blind man, he had a pretty good idea of what people wanted to see. I know my eye was pressed up tight against the peephole.

Chilly sat there gaping, looking dumb as a salamander about fire. You kind of got the idea that he was picturing himself wearing that crown and having people all the time bowing and scraping before him. I'd never seen a grown man look so dreamy. With all my heart I wanted to be long gone before he came back to earth. There wasn't any telling what he might do if he didn't get his hands on that crown.

"That real?" Goose Nedeau asked, breaking the spell.

"If it ain't," Chilly blustered, rushing to the crown's defense, "I don't know what is. Chief, I'd say you got yourself a hand of cards."

Chilly tore himself away long enough to dash upstairs to collect the chief's sacred medicine bundle. Soon as he took off, I found my right hand grabbing the pouch holding that crow's leg. Somehow it made me a smooch more confident to feel it in my palm, though when I held it up to my ear, it was quiet as midnight. Maybe it was still taking in the crown too.

The old deerskin bundle that Chilly brought down was the one I'd spied stashed atop the wardrobe many a time but had never been brave enough to peek inside. Naturally, it couldn't hardly compete with a beaver pelt for pretty, and though the two bundles were about the same size, whatever was inside the deerskin was twice as lumpy, with bulges all over the place.

The princess accepted it from Chilly as if handling something alive and passed it on to her father, who ran his fingers over the bundle as if knowing its every bump by heart. He talked to it some too, and, using both hands, lifted it up, sniffing deep as my ma did when burying her nose in my hair after bath night. It didn't look as though he'd ever get his fill of the smells inside that hide, and all the while he sniffed, his shoulders went up and up, got straighter and straighter, till he sat there tall as the young man he'd once been. I guess it's safe to say that as far as the chief was concerned, that sacred bundle was worth a whole wagonload of gold crowns from Europe. Seeing him shed years like that—it gave me the grit to go on.

When his nose finally had its fill, the chief set the bundle down gentle and spoke to the princess, sounding satisfied but impatient all in one breath.

"My father asks," the princess relayed, "what's taking so long."

"Professor," Chilly called out, his eyes still on the crown, "bring us a fresh deck."

The Professor brought over an unopened box and set it before Chilly, who cracked the seal and pounced on them cards, shuffling and twirling them for all he was worth. He couldn't help showing off his skills, even if he was dealing to a blind man. Watching him carry on so shameless brought to mind how little I'd seen when I'd first met up with him.

The chief, he sat there patient as moss. I didn't have any way of knowing for sure, but I liked to think there was a faint little something of a smile tickling his lips as he thought of me curled up behind him. He wasn't the only one trapped in amber either. Every gambler gathered round that table seemed struck dumb by the sight of the crown, especially Chilly, who seemed to drink deepest of the sight before us. Maybe that's why he got his fill first. Rousing himself, he looked around and didn't take kindly to having all those grubby eyes gawking at *his* crown. He broke the trance by wisecracking, "Boys, I learned everything I know from my ma."

"She must have been quite a lady," remarked Goose, who was so desperate to get a view of what had made everyone quiet that he'd fumbled out his specs.

"Oh, she was," Chilly said, making the cards fairly hum. "The only reason she married my pa was 'cause he had enough sense to let her do all the voting."

The banter earned a mean laugh or two, though not from me. I had a chore to do. Quiet as stardust and with my heart whirring as if it had wings, I tucked the pouch in a vest pocket below the one holding Chilly's watch and slid off my shelf to the floor. Running my fingers across the floorboards, I lifted out the ones that Ho-John had loosened up and leaned 'em against the wall. I wasn't real fond of opening up a hole in the floor again, 'cause there wasn't any telling what might slither up through it, but I didn't see any way around it either. When the time came for skedaddling, I didn't want to be fumbling with boards. I'd have lifted 'em out earlier except that till now I couldn't be sure that Chilly might not decide to pay me another visit to rattle me by the neck some more. But once the chief had pulled in, I knew Chilly wouldn't risk coming anywhere near me, not even if he discovered his pocket watch was missing. That's how I had told the chief to play her too. Let Chilly shuffle those cards to his heart's content, I'd said. It'd give me a chance to set things up on my side of the wall.

With the boards removed, I climbed back onto my shelf as careful and quick as could be. Only trouble was, I put more muscle into the *quick* than the *careful* and brushed against some crockery. One that was full of pickles crashed to the floor.

The voices out in the parlor hung up as if expecting a large timber to fall atop them. Chilly covered up by declaring, "Goose, you've got the clumsiest rats I've ever heard."

Tense as everyone was wound, that little joke set them to slapping their knees and roaring with laughter, which gave me a chance to settle onto my shelf, this time paying more attention to the careful than the quick.

The way Chilly went right on talking could have charmed swifts out of the clouds, so it wasn't long before the crowd forgot they'd heard anything smash at all. Back at the peephole, I could see that Chilly had the cards marching around fancier than a Fourth of July parade. All the while he shuffled, he talked, and all the while he talked, his eyes stayed glued to the chief's crown.

CHAPTER TWENTY-SIX

AFTER CHILLY HAD HEATED THE CARDS UP to his liking, he slapped the deck on the table to be cut, but the chief shook him off with a wag of his head. The way he stuck up for himself cheered me no end, though my smile went flat fast as the princess spoke out, saying, "My father doesn't want new cards."

My head snapped back and my tongue went all thick, 'cause this didn't fit any plan I'd laid out. Go for a new deck, I'd advised. Less likely to be marked, I'd said, though around Chilly there weren't no guarantees about such things. But the chief didn't play it that way at all, which blew to smithereens any chance I had of helping him. An old deck threw all the advantage to Chilly, 'cause he wouldn't even need me to work the telegraph but could read the back of the marked cards himself. The chief's request paralyzed everyone else in the place too, with nary an eye stuck anywhere but on Chilly.

"Why's that?" Chilly's smile had frosted up on him. "Don't he trust me?"

Or me? echoed inside my head.

Chilly's question was full of gunpowder, but the princess answered real level, "Of course he doesn't trust you, but this has nothing to do with that. My father had a vision that said the cards shouldn't be new. They feel too stiff."

Grabbing up the new deck, Chilly flung it over his shoulder hard enough to break glass. Next he leaned forward to take a good squint into the chief's eyes. It appeared to be hard work, staring down a blind man, though Chilly kept at it till satisfied that he'd done it up good and proper. Sitting back down, he turned huffy.

"Who am I to go against a man's vision," Chilly reasoned, amused-like. "Professor, bring us some used cards. I like a deck that's been limbered up some myself."

So the Professor ducked over behind the bar and brought out the satchel stuffed with the decks that Chilly and Goose spent their afternoons marking, and all I could do was stay curled up in the dark, praying for the best. What's more, the chief surprised everyone by grabbing the top deck in the bag and tossing it toward Chilly. He never even lifted it to his nose for a sniff.

"You're acting like a man who's had himself *some* vision," Chilly said, opening up the deck. "Would you like a shot of whiskey to help it along?"

"No whiskey." The princess didn't bother to ask her father about how to answer. "That's how you got the medicine bundle the first time. And no shuffling," she added. "Just deal 'em."

She spoke up extra loud on that last bit, as if talking to someone outside the room, which she was—me. The time had come to let loose some caws.

A twitchy silence grabbed hold of the parlor as Chilly let the cards fly, so there wasn't going to be any trouble over my being heard, provided I could find the strength to do what needed doing. What took care of that was dragging out the chief's leather pouch once again. The instant I touched it, a jolt shot up my arm to the back of my mouth, knocking loose a "caw-caw-caw" as high and crisp as any of the chief's.

Chilly stiffened up as if snakebit, not knowing whether the crow had come calling for him or the chief. The feverish red covering his cheeks flashed white, and he crimped the corner of the cards without even knowing it. Low and ghostly, he pleaded, "Not now. Not here."

Eyebrows went arching all over the place, but nobody

but me, the chief, the princess, and maybe Goose, who was turning ten shades of pale himself, had any idea of what had grabbed hold of Chilly. But *we* knew he was afraid his luck had been shot through the heart. Growling low, he reached for his lucky pocket watch, to ward off whatever the crow was up to. And that's when everything he'd ever done wrong his whole life long caught up to him, 'cause of course all he found was an empty pocket.

When he realized his watch wasn't where he expected, his fingers brushed over his back pockets, side pockets, and hidden pockets. The quicker his hands dodged around, the farther I shrank from my peephole, until finally he lurched back from the table as if scalding water had been dumped on his lap. By then he was searching all over himself, kicking his chair away from the table to check the floor and bellowing for all he was worth, "Goose! A man can't gamble proper with all this noise. Do something!"

Right away Goose passed the buck by shouting, "Ho-John! You know we don't tolerate crows around here. Do your job and get rid of that blame thing!"

Men and chickens were bumping and stumbling backwards from the table fast as they could, not knowing what to make of Chilly's contortions. The only ones to hold their ground were the chief, who pulled the crown closer, and the princess, who kept a firm grip on her father's shoulder.

"Ho-John!" Goose screamed.

There wasn't any answer from Ho-John, except for the clanking of his chains as he left the kitchen to scare off the crow. The back door creaked open and woke the dogs, who commenced to yipping and baying the instant Ho-John laid into a skillet with a wooden spoon. After a minute or so of deafening bangs on that pan, Ho-John took a rest. Not the dogs.

"I can't concentrate with such a ruckus," Chilly declared loudly, still patting down his coat and pants pockets.

"Ho-John!" Goose shouted above the din.

A half minute later the dogs fell quiet without a yelp. Plenty of men believe a good swift kick is the best way to learn a hound some manners, but Ho-John put his faith in lullabies. As soon as the dogs hushed, you could hear him singing low and scratchy.

"Finally," Chilly muttered. To get ahold of himself, he crossed his chest three times and drained his whiskey. That settled him some, after a shudder. Sitting back down, he scanned the faces of the men hanging back from the table. They were as pasty faced and round eyed a bunch of rabbits as could be imagined. One loud clap could have sent 'em all scampering back to their burrows.

Well, Chilly may have been in a tight fix, but he was still Chilly Larpenteur, which meant he knew how to bluff when he had to. Scowling, he said to the room at large, "Ain't we putting on a show tonight?" Then he laughed and added with a wave of his hand, "Come on back, boys. I think a wasp or something crawled down my shirt, but I'm all right now. Raring to go. Hold on to your war bonnet, Chief, 'cause here they come."

After all that, Chilly didn't bother arguing about shuffling, nor did he even try to sneak something into the deck. He just launched into flinging cards as if someone had stomped on his toe. But he slowed down right fast. You see, the chief wasn't picking anything up, nor even letting the princess handle 'em. Laying his hands atop the pile, he hid what Chilly had dealt out from everyone including me. It appeared that the chief wasn't satisfied with any part of my plan and had ideas of his own about getting back his sacred bundle. I nearly wore my neck out, fast as I was shaking my head no, but there wasn't much I could do to stop him, other than caw again, and all of a sudden I felt too weak to manage it. About all I had the strength for was leaning closer to the peephole to see what came next.

"They won't bite," Chilly teased, 'cause he wanted the chief looking over those cards worse than anyone. Without that, the telegraph was a bust and he was high and dry, couldn't even read their markings, not with the chief's hands covering them.

"My father likes them where they are," the princess declared.

Hearing that made me feel as though I'd swallowed a tack.

"Ain't he planning on even giving them a sniff?" Chilly asked.

"No."

"I guess a man's entitled to lose any way he wants to," Chilly grunted, his good humor going threadbare fast.

Without another word, Chilly scooped up his cards and got busy admiring them. Any other day he would have held his hand tight to his chest and sighted 'em up by squinting down his nose. But not now. Today he fanned his cards so that the gents behind him could study his hand as if they were playing it. I'm bound to think that Chilly sort of invited their attention to create a little diversion, 'cause while everyone was craning to see what he held in his left hand, his right hand was busy dipping down his boot and up his sleeves for hold-out cards that he slipped on top of the deck, smooth as silk.

"Cards?" Chilly sounded pleasant as Sunday dinner.

"We'll play these," the princess stated.

"You can have some new ones if you want 'em," Chilly offered, all generous. "I wouldn't want these gents to think I was taking advantage of you."

"My father's happy with these."

Chilly raised his eyebrows some at that, straining to act amused, but it was a fainthearted job. You could tell he was more than half sunk by my caws and his missing watch. Any satisfaction I'd taken from his predicament was dwindling fast—not that I felt sorry for helping to put him in such a tight spot, but just that it didn't seem smart to gloat on it. We weren't out of the woods yet.

"Pleased you like 'em," Chilly huffed. "I'm not quite so fond of mine. But I think three new ones ought to do me fine."

Discarding three, he dealt himself the cards he'd sneaked atop the deck.

I opened my mouth to try cawing again, but nothing came out, not even when I squeezed the chief's pouch. What made me so mute? Maybe the way Chilly flashed a look at my peephole that could have sizzled bacon. Desperate, I lifted the leather pouch up to my ear, thinking it might tell me what to do. I had the right idea there; the pouch did try to tell me something. But whatever was inside that bag spoke Indian, which I couldn't understand a word of. I shook it some, to try and wake it up, and pleaded with it silent-like to switch over to English, but that didn't get me anywhere. To block out the jabbering, I tucked it away again. And all the while, Chilly was sliding his new cards into his hand and fanning them apart. One of the gawkers behind him whistled low in appreciation of what handsome additions they were. I felt a bead of sweat trickling down my armpit.

By rights, the chief should have shown his hand first. As the dealer, Chilly should have gone last, but he must have still been rattled by my cawing 'cause he couldn't be bothered to wait. With a coarse laugh, he announced, "Sorry, Chief." And he spread his cards face-up on the table, which meant he couldn't go making any changes to them once the chief showed his. At least I'd helped the chief out that much. Though if you'd asked me, I would have said it was an outstanding case of too little, too late.

Chilly had packed his hand with three kings on top of a pair of eights, which made for a full house. Those three kings were some of his favorite royalty, as a matter of fact. I'd seen them come visiting Chilly's hand a half-dozen times this past week alone. He leaned across the table to collect the chief's crown, cackling all the way. I nearly called out "No" to stop him, but someone else beat me to it.

"Wait!"

That was the princess. Chilly hung up, maybe expecting to hear her beg for another chance, but that's not what he got. What he saw next reddened his face brighter than a blacksmithy's forge could have managed. When the chief lifted his hands, the princess gave his cards a flip, revealing four aces.

And a joker.

The joker was a wild card, so it counted as an ace too, making five aces.

I'm not entirely sure a royal flush would have whipped such a crowd of aces. Maybe the only hand strong enough to do that would have six aces in it, and even Chilly Larpenteur hadn't figured out a way to slip that many into a game of five-card.

CHAPTER TWENTY-SEVEN

A BAG OF MARBLES WOULD HAVE BEEN more talkative than the men around that table. Goose kept pawing at his bloodshot eyes as if he couldn't trust what he was seeing, and the Professor wore a skinny, sideways smirk that said he was enjoying himself for the first time in weeks. As for Chilly, he appeared to have just discovered the sky was falling. He couldn't get a word out.

What we'd seen didn't make sense, not unless the chief had somehow or other cheated. Or had even more powers than he'd told me about. Or . . . well, that pretty much covered it, but at the moment I was feeling too giddy to care which way he'd done it. So long as Chilly got his just deserts, I was well satisfied. If the chief had the power to turn deuces into aces, so be it. And if he was cheating, then let a lightning bolt blast me to ash for trying to help him, 'cause, well, I'd cast my lot and was sticking to it, even as Chilly's watch ticked away like a second heart above my own.

The chief's hands groped across the table toward his sacred bundle. Once his fingers found it, he picked the bundle up careful as a sleeping baby and set it down next to the crown. Wrapping up his prizes took the chief a bit, and all the while he was fumbling with them, Chilly's cheeks were glowing like a chimney fire, his knuckles pressing down so hard on the table that they looked about to burst.

But not till the chief started to stand as if to leave did Chilly find something to say. "Where in tarnation do you think you're headed?"

He sounded off his feed but still a force to be reckoned with.

"Home," the princess told him.

"Not yet, you're not," Chilly declared. "Goose, Professor, help the chief back down."

Goose and the Professor stepped forward, more than a little sheepish about having to bully a blind old Indian and a young girl, but the princess and her father eased down all on their own, looking proud but mighty outnumbered. I covered Chilly's watch with one hand and the chief's pouch with the other, trying to keep both quiet.

Then Chilly stroked his goatee some and sized up the chief for a longish spell, during which the chief held himself straight and speechless. Everyone else in those parts might as well have been cut from wax—me included. After a while, Chilly leaned back to chuckle.

"Wasn't that slick?" Chilly asked the room. "I ain't for sure positive how he pulled it off, and I ain't going to hold my breath waiting for him to spill it. I'll just say he has my admiration. But admirations only stretch so far." Slapping a hand on the table, he leaned forward and demanded another hand of cards. "For the crown. You can keep that old bundle of yours."

After relaying all that to the chief, who answered softly, the princess said for him, "What do you have to bet?"

That strung Chilly up good, for a gambler couldn't very well force someone to gamble for nothing. He wouldn't have been any better than a highwayman if that was his game, and there wasn't any way Chilly would suffer being lumped together with riffraff so low as that. To hold his head up, he'd have to put something on the table that matched the chief's crown for price. Chilly knew it, and the chief knew it, and so did every hanger-on in that room.

"Why, I've got a whole passel of valuables," Chilly bragged, steamed that anyone would dare think otherwise. "Ought to be something I can find to suit your fancy."

That's when Chilly started rooting through his pockets for something besides his watch. First off he plunked down a solid silver snuffbox, but the chief wasn't having none of that. The princess said he didn't trust anything with square corners. Chilly thumped the side of his head as if he couldn't have heard right, but then, without comment, he lifted the diamond pin off his shirt front and tossed it on the table. When the chief rubbed the diamond between his thumb and finger, it spurted out of its setting like a slippery melon seed, skittering across the table. The chief said—through the princess, of course—that he had plenty of seeds and didn't need any more.

Chilly dipped deeper into his pockets and came up with a gold cigar clipper and a pair of gold dice, but everyone could see that Chilly's pile of loot didn't come close to matching up with the chief's crown. And now that the chief had his sacred bundle back, he wasn't proving so easy to boss.

"What else then?" the princess asked.

Chilly stomped off to our room and come back with a silk sack of gold and paper money that had been hid I don't know where.

"Count it," the princess said for her father.

So Chilly laid it out in rows and stacks, coming up with nearly a thousand dollars. He may have never learned to read or write, but when it came to tallying money, he rattled off numbers as if he'd been born and raised in a bank. I couldn't even begin to speculate on what amount of those stacks was my share of our winnings, not that I felt particularly proud about it.

"Nothing more?" the princess asked.

"Well, I don't know what else there might be," Chilly said, so put out that one of his cheeks took to quivering on him.

When the chief heard that news from the princess, he laughed from the belly, which started him coughing. After his throat finally settled down, he spoke to the princess, who said, "Put up this inn, with everything else, and he'll think about one more hand."

Goose Nedeau sagged backwards a step at that reckoning, but nobody paid his stumble much mind. They were too busy watching Chilly, who sat there flaring his nostrils and trying to pace himself so's he wouldn't explode. (Now's probably as good a time as any to mention how I feel about explosions—deathly skittish.) After a bit, Chilly couldn't take it no more and told 'em, "I don't own but half of this place."

That widened the eyes round that table plenty. Except for Goose and the Professor, there wasn't a gent present what knew that Chilly had any say in the inn. You could see they didn't take kindly to the notion either, not considering all the money they dropped into Chilly's lap so regular. As that news sunk in, several of the gamblers began warming up to the chief and princess, who were conferring.

"Which half's yours?" the princess asked at last.

"The good half," Chilly declared.

That set off more jabbering, until the princess hushed everyone by announcing, "If the good half includes the hounds out back, my father says yes."

"Done," Chilly growled, not caring one whit about Goose's objections that the dogs were his.

Throwing himself back from the table, Chilly charged upstairs to collect a curled-up sheet of yellowed paper and the silver box where he stowed other gamblers' good-luck pieces. Tucking the box into the crook of his arm, he tossed the paper, which must have been the deed to the inn, atop everything else already before the chief as if daring him to ask for more.

Me, I lay there wishing I could close my eyes, 'cause I surely couldn't stand to face whatever might be coming down the pike next.

"That's the whole shebang," Chilly announced. "My half of this inn and everything else I own in this world. Win the next hand and it's all yours."

"What about that?" The princess nodded toward the silver box Chilly still held.

"You wouldn't take away a man's good luck, would you?"

"That wouldn't bother me," the princess answered. "But let me ask you this: will you let us leave when this hand is over?"

"On my word as a gentleman."

I had to muffle a cough when I heard that promise.

"Then keep your good luck," the princess said after talking to her father.

Holding up his box, Chilly raised its lid and poured everything inside it onto his side of the table. Thirty to forty lucky charms came tumbling out, everything from the clamshell named Sherry-Ann to those false ivory teeth, with three or four rabbits' feet in the mix, along with a walrus tusk and chinese coins, rear molars, jug corks, pictures of sweethearts, and, well, I don't think I can go on naming 'em all without losing my mind. Chilly stood behind that mound, brimming with confidence, beaming with vigor, 'cause he'd found a way to replace his gold watch.

And all that while the chief's pouch lay still as a forgotten promise in my vest.

CHAPTER TWENTY-EIGHT

AND THEN CHILLY STARTED FEELING HIS OATS. He wanted a new deck of cards to change his luck, and once he got the new deck, he had to get acquainted with it. That took several minutes, but the better he got to know those cards, the more swaggery he swelled. Finally, when he had everything in that deck stacked the way he wanted it, he said real theatrical-like, "Long as we don't hear any more crows, I'm set." Speaking up loud enough for even a bird perched on the roof to hear, he added, "Any more crows come calling, I ain't resting till I've loaded every last one of them with enough lead to sink the *Rose Melinda*."

That pinched me pretty hard, 'cause something was stirring in the chief's pouch, making me think I was due for another caw, but the princess saved me from having to try by saying, "It's too late at night for them to be out."

"Glad to hear it," Chilly said. "That just leaves me with one request, Chief. It's a small one, and I hope you'll honor it."

The princess told her father, who nodded for Chilly to spit it out.

"This time around," Chilly began, "I want you to hold your cards like an honest-to-goodness poker player. No more of this leaving 'em lay. Seeing someone play that way gives me the willies."

The crowd wasn't all with Chilly on this one, not after learning about who owned the inn, though plenty felt the same as Chilly and wanted the chief to act proper. Others sided with the chief, claiming he ought to be allowed to play his hand any way he saw fit. Arguing broke out here and there, but the chief squashed all that by having his daughter say, "He can see his cards through his fingertips."

"Don't matter," Chilly maintained. "Holding 'em in your hand is what's proper."

One way or another he planned to get me a look at what the chief got dealt. Judging by how the chief kept shaking his head stubborn-like, I got the idea he was holding out, trying to protect me, but it never came to blows. The pouch in my vest pocket came to life before that could happen. At first the crow in that pouch spoke out in a voice that a raindrop could have drowned out, but don't go thinking it was satisfied to stay quiet. No, it had inherited the same kind of tongue as Buffalo Hilly and never took a rest but instead croaked louder and louder. Whatever it was blimblamming on about didn't do me any good 'cause dang if it wasn't stuck on speaking Indian. I tried to muffle it with my hands, and when that didn't work, I lifted it up to my mouth for a good shhh. Didn't matter. It kept right on twaddling away, marking me for a dead man soon as someone on the other side of the wall heard it.

"Not now," I hushed.

Loud as it was getting, I was going to be discovered any instant. Rolling over for a peek out the hole, I fully expected to find an eye peering back at me. No such thing though. Nobody out in the parlor had budged, not an inch, 'cause the princess was leaning over her father's ear, pretending to whisper to him behind a cupped hand. But really the only voice talking belonged to the crow in the pouch just a couple of feet behind them. The chief listened long and hard, even talked back twice, but the pouch kept on insisting till finally the chief threw up his hands as if fit to be tied and passed on some news to the princess, who said, "He'll hold his cards up on two conditions."

It appeared the pouch had convinced him.

"Just name 'em," Chilly said, all sunny.

"We pick the deck," the princess answered, "and no shuf-fling."

Right away Chilly knew he was up against the chief's visions again, so it wouldn't be any use trying to talk him out of it, not if he still wanted a chance to win that crown. Besides, now that he'd settled down a bit, he must have realized that it didn't matter what cards he dealt himself. They weren't the ones he planned on finishing with.

"Professor," Chilly barked, "bring back that satchel."

So all over again the chief latched on to whatever deck was on top and slid it across the table toward Chilly.

"Gentlemen," Chilly called out, "one more hand. All my worldly possessions against the chief's crown."

"*Tsa kic ti.*" The chief nodded in agreement.

The princess didn't have to bother passing on what her father had said. Everyone got the gist of it. The chief was ready to play cards.

This time when Chilly dealt, the cards snapped out of his hand and skidded across the table as if landing on ice. I watched with hawk eyes and have to say it surely looked like he was playing square. It was the top card that went flying every time, not the second from the top, or the bottom, or anywhere in between.

That didn't mean much though. No matter how many good-luck pieces he'd stockpiled, Chilly's old reliable had always been hold-outs. That was the way he tried to steal the first hand, and it appeared to be his choice for the second too.

And all he was waiting on, before pulling out those extra cards, was news from me concerning what the chief held in his hand.

Good as his word, the chief picked up his cards and fanned them out so the princess could see 'em. That also made it time for me to start operating the telegraph. Just thinking about it made me gulp so loud, I'm surprised there wasn't a whole new go-around about the rats in Goose's walls. But everyone stayed focused on Chilly and the chief, hoping to catch one or the other of them cheating.

What happened next isn't anything I care to try explaining twice; once is strain enough. One by one the cards marched into the chief's hands, and I nearly dropped the leather pouch and thumped my head on the upper shelf watching them arrive. Four aces in a row showed up, followed by—you guessed it—the wild old joker, same as before. It was a feat that had to rank up there with walking on water and spinning straw into gold. Rubbing my eyes didn't change nothing either. What's more, when the princess told the chief what he'd been dealt, he nodded once as if that's what he'd expected to hear.

But just as puzzling was Chilly's reaction to those cards. He took a long, shameless squint at their backs, scowling all the while as if peering into a fogbank 'cause apparently he couldn't read their markings. Finally, he up and said, "I hope you got something pretty, Chief. This time you're really going to need it."

The chief answered through the princess, "Pretty as my mother's smile."

"You wouldn't have another crown to wager on that, would you?"

That got quite a rise out of the crowd, who figured Chilly was joking, but I wasn't so sure. His voice had a terrible, ragged edge to it, and the way his eyes kept skipping up toward my peephole told me he was waiting to hear from his telegraph operator. Well, he'd be waiting a blue moon before I sent him any news about all the aces congregating in the chief's hand.

"Only if you've got another inn," the princess answered, which drew an even bigger snort from the crowd.

As for what Chilly was holding, that was between him and the devil, 'cause this time around he pressed his cards so tight against his chest that no one else could see them. All I knew for positive was that my pantry shelf was getting smaller and more cramped by the second. There didn't hardly seem to be enough air to breathe either. I had me such a sinking, achy feeling about what Chilly might have slipped himself that I squashed the chief's pouch up against my ear again, but wouldn't you know, now I couldn't hear a single word of

Indian coming out of it. About the only thing I could hear was the ticking of Chilly's watch.

The princess's comeback set Chilly to arranging and rearranging his cards like some old auntie with a bouquet of flowers that won't behave. He cast my peephole a steely glance over the top of his hand before announcing, "Chief, I've been studying these cards so long, my toes have all gone to sleep on me." And he stomped twice on the floor, as if trying to wake up his foot, though I'm the one he was really talking to.

"Careful," the princess warned. "You'll upset the rats again."

Everyone had a good chuckle over that till Chilly trumped her one higher by saying, "I always figured I'd wear me a crown someday."

That got an even bigger rise out of the crowd, but when all the guffawing died away, the princess shot right back, "Too bad it won't be today."

Her answer stirred the crowd up so much that Chilly had to signal for quiet. The hand he held up was the same one that had been busy as a bee adding hold-outs to the cards in his other paw and ditching the cards he didn't want somewhere under the table—all of it done right under every nose in that room without raising an eyebrow. The man was a marvel.

"Talk's cheap," Chilly said. "Let's see them cards."

A hush fell over the entire world, or at least the part of it that I could hear. It reminded me of how everlastingly quiet my brothers and sisters had gone when Pa had walked me down to the steamboat that had carried me away from home. Everything was leading up to something that couldn't be reversed.

"You first," the Princess said.

"How about we spread 'em out at the same time?" Chilly answered.

The chief agreed to that.

"One," Chilly counted.

"*Due tsa,*" the chief counted.

"Two."

"*Dopa.*"

"Three."

"*Dami.*"

They laid 'em out.

When they were done, there wasn't a pair of eyes that wasn't bugging, except for the chief's, which were white and blind as ever.

Chilly had packed his hand with four aces and a joker, same as the chief. Lumping their cards together made for eight aces and two jokers . . . in one deck.

I guess Chilly wanted everyone to know that he could best

the chief at his own game. What he hadn't figured on was the chief playing the same game all over again.

When Chilly saw the chief lay out four aces and a joker too, he looked gut shot. His face went all white and billowy as a sail, and he stared straight ahead at my little peephole. I hope I never live to see eyes burning toward me like that again. Fiery comets couldn't sear you no hotter.

CHAPTER TWENTY-NINE

I TURNED ALL EGGSHELL—a single tap could have cracked me into a thousand pieces. Tight as I was gripping the chief's pouch, I must have been hoping for advice but none got delivered, leastways not in English. Think that didn't make me want to cry? No time though.

Chilly had shoved back from the table, sending his chair tumbling as he straightened up and grabbed at his vest. His eyes were dancing wild, and he could only have been reaching for one thing: his pocket pistol. A second later he was pointing a barrel big as a cannon at President Washington's portrait and me behind it.

I rolled off my shelf without a worry about knocking any crocks loose. Inside the chief's pouch, it felt as if a pair of wings was beating, trying to get out. When I dropped through the hole in the floor, I banged my hip a good one but bit back any whimpers, 'cause Chilly was bellowing, "I been double-crossed!" He sounded as though run through by a Pawnee war lance.

There followed a bunch of other shouts, most of which came all at once and went along the lines of this:

"Look out!"

"Crazy fool!"

"Ha ka ta!"

"I'm done!"

Judging from the thumps and crashes I heard, gents and Indians must have been diving for cover everywhere.

All that went mum when Chilly fired his pistol, giving my ears the rings worse than a bell tower. Crockery exploded above me. Pickle juice rained down. I fell all the way to the ground and took off crawling.

Fast as my arms and legs were moving, you might have mistook me for a centipede, if there'd been enough light to see by. Bumping into Ho-John's cache of runaway supplies, I raised my head too high and cracked against a timber. The conk laid me flat for a second or two, though not for long, not with Chilly roaring behind me, "He's gone!"

The hole in the pantry floor wasn't a secret any longer, which I felt mighty bad about, considering the fix it would leave Ho-John in. But Chilly's shout sent me rolling again, for fear he'd reloaded. When I reached the edge of the house,

I scrambled out and tore off into the darkness. Once I hit the road, I headed for the levee and the nearest steamer. If only someone would get me out of St. Louis, I'd do anything they wanted of me—wash dishes, scrub spittoons, even haul wood. I wasn't going to worry about slivers or deep water or nothing. I'd be brave if I had to.

As I went pounding down that dirt road, Stavely's Landing and home popped into my head as if cast there by a magician. A whiff of Ma's cooking rolled right up my nose without the slightest hitch. This was to the good, 'cause it was fast becoming clear that planning ahead wasn't one of my strong suits. What had I been thinking of doing after helping out the chief? Well, I hadn't considered it one iota. Too wrapped up in everything else, I guess. Lucky for me that running home didn't take any foresight at all. Where else would someone stand up for me, whether I was right or wrong, and get around to boxing my ears only later, after all the company had left? Home was the place where I had a cabin full of brothers and sisters all looking up to me for no better reason than that I'd been there the longest. It was also where I had a ma and pa who'd mostly done their best by me without any pay and not too much thanks either. That's why every puny muscle I owned was pulling me there.

But home was a long ways off. A hundred and sixty-some miles off, and every one of those miles was dark and full of woods and poisonous snakes and mangy dogs and half-starved panthers and ornery homesteaders and whooshing thunderstorms and lonesome wood ticks and . . . The list wound around me tighter and tighter, faster and faster, till I could barely suck down a breath. One hundred and sixty-some miles looked to be the distance to the ends of the world.

And not far behind me, Chilly was screaming and cursing and breaking things like a man who was three-quarters volcano and one-quarter jaws of hell. I'd barely got a stone's throw from the inn before I heard its front door slam open. Checking over my shoulder, I saw Chilly come busting outside, with the Professor right on his coattails.

Well, if I was ever going to make it home, I had to do something and do 'er pretty quick, so I dove into a patch of woods along the creek. When I struck an old oak about four steps in, I gave up running and started climbing. Hiding in its limbs seemed safer than sounding like some bear thrashing through the brush. Needing both hands for pulling myself up, I stuffed the chief's pouch in a vest pocket and shimmied upward till the air went so thin, I couldn't hardly breathe. At first I didn't dast check how high I might have gone, but finally I chanced a peek and found I was barely off the ground. Four or five feet at the most.

So upward I struggled again, going mostly by touch and

smell, 'cause my eyes were nailed shut tight as coffins. The next time I looked, I found myself about as high as Ma and Pa's cabin roof. There I stayed, figuring if it wasn't high enough, they could have me, 'cause one foot higher would have done me in, fast as my heart was whim-whamming away. And the sound of Chilly's watch in my ears? Loud as a blacksmith clanging on a horseshoe. I'd barely got a good hug on the tree's back side before Chilly and the Professor come charging along. I swear they didn't look any bigger than sugar ants way down below me as they peered every which way in the dark.

"I ain't got the foggiest how that old Injun did it," Chilly was roaring, "but when I get my hands on that boy I'll find out quick enough."

"You sure Zeb was in on it?" the Professor asked, clearly not so quick to judge.

"Why do you think he took off running?"

"Maybe 'cause you was shooting at him. 'Sides, the boy couldn't have had anything to do with all them aces. How you going to explain them?"

"I can't," Chilly growled. "And that's my point exactly. There's a whole lot more going on here than I can figure, like how come a deck from that satchel wasn't marked ten ways from Sunday. Answer me that."

"You'll have to ask Goose," the Professor came back. "He's the last one I seen tinkering with them cards."

"That old fool! And why didn't that worthless boy warn me a lick?"

"Maybe the wire broke."

"Don't give me none of that. Just fetch them hounds. When I get my hands on that boy, I lay I'll get to the bottom of all this."

If my blood hadn't already been standing still, hearing that would surely have brought it to a halt. They were going to have me treed in no time. Sitting where I was, I'd already done half the job for 'em. And every tick of Chilly's watch seemed to be calling out, *Here I am!*

"You want Ho-John too?" the Professor asked.

"Can you name me anyone else can handle those mutts?" Chilly spat out. "'Course I want him, and I want him tonight. Not sometime next week. Just send 'em out here, then go help Goose hold on to that Injun."

Once the Professor was gone, Chilly kicked dirt and thrashed about and called out my name some, sounding as if he had the sweetest, most special treat for me in all creation. Pretty soon the hounds started baying, and Ho-John in his chains was herding them down the road. All of a sudden my blood started moving again.

"We're after that boy," Chilly shouted above the dogs.

"Need something to sniff up," Ho-John said.

"Well, go get it," Chilly yelled. "Do I have to do all the dang-blamed thinking around here?"

Off Ho-John shuffled, leaving Chilly behind to lay out everything that had ever gone wrong his whole life long. It was quite a list and mighty impressive, ranging from his pa running off with that duchess to his ma being strict as a judge about his upbringing. Chilly was cussing out the crow that'd been plaguing him and wondering how it'd made his precious watch disappear when Ho-John came hurrying back with my blanket in one hand and a lantern in the other. I cracked open my eyes enough to see that the lantern threw shadows everywhere, especially across Chilly's face, which looked long and mean as an ax head. The dogs buried their snouts in my blanket and got the idea right away. Drat my luck but they had to be the most intelligent pack of hounds I'd ever run across. First thing they did was make a beeline for the oak tree I was clinging to the back side of.

There they were, howling and bouncing higher and higher off the oak's trunk. And there I was, clenching my teeth and squeezing my eyes shut as if that would somehow hide me better. But what saved me in the end was Ho-John.

"Ain't nothing up that tree," he called out. "They just re-membering some old coon they had up there last week."

If Chilly had been paying attention to anything but the chief's crown, he'd have known that Ho-John was laying out a bold-faced lie. Nobody had had those dogs out in the woods since the telegraph had been up and running. No, what Ho-John was doing was saving my skin, even after I'd sunk his escape plans, and I daren't even sing out a peep of thanks.

"Well, get 'em moving," Chilly shouted. "We ain't got all night."

So Ho-John handed off the lantern and waded into the brush, where he lifted the lead hound up in his arms gentle as a lamb and carried him back to the road. Setting the dog down, he gave him a slap on the rump. The hound took off baying, with the rest of the pack close on his heels. Ho-John rambled after them, remarkable fast for a man shackled by irons. Chilly brought up the rear, swaying the lantern from side to side, searching for sign while cursing a blue streak and trying to keep up.

I stayed way up that oak, trying to remember how to breathe. Once I got my lungs working, I tried backing down from my perch, 'cause it wouldn't be long before Chilly figured out they'd missed my track and come doubling back. Trouble was, I couldn't bring myself to let go of the tree trunk. The idea of climbing down churned me worse than going up had;

the only thing I could sell myself on was jumping off all at once. 'Course, I might break a leg or arm, but that couldn't be any worse than staying put till Chilly doubled back, could it? I was still arguing with myself about that one when a whole new row broke out at the inn as a crowd pushed and shoved its way through the front door. There wasn't enough light to see much by, but I could hear Goose carrying on.

"Now hold on, now!" Goose shouted. "Not so fast now! Who elected you sheriff?"

The men answering him were facing away from me, so their voices didn't carry at all. Whatever they were shouting back sounded plenty hotted up though.

"And I say," Goose answered, "that this old redskin stays here till Chilly gets back."

That was when the grabbing and cussing started. There was yelling too, plenty of that, along with a bottle or two that got broke. Then came a gunshot. That got hold of everyone's ears real good and put the squabbling to rest.

Then one voice started laying down the law to all of them about something or other. I couldn't make out the words exactly, but you could tell by the tone that whoever was talking sounded like a judge or turnkey or constable or someone official.

"Ain't no good going to come of this," Goose warned, kind of whiny and defeated-like.

The man barking orders turned my way, and now I could hear him perfectly clear. "If it takes Chilly Larpenteur down a peg or two, that recommends it to me. You and Chilly keep this inn and give this blind old man the rest. That sounds fair enough, considering how you tried to cheat him."

It was the Professor talking, and there was a whole lot of agreeing from the crowd. Hardly anyone was bothering to tag along with Goose's view. Actually, I think he might have been entirely alone in the matter. I guess they were all plenty tired of Chilly's winning every time, especially now that they'd learned about the telegraph.

"You two better get going," the Professor advised.

A couple of people stepped away from the crowd, untied a pony from out front, and started down the road toward me. Goose tried to stop 'em till the Professor sicced a couple of men after him. Before long I saw it was the princess and the chief who were headed my way.

The oak where I was holed up had a large limb stretching out a mile or two above the road. Dropping down to my hands and knees, I summoned every wisp of courage I could manage and crawled along it, nearly losing my grip and plummeting to a pulpy death a half-dozen times at least. But I managed to hang on long enough to *pssst* as the pony passed beneath me.

They came to a stop, the princess searching around for me.

"Way up here," I whispered.

Looking upward, the princess said, "Excuse us, but we're running for our lives."

"What do you think I'm doing?" I groused, kind of tart-like.

"You can't run very far sitting in a tree," she pointed out.

But the chief cut us both off. *"Tsa ki ha!"*

Following that, the chief and princess gnawed at each other a short minute before the princess took a deep breath and said, "My father wants to know if you're done with his pouch."

"Not exactly."

"What else do you need it for?"

"To help me get out of here."

When the princess passed that on, the chief gave a quick answer back.

"Swing down and ride with him," the princess ordered. "So you won't leave a trail for the dogs."

"But you're headed right for Chilly," I said.

"Not for long," she told me.

I thought it over a tiny bit and didn't see as I had much choice in the matter.

"All right," I grumbled. "I'm coming down."

The princess walked the pony forward a step or two. Dying ten times over, I dangled myself off the branch till my toes could touch the horse's rump—maybe that limb wasn't so high up as I'd thought, though it was plenty high for my tastes. Laying one hand on the chief's shoulder for balance, I dropped down, feeling as though I was falling off the evening star.

And that's how I got away: on the back of a broken-down old Indian pony, hanging on to the shoulders of Chief Standing Tenbears while fighting off sneezes due to horsehair and war bonnet feathers that kept tickling my nose. Soon as I handed the chief his pouch, he started chanting a song that sounded happy as a basket full of larks.

CHAPTER THIRTY

WE STUCK TO THE ROAD AROUND A CURVE and up and down a dip, but then took to the woods on an old deer path. Narrow and grown over as that trail was, I never would have noticed it, not even come daylight, but the princess picked it out easy as one-two-three.

Not too long after that a clingy drizzle started falling. It fit my mood like a black glove, 'cause I couldn't quite shake the notion that Chilly would sooner or later track me down. And when I got tired of trying not to fuss about what'd happen then, I switched over to feeling glum about Ho-John and how I'd sunk his chances. Once Chilly sat down and figured out how those pantry floorboards had got loosened, he'd be shouting for Ho-John's head. Oh, I tried to tell myself it had been an accident, that I hadn't meant to drag anyone else down with me, but that didn't smooth the waters any. All round, it was a pretty gloomy ride, especially after the princess got it in her head to start acting all chipper. What improved her mood so was the drizzle.

"It'll knock down our scent," she said.

Well, I knew that. I was about to tell her so too when the wind gusted, carrying the baying of Goose's hounds. My haunches went tight as springs above that pony, but soon as the wind died off, their barking faded away and I breathed easy (in between struggling not to sneeze). Then the wind came snaking back, this time from a different direction and carrying Chilly's shouts: "Ho-John? Ho-John!"

He sounded close enough to grab my ankle, though I couldn't spy him anywhere near 'bouts. By and by, the princess spotted the tiniest twinkle way off through the woods, and we figured that for his lantern.

"Ho-John!" Chilly was yelling. "Don't you go running on me!"

Then the wind shifted directions again, covering up Chilly's voice with the creaking of tree limbs and the rustling of leaves and even the ringing of church bells clear from town, but hearing him that brief bit made the chief order the princess to hold up. He adjusted his warbonnet that way he did when listening to what the crow was saying. After a little, the chief whispered a question to the pouch, which he'd dropped atop his head the instant I'd handed it off to him. Still hanging on to the chief's shoulders, I heard the pouch reply in Indian. It didn't sound none too happy. Back and forth the chief and crow went till the wind swung around, blowing Chilly's threats our way again.

"You ain't going nowhere, Ho-John," Chilly yelled. "Not with those dogs giving away your every move."

I asked the princess in a low voice what the chief and that crow were going on about, hoping they were figuring out some way to give Ho-John a hand, but that wasn't the case at all.

"They're talking over which way to go," she said.

"But Ho-John's in trouble," I pointed out.

"And we aren't?"

"I think maybe I need to go help him."

"What could you do?" the princess scoffed.

The way she made my rescuing Ho-John sound laughable gave me the pluck to say, "Maybe I can distract Chilly."

"By getting yourself get caught?"

"I hope not, but if that's what it takes . . . " The words trailed off on me, as happens when you're not exactly sure how brave you're prepared to be.

"Well, don't let us slow you down," she said, though maybe with a touch of admiration. The only reason I say that is because she begrudgingly added, "We'll wait up the trail for a while."

"Fair 'nough," I told her.

Sliding off the back of the pony felt like going down in deep water for the third time. The woods were already mucky dark and the drizzle had soaked me to the skin, so I might as well have been sinking into the river. I'm sorry to have to say it, but I hung on to that pony's bristly tail till the princess walked him out of my grasp. Within seconds they'd disappeared down the trail, the chief and crow whispering all the way. That made it just me and the trees, the nearest one being a hickory with branches that seemed to be clawing at me, but even that wasn't enough prodding to move me toward that tiny light way off in the woods. Both my feet liked it right where they were, even when I tried reasoning with them. Pleading didn't work either. I was just about to try ordering them forward when Chilly shouted, "Wait up now, Ho-John. If you got any idea what's good for . . . "

But then the gust died off and I couldn't make out the tail end of his threat. When the wind came back next, it'd swung around behind me, and I figured there was a chance it'd carry my voice to Chilly without my having to convince my feet to budge an inch. That was all the encouragement I needed to bawl out in a hurry, "Chilly! This way! I got Ho-John! Right here! Can you hear me? If you can . . . "

My voice was hoarse by the time the wind shifted away, but at least my plan appeared to be working, 'cause that lantern light started growing a touch bigger and Chilly was answering me. "That you, boy? Just stay right where you are. I'm coming. Don't you move a foot."

Then the wind sashayed back my way, which meant it was my turn again to cut loose. "Over here!"

Back and forth we went as the wind played its tricks, blowing this way and that and occasionally dying to a whisper. Chilly and his lantern drew closer and closer, while the night kept on swallowing more and more black till it felt about to smother my soul—if Chilly didn't find it first. The only thing that kept me going was the thought that Ho-John might be getting away, so at least some good would come of my suffering an end too terrible for words.

"Consarn it, boy! Where'd you get to?"

Mixed up with all his bullyragging was the occasional wind-carried sound of the hounds far and gone away, which gave Chilly pause and made him yell for me all the louder, his temper just shaking and blasting, 'cause even with a lantern he couldn't follow the deer trail we'd been on and kept bumbling into thickets that tore at his sleeves and pants. Nearer he prowled, till he wasn't but twenty or thirty yards distant. His raging face and tangled hair were flashing in and out of the light as he swung the lantern to and fro.

"Boy!" he bellowed. Then lower, to himself, he added, "When I get my hands on you . . . "

Still as a moth, I pressed against the trunk of that nearby

hickory and tried to shut my eyes, though—wouldn't you know—this time they wouldn't close for nothing. What's more, my lower jaw set to trembling, my hands hung limp and useless at my sides, and something tinier than a cricket was chirping in my throat. I could feel a faint coming on fast, but before it hit, the wind whipped around one more time, bringing with it the hell-bent yipping of hounds. It sounded as though the chase was over and they'd treed someone.

That stopped Chilly cold. He spun around twice right where he stood, not knowing what to think about the change in the dogs' barking. Into the wind he shouted, "Boy!" And then, "Ho-John!"

I squeezed against that tree trunk for all I was worth. Chilly had slogged so close by then that I hadn't dared a peep for several minutes. And then, maybe because Chilly's gold watch was still ticking in my vest pocket, my luck held and the wind kept right on carrying the yelping of the hounds to Chilly.

"If I ever . . . " Chilly threatened. "Boy!" Holding the lantern high, he inched all the way around again, peering into the gloom as he called, "You know what needs doing. Come on in now." He kept turning. "Won't nothing bad happen to you." Then under his breath, "Excepting when I get my hands on you."

And all the while the hounds went wilder and crazier till

Chilly couldn't stand listening to them no more and shouted, "Urgggg!" Giving up on me, he started punching his way back out of the thicket I'd lured him into. He was heading back toward the dogs.

The wind held steady for another couple of minutes—going on centuries—pulling Chilly away from me. And off to the west and south, a thunderstorm reared its head, sparking the clouds up good and whipping the wind even harder. I hung on to the hickory, waiting, waiting, and when Chilly was a good hundred yards gone, I bolted for the chief and princess. By the time I caught up to them, the drizzle had turned to sheets of rain and there wasn't nothing but falling water to be heard. It was such a lovely sound and the downpour had soaked me so completely that I figured it was safe to cry. Nobody'd notice.

And so I did, 'cause I was so relieved to have done something right and lived to tell about it. Just then, a stab of lightning turned the woods into daylight, showing me the chief and princess holed up under a tree. Standing right beside them was a third person who was so large and round in shape that it looked sort of like Ho-John.

CHAPTER THIRTY-ONE

I NEAR JUMPED INTO HO-JOHN'S ARMS but held off, not sure if my eyes had been playing tricks on me. That flash of lightning hadn't lasted but two beats before everything flicked back to black. What if I'd only been seeing what I wanted to? Maybe someone else was blocking the trail we'd been headed down. I was busy wishing for a white stallion to hop aboard and thunder away on when a second stab of lightning split open the night, revealing Ho-John right where I'd thought he'd been—half drowned beside the princess and chief.

"But the dogs . . . " I sputtered, flopping an arm in the direction Chilly had gone. 'Course, by then the second flash had faded and nobody saw my gesture.

"I found them a real raccoon in a tree," Ho-John said from the darkness, "and left them to it." He shuffled forward a step to drop a hand on my shoulder. "Seems you've done yourself proud all over the place."

Hearing that swelled me up, till I had a thought. "But how'd you ever get away from Chilly?"

"Seems the back of his head ran into a tree branch," Ho-John said. "And when he came to, me and the dogs were gone."

I think there might have been a smile to his voice, though I was only guessing—I'd never heard one there before and in the dark I couldn't be sure.

"And now where you going?" I asked.

"Circling back to town. I know where there's a skiff might get me across the river."

"On such a night as this?" I gulped. "On your own?" I couldn't fathom taking a tippy boat over deep waters in the dark with the wind just a-whipping and rain coming down like needles. But I seen that he meant to do it, which didn't leave me but one thing to say, though I wished I could have managed to get it out a little louder and braver sounding than I did. "I could go with you."

"Skiff's only got room for one," Ho-John answered, which sounded like a barefaced lie and for which I was eternally grateful.

"Well, at least let me give you some good luck."

"You got some to spare?"

Pulling Chilly's gold watch out of my vest pocket, I pressed it into Ho-John's thick hand.

"What's this?" he asked, deathly serious.

"A gift from Chilly."

Then came a pause. In the dark I couldn't tell Ho-John's mood, but I got a feel for it when he said defiant-like, "'Bout time he gave me something." Then he started talking faster. "You take care of yourself, Zeb. And mind you stay out of trees. There won't always be a Ho-John around to pretend you're not there."

"I'm beholding to you for that," I answered, choking a little on the words.

"Not anymore you're not."

Then the time for jawing was done. Ho-John started off toward the river, which had to be the riskiest possible direction for him to head, except that's where the skiff must be. I heard his shackles rattling and knew he wasn't going to sneak past anyone too easy, nor outrun anyone either, not unless it was Goose Nedeau. And how handy could they be for swimming if his boat got swamped?

"Wait," I said. "What about those chains?"

"What chains?" he answered, loping away.

I'm guessing that was the power of freedom talking, which left me convinced that he'd find some way to shed his irons, 'specially now that he had Chilly's watch. The last I saw of him was thanks to a lightning bolt. He was dodging and weaving through the woods fast as he could move.

When I turned to ask the chief and princess if they thought he'd make it, I found them moving off in the opposite direction. I had to run to catch up, and soon as I did, I latched on to the pony's tail as if it was a lifeline. My plans may have been sketchy, but I knew without a doubt that they didn't include being left alone in those woods.

CHAPTER THIRTY-TWO

———◆◆◆———

WE PUSHED ON THROUGH THE WOODS for most of an hour, which
stretched out longer than a lifetime of pins and needles. Every
step of the way it felt as though Chilly was going to grab me
by the hair any second and drag me back to the inn. But when
the storm eventually veered away to the southeast, pulling
the rain with it, and we still hadn't been caught, I dared to
feel a little tug of hope.

Whenever there was a fork in the trail, the princess picked
the way that took us farther and farther from any sign of civilization. It wasn't long before church bells from town sounded
tiny as harness bells over a hill. We didn't stray close to any
cabins, though once I saw a candlelight shimmering through
wetted-up branches and another time I heard voices arguing
about who had to sleep in the loft and a third time we hit

some wood smoke that smelled so cozy and homelike that I nearly sat down right there.

Finally the trail met up with a meadow. That's where we stopped, right on the lip of the woods.

The first thing the princess did was order me to help her pull a travois out from its hiding place under some cut spruce boughs. Shaped like a V, the travois was built of two lodge poles lashed together with rawhide. Tepee skin had been stretched across the poles to make a carrying shelf. Everything the chief and princess owned in the world appeared to be heaped on that sled, and kind of slapdash too, as though done in a hot-coal hurry.

It took all three of us to hook up the contraption. The point of the V was tied to the pony's back and the other two ends were left to drag on the ground, sort of like a wagon without wheels.

Satisfied that everything was in place, the princess said to me, "We wait."

"For anything in particular?" I asked.

"Birdman."

If she was going to dole out a pinch of this and a dash of that, I decided not to give her the satisfaction of asking for more, though I did at least mumble a thank-you for saving my skin.

"Your *worthless* skin?" she asked.

"That's the one," I agreed, which earned me a chuckle from the princess, along with a nod, as if to say, *You're welcome.* I was encouraged enough to ask something that'd been eating away at me since the inn. "Where'd all them aces come from?"

My question broadened her smile enough for me to see her teeth, which told me I could repeat myself till the cows came home—she wasn't going to answer.

So there we waited for Birdman, whose very name dropped the jitters on me. I couldn't help but picture some fierce Indian warrior painted green or blue with black feathers glued all over creation.

Somewhere in there a breeze swept the last of the clouds away and stars came winking out. A touch of moon drifted along. Not much, just enough to help see anything that was shiny.

Before long a shiny head did come bouncing across the meadow toward us, but it wasn't attached to a green or blue or feathered brave. It was mostly bald and belonged to the Professor, who was riding a fine bay. Soon as I recognized him, I spun about, searching for a tree to climb up or hole to crawl down, 'cause naturally I figured that Chilly had sent him after me. But he doused my fears quick by calling out, "Hold your horses, Zeb. There ain't nothing to combust about."

Not till then did I catch sight of Venus and Aphrodite,

clucking and pecking inside wooden cages that were draped over the horse's flanks. Seeing those chickens, I finally pieced together who Birdman was—the Professor, of course.

There was a rolled-up blanket and carpetbag tied behind his saddle, so it appeared he really wasn't hunting for runaways but was on the move just like us. Doing my level best not to act surprised, I said with a voice that had a touch of squeaky door to it, "What brings you—" Clearing my throat, I tried again. "What brings you calling, Professor?"

"The chief."

"You've got doings with each other?" I'm afraid my voice floated upward on me.

"We better have," the Professor said with a chuckle. Growing serious, he added, "Zeb, I'm thinking you'd be smart to steer clear of Goose Nedeau's place for a decade or two."

"I reckon I can manage that," I said. "They done looking for me yet?"

"Not hardly," the Professor said. "Chilly came rampaging back to the inn just as I was taking my leave. Goose's hounds were howling at his heels, and he aimed to put their noses to the ground as soon as he could find someone to handle 'em. So you best keep right on going. From what I heard Chilly shouting, that's what Ho-John's doing."

"Where *you* headed now?" I asked, ripe for suggestions.

"Guess I'm pointed California way. Going to get me some of that gold lying around out there."

"Sounds like a long ride," I pointed out, kind of hoping he'd stay with us in case Chilly showed.

"I was figuring on using a boat."

"How you affording such a thing as that?"

The princess answered that question by dipping into her father's beaver-pelt bundle and digging out Chilly's diamond pin, gold dice, and gold cigar clipper, along with a handful of cash. She pressed all of it into the Professor's hands.

"So it was you behind all them aces?" I cried out, finally understanding how the chief had come by the winningest hand in the history of the West.

"'Fraid so," the Professor confessed. "Me and the chief had it all planned out. Not that the chief wasn't grateful for your help, but when it comes to his medicine bundle, he's not about to take any chances. So I agreed to stack some decks for him. I do believe that Chilly's going to be seeing them aces till his dying day, which is why I'm on the road. Once him and Goose get a chance to put their heads together, they'll figure out my part in it. Adios, Zeb. And mind what I said about Chilly Larpenteur and your neck. He ain't the kind of man with a short memory and he ain't no dummy."

Giving his horse a giddyup, he left, cutting back toward

town and a steamer pointed toward New Orleans, then a clipper headed for San Francisco, with maybe a stop or two in
South America on the way. I reached out to tug on his pant
leg and beg to go along, but I came up short when I spied the
Professor's chickens taking aim at my hand with their beaks.
Gathering myself, I was about to overcome my fear of birds
and try again when something else occurred to me: hadn't I
once felt this same kind of tingly excitement over the prospects of hooking up with Chilly Larpenteur? Guessing that
taking off with another gambler couldn't be called anywhere
near smart, I stepped back, letting the opportunity pass. So
maybe I'd learned one lesson. The question was, how many
more did I have waiting ahead of me?

CHAPTER THIRTY-THREE

❖

Soon as the Professor was gone, the chief had himself a pow-wow with his pouch and daughter, who argued back till he got short with her.

"We'll take you home now," she announced, sounding sulky about it.

"Come again?" I said.

"You heard me," she grumbled.

"And just how do you know that's where I want to be going?" I came back, snippy-like 'cause I wasn't about to fess up that home was exactly what I'd been pining for. The only other option I seemed to have was throwing myself on my Great-Uncle Seth's mercy, which remained about as appealing as when I'd first met Chilly. I just couldn't sell myself on it.

"The crow in my father's pouch looked inside you." She

sounded awful put out, as if there didn't seem to be any end to the places that crow spirit could see.

"He's sure it was me?" I asked, shocked that not even my innermost feelings were safe from that bird.

"Yes," she complained. "And he saw us lead you home too."

"He can look into the future?"

"And the past. He doesn't give us any rest at all. He says we take you every step of the way home. To get the picture of the two-humped horse from your mother."

"Why's that thing so goldurn important?"

"My father wants to take it with him when he dies, as a gift for his father, whose name was Two Humps."

"Two what?"

But I'd heard her right. It turned out that Two Humps had got his name on account of a vision he had of a horse with two humps that led his youngest son—meaning the chief—home. Except that it had never happened, leastways not when the chief was a boy, which made him ashamed as a blue goose, what with all the other children rawhiding him day and night and claiming his pa's real name should have been No Humps. The chief and his pa had words about it too, the strongest kind of words, but Two Humps stuck with his vision to his dying day.

The princess said that a bunch of years passed. The chief grew into a man and held on to his father's sacred medicine bundle, partly 'cause nobody else wanted it and partly to prove that he believed his father's vision, even though some doubts had begun to sprout here and there. He had himself a vision too—of a crow who helped him find things. Just like his father's, his vision failed to come true. Oh, he went and bagged himself a crow and put its leg in a pouch, just the way the village elders told him to, so that the crow spirit would have a place to stay if it came to visit. But nothing come of it. The chief couldn't find dark on a moonless night, or so his neighbors claimed. He tried to be philosophical 'stead of bitter about all this, but he never gave up either. Anytime he saw a crow, he tried to strike up a conversation, and if a stranger passed through the village, he was sure to ask for news of a horse with two humps.

More time spun by. A white-man's sickness hit their village, wiping out neighbor after neighbor till Standing Tenbears got named chief for just surviving. Somewhere in there he grew old and his eyesight began to fail, making him take a young wife to help him see. According to the princess, they had a beautiful daughter who made them happier than sunrise on the prairie. When the princess was eight or nine, a bearded man came looking for people willing to travel with him to meet the kings and queens of Europe. The chief asked if there were any two-humped horses over there. *Why, only all over the place,* the bearded man said. When the chief asked about talking crows, he learned they were common as boots.

That settled it. He was headed to Europe with his wife and daughter, to prove that his vision, and his father's, had been true. But there wasn't anything to recommend the trip from the start. The princess's mother got sick and died on the crossing, and then the gent who'd brought them over disappeared somewhere in France, taking everything but the chief's spirit pouch and the sacred medicine bundle of his father's. He'd have probably grabbed them too if the chief hadn't always slept with them at his side.

So there the chief and princess were, stranded in a strange land and penniless. And they hadn't even hit rock bottom yet, nowhere near it, 'cause right about then it started snowing heavier and heavier behind the chief's eyes. In a matter of days he went totally blind.

But just before his vision was completely gone, a ray of sunshine struck. Buffalo Hilly happened upon them with a camel, which was the last thing the chief ever saw. And then came another miracle. The instant his eyesight was completely whited out, the crow spirit in his pouch started telling him what it saw. When Buffalo Hilly said he'd been invited to visit the king of Prussia, the chief and princess tagged along, knowing the camel would sooner or later lead them home, exactly the way Two Humps had foreseen.

Just hearing of such tribulations brought a lump to my throat, and not some little speck of a one either. I didn't even bother asking how the chief planned on getting a page from Ma's dictionary to his dead father. No doubt he'd find a way. All I knew was that they really were going to help me get home. The relief I felt could have filled an ocean.

When the princess and the chief waded out into the damp meadow, I followed along without any back talk, except to say, "The river's the other way."

"So's Chilly," the princess answered.

Seeing her point, I shut myself right up, figuring that every road headed home if you took the right turns. And besides, how lost could I get traveling with Indians? They'd been back and forth over this land a lot longer than me and mine.

We crossed the meadow with the princess up front leading the pony and travois, which the chief was stretched out atop with all his worldly possessions. I brought up the rear, feeling so lightheaded that I halfway convinced myself that if I ever did get home, I'd just tell Ma and Pa it'd been a busy few weeks and leave it at that.

But I was only lightheaded, not completely headless, so we

hadn't gone too awful far before it dawned on me that such talk wasn't going to wash. My folks would have a whole lot more questions than I had answers.

Not long after I struck that notion, I started lagging farther and farther in back of the pony. Oh, the chief and princess might walk me home across that hundred and sixty miles of wilderness, all right, but what could they do to change my ma's and pa's minds about apprenticing me out? The chief, with the help of that crow, might be able to see through mountains, but could he move 'em?

Maybe a letter home was the thing to do after all. That way I could let them know the earth hadn't opened up and swallowed me whole, and that even though I hadn't exactly hooked up with Great-Uncle Seth, I was doing just fine and . . . Slower and slower I dragged across that wet meadow, fretting every bit of the way about what I could pack into such a letter, until finally I was creeping along worse than Methuselah toward the end of his years. The chief and princess even had to pull up to wait for me.

"Is that the fastest you can walk?" the princess wanted to know.

"Some days."

"My father says you'll be an old man before you get home."

"You know," I said, coming to a stop, "I've been thinking

about that. Maybe home isn't where I ought to be heading."
Something desperate swooped over me then, and I think that I
heard a trumpet blowing off in the far-gone distance as I spied
the shadow of a possible answer to my woes. Even from the
first I knew it was a slim chance, but when it comes to fools,
I guess one size fits all. "There any way I could hook up with
you?" I blurted. "Maybe learn about visions and such?"

"What makes you think you could handle visions?" the
princess scoffed.

"Got my middle name from an uncle who's a wilderness
preacher," I told her, hopeful-like. "Maybe such doings run
in the family?"

She wrinkled her nose some at that but passed it on to
the chief, who gave back an answer I wasn't anywhere near
expecting.

"Let's make camp," the princess translated for him.

And that's what we did. In the middle of that soaked
meadow the princess somehow or other got a fire started and
put a stew on to cook. When the princess and chief finally
got around to putting their heads together, the princess got
her back up and her cheeks went all starchy, for she and her
father were disagreeing up a storm. In the end, the chief won
out and the princess lifted her chin formal-like to remark,
"My father wants to know if his pouch talked to you."

She made it sound as though I was far too lowly for such a thing to ever happen.

"Some," I answered back, taking exception to being lumped together with grubs and worms. "But it would have been helpful if I could have understood it."

The princess acted as if what I'd said only proved her right and passed it on to her father with a flourish. Her high tone put the chief on the warpath. After a flurry of words that sounded all stones and sparks, he had her ask what was wrong with how the pouch had talked to me.

"For one thing," I said, "I don't know Indian, and it wasn't bothering with any English."

The princess had no more than passed all that on than the chief seized up as if he had a fish bone stuck in his craw. When the princess tried patting him on the back, he waved her off. He wasn't choking, just laughing. When he explained the joke to his daughter, her face went crab-apple sour and her voice fell flat. Seems that it had been the crow who ordered the chief to hand the pouch over to me. That had gone against the chief's better judgment, but the spirit had declared that I was the one in danger and if they ever hoped to get that picture of the two-humped horse, they had to get me some help. Except that the crow hadn't foreseen that I couldn't understand a word of Indian. This from the same spirit who'd helped guide them home all the way from Europe? That struck the chief as about the rip-roaringest thing he'd ever heard.

The crow must not have been so amused though, for all of a sudden the chief sobered up as if he'd gotten new marching orders. Right away he spewed some words at the princess, who asked me, "Are you willing to learn our language?"

The resentful way she laid that out, I could tell this wasn't any time for funning. So I squeezed on it some and come to see that maybe here's where I'd been heading all along without even knowing. It appeared I had something of a gift for talking with crows. How else could I explain being able to hear the one in the chief's pouch? And if that was the case, where else was I going to get a chance to put such a talent to use, other than with the chief? What's more, Ma and Pa couldn't argue with it if I ever got around to writing them a letter, not if I worked in how I was planning to hook up with Uncle Clayton somewhere out West and learn what he had to teach me about preachering. So it looked as though the die was cast, and I was dreadful glad of it, what with all the bridges I'd left smoldering behind me.

"I don't see why not," I told 'em.

When the princess passed on my answer, the chief puffed on his pipe real strong. For two or three hours he went at it, conferring with the pouch now and again, but otherwise taking time off only to hack and cough. I asked the princess what her father was up to, but she shhhed me, saying the crow was having a look around. Finally the chief cupped a hand around his ear to hear the pouch, then spoke to the princess, who looked crushed but managed to say, "You're hired. On one condition."

"What's that?"

"You'll have to ask your parents for permission."

"Now hold on just a gosh-darn minute. . . . "

"The crow's seen you talking to them in a vision."

"He has?" My toes ran cold.

"You tell them the truth and everything is fine."

"It is?"

"He saw it," the princess insisted, though in an almost gentle kind of way.

"Were they mad?"

"Of course they were," she said, flaring up a bit only to simmer down and add, "but they get over it."

Maybe that was what I'd been needing to hear all along, 'cause it settled me down considerably. I was even calmed enough to make a long speech to the chief and the pouch, telling them how thankful I was that they were willing to take a chance on me, though deep down I think what I was most grateful for was having someone willing to stand beside me when I had to face Pa and Ma. But the main thing was, I was headed home to set the record straight and that just felt right all over, no matter what the consequences.

And then something no heavier than a shadow landed on my shoulder. Turning my head sideways, I found myself eye to eye with a glossy black crow who appeared to have something to say. Now all I had to do was learn how to listen.

THE END

AFTERWORD

In 1849, if you were a twelve-year-old boy of European descent and if your parents believed in the importance of knowing how to make or fix quality things, then you might have ended up apprenticed to a master craftsman (most girls did not serve as apprentices). However, the practice of individual craftsmen training young boys was dying out. In another ten or fifteen years, by the end of the Civil War, apprenticeships would be almost entirely gone. Why? The biggest single reason was the Industrial Revolution and the changes that it brought about. Material goods were more and more likely to be turned out by a factory and less and less likely to be hand-crafted. The spread of factories made it harder for craftsmen to make a living, and as a result, the number of craftsmen and apprentices dwindled.

Another factor that contributed mightily to the downfall of

apprenticeships was the rapid spread of Europeans across North America. New towns sprang up everywhere, and these towns had many available jobs. It became relatively easy for apprentices to run away. They could break the terms of their contracts with craftsmen and still be able to find employment in a new city that was in need of workers.

The most famous example of such a runaway was one of the United States' Founding Fathers—Benjamin Franklin. Apprenticed as a printer to his own brother in Boston, Franklin broke the terms of his apprenticeship and ran off to Philadelphia, where he started his own print shop. Years later he went on to write about it in his autobiography, which was published after his death in 1790 and became a bestseller of its day, going through fifty-five reprints in the next thirty years. Certainly his story must have influenced other young apprentices to follow his lead and start their own adventures.

It is safe to say that one occupation that didn't have a formal system of apprenticeship was that of the riverboat gambler. However, such gamblers would have certainly been willing to take advantage of a naive young boy setting forth on his own. They were willing to dupe almost anyone for their own personal gain. Cheating was their way of life, and the telegraph described in this story was only one of the ways they rigged games of chance. In the years leading up to the Civil

War, gamblers thrived on steamboats and in river towns, living off the huge influx of people and money along the Ohio, Mississippi, and Missouri rivers. That was where the action was.

If you had been a twelve-year-old Indian girl in 1849, you might have found yourself leading as nomadic an existence as the princess in this story. The Indian tribes at the center of the continent were suffering mightily as tens of thousands of European settlers arrived each year. The pressure to force Indian people westward had been mounting since the founding of the first European colonies. The basic reason behind this colonial expansion? Land for settlers. By 1849, European settlers in the United States outnumbered Native Americans by roughly thirty to one. But fifty years earlier, in 1800, the ratio had been only five to one. Fifty years before that, the ratio had been close to one to one. Go back another fifty years to 1700, and Native Americans outnumbered Europeans by perhaps five to one.

In her own words, a young Indian girl named Zitkala-Sa of the Yankton Sioux tribe, which now lives in South Dakota, remembers the impact of Europeans on her life in the later 1800s:

Late in the morning, my friend Judéwin gave me a terrible warning. Judéwin knew a few words of English, and she had overheard the paleface woman talk about cutting our long, heavy hair. Our mothers had taught us that only unskilled warriors who were captured had their hair shingled by the enemy. Among our people, short hair was worn by mourners, and shingled hair by cowards!

We discussed our fate some moments, and when Judéwin said, "We have to submit, because they are strong," I rebelled.

"No, I will not submit! I will struggle first!" I answered.

I watched my chance, and when no one noticed, I disappeared. I crept up the stairs as quietly as I could in my squeaking shoes—my moccasins had been exchanged for shoes. . . . I found a large room with three white beds in it. . . . On my hands and knees I crawled under the bed, and cuddled myself in the dark corner. . . . From my hiding place I peered out, shuddering with fear whenever I heard footsteps nearby. . . . What caused them to stoop and look under the bed I do not know. I remember being dragged out, though I resisted by kicking and scratching wildly. In spite of myself, I was carried downstairs and tied fast in a chair. . . . I cried aloud, shaking my head all the while until I felt the cold blades of the scissors against my neck, and heard them gnaw off one of my thick braids. Then I lost my spirit.

This young girl had to change her name as well as her hairstyle and became known as Gertrude Bonnin. The quotation is taken from "The Cutting of My Long Hair," collected in *American Indian Stories* (published by Rio Grande Press in 1976) and reprinted in *A Braid of Lives: Native American Childhood* (see section on further reading).

The princess and the chief's tribe was a neighbor of the Yankton Sioux. From the time of Zeb's story onward, all Indians west of the Mississippi were slowly being confined to reservations, making it harder for them to travel about and live off the land as their ancestors had. The princess would not have been raised on a reservation, but her children might have been and her grandchildren definitely would have been. Once forced onto reservations, Native Americans everywhere suffered the same traumatic loss of culture described above as Europeans tried to convert them to Christianity and the white man's ways.

As for visions and dreams, they played a central part in the religion of Native Americans at the time of Zeb's story. The members of many tribes went on vision quests as young adults in hopes of finding a spirit who would protect and guide them. They prepared for this by fasting for several days. Often the vision they received was of an animal, on whom they were later able to call for the kind of help that an outsider might label as magic or a miracle. Certainly Chief Standing Tenbears benefited from the power of such a spirit.

By 1849 the total population of the United States was twenty-three million, of which roughly three million were slaves of African descent. What was it like to be a slave? First, all were the property of another person. Just as people today can own a house or car or big-screen TV, people back then could own other people. What if you were someone else's property? The best you could hope for would be to have a humane master— one who treated you kindly—but many weren't that lucky. To get more work out of their slaves, some owners resorted to whippings and beatings.

Slaves rebelled against such treatment in many different ways. Some resorted to armed uprisings, such as Nat Turner's slave revolt in 1831 in Virginia, which had to be put down by federal and state troops. Self-mutilation—harming oneself— was another form of rebellion, for this deprived the owner of work from the slave. A carpenter slave in Kentucky was reported to have cut off one of his hands as well as the fingers of his other hand to prevent himself from being sold down the river. Finally, running away from their masters was a common form of rebellion. Those who tried escaping slavery this way either joined groups of slaves hiding in wilderness areas or made for the Free States, where slavery was outlawed (basically, any state north of the Ohio River was a Free State). How badly did slaves want to be free? One woman in North Carolina ran away from her owner sixteen times, which of course meant that she was caught and punished just as often.

St. Louis was the boomtown of the era. In the century before this story, it was ruled by three different countries—Spain, France, and the United States, who acquired it as part of the Louisiana Purchase in 1803. By 1849 it truly was the gateway to the West, a sprawling, rambunctious meeting place for a wide range of people and cultures. Roughly half of its 1849 population of seventy thousand people had been born in other countries, and of the half that were native-born Americans, a majority of them came from other states. Also included in St. Louis's population were 2,700 slaves and 1,300 free blacks. Native American tribes, such as the Osage and Illinois, had been pushed out of the area, but they remained regular visitors to the city, often camping on the banks of Chouteau's Pond.

But not all movement was westward in America. There was also a tiny but newsworthy trickle of Indians who traveled eastward. Sometimes they went to the nation's capital to meet the president. Other times they traveled across the Atlantic Ocean to Europe.

In the 1820s a group of twelve Osage Indians, including a man named Big Soldier, left St. Louis for Europe. They traveled widely, seeing France, Belgium, Germany, and Switzerland. They attended operas, were mobbed by crowds of curiosity seekers, were taken advantage of by greedy promoters, and were wined and dined by King Charles X of France. The "Noble Savage," as North American Indians were sometimes romantically thought of by Europeans, excited the imaginations of royalty and commoners alike.

Certainly the attitudes of Europeans toward Indians were contradictory. Europeans may have invaded and taken Indian lands, but sometimes they deeply admired the Indians' close ties to nature and their customs, which were viewed as exotic. It was documented that Indians traveling across Europe received gifts from their hosts and that these gifts became prized possessions upon their return home. Travelers to Missouri in the 1840s recorded that Big Soldier, one of the twelve Osage who had traveled across Europe twenty years before, proudly showed off a French bronze medal given to him on his trip. The medal bore a portrait of the French general Lafayette.

Big Soldier spoke of the general with affection and treasured the medal above all his possessions.

Did an Indian ever receive a golden crown from a European monarch, as in this story? Not that was recorded. When gifting Indians, Europeans were far more stingy. They were most likely to part with what they thought to be cheap trinkets than anything they valued. Yet being of European descent myself, I like to think it possible that at least one prince or king, overcome with brotherly love (and perhaps too much wine), might have bestowed a crown on a visiting Indian chief— a gift from one blue blood to another. Such a generous gift might have been made by a kinsman of someone like Prince Maximilian of Germany, who traveled through St. Louis in the 1830s and lived for a time among the Mandan Indians of the upper Missouri River. Writing of his travels, Prince Maximilian said, "Wonders passed us as in a dream."

As for traveling medicine shows, they were descended from quack doctors called mountebanks who for centuries had sold elixirs and cures across Europe. In America such con artists flourished in colonial times and by the late 1800s had become wildly popular. They peddled tonics, which were mostly alcohol, and provided entertainment.

Whether or not there was ever a medicine wagon pulled by

a camel is unproven, but in the later 1800s medicine shows often used animals such as elephants to help draw crowds. In this way they were a forerunner of the traveling circuses eventually made famous by P. T. Barnum and the Ringling brothers. As to whether there were camels in North America by 1849, the first camel to reach North America was believed to have come in the early 1700s to Virginia. And it is well documented that in 1856 the U.S. Army imported camels to Texas to help settle the West, an experiment that failed but spawned a host of colorful stories about the sightings of camels in the wilderness. It certainly seems possible that an enterprising showman such as Dr. Buffalo Hilly, who had traveled to Europe and possibly beyond, could have brought home a camel to pull his wagon.

Did medicine shows include Indians? Oh, yes. People of the time were eager to be treated by the potions and cures that Native Americans had learned from tribal elders or seen in visions. Patent medicine companies, such as the Kickapoo Indian Medicine Company, became successful because of it. Traveling medicine shows included Indians for the same reason. Although many of the traveling shows and patent medicines were later proven to be run by white men who were con artists, there were still patients who claimed remarkable cures thanks to them. Perhaps such patients had been treated by medicine men as talented as Chief Standing Tenbears.

FURTHER READING

Some of the books I consulted in preparing to write this story include the following:

BOOKS ABOUT ST. LOUIS

Primm, James Neal. *Lion of the Valley: St. Louis, Missouri, 1764–1980.* 3rd ed. St. Louis: Missouri Historical Society Press, 1998. An encyclopedic look at the great city.

Ross, Oscar Mervene. *The History of St. Louis, 1848–1853.* St. Louis: Washington University, 1949. A master's thesis written and stored at Washington University in St. Louis. It brought to life the early city of St. Louis for me. My thanks to Washington University for sharing this gem. (A master's thesis is a lengthy research paper by a college student working on an advanced degree.)

Books About Steamboating and the Mississippi River

Bissell, Richard. *My Life on the Mississippi, or Why I Am Not Mark Twain.* Boston: Little, Brown, 1973. Worth reading for a perspective on Mark Twain.

Larson, Ron. *Upper Mississippi River History: Fact–Fiction–Legend.* Winona, Minn.: Steamboat Press, 1998. An entertaining look at the folklore and history of towns along the upper part of the river, as well as the art of steamboating. This one is a favorite of mine, in part because the author has captained modern-day riverboats and in part because he hails from Winona, the river town where I grew up.

Petersen, William J. *Steamboating on the Upper Mississippi.* Iowa City: State Historical Society of Iowa, 1968. A comprehensive look at the days of steamboating on the upper Mississippi.

Twain, Mark. *Life on the Mississippi.* New York: Signet Classic, 2001. Mr. Twain's exaggerations in this book as well as in *The Adventures of Huckberry Finn* and *The Adventures of Tom Sawyer* were a constant inspiration.

Books About Apprentices

Rorabaugh, W. J. *The Craft Apprentice: From Franklin to the Machine Age in America.* New York: Oxford University

Press, 1986. An in-depth look at the demise of apprenticeships in the 1800s.

Books About Gambling

Devol, George H. *Forty Years a Gambler on the Mississippi.*
New York: Reprinted by Johnson Reprint Corporation,
1892. A biography written by a riverboat gambler about
his days of cheating and glory.

Books About Medicine

Armstrong, David. *The Great American Medicine Show.* New
York: Prentice Hall, 1991. A well-illustrated history of
medicine shows in America. The pictures alone are worth
a look.

Dunlop, Richard. *Doctors of the American Frontier.* Garden
City, N.Y.: Doubleday, 1965. You'll never squawk about a
trip to the doctor again after reading this one.

Books About the Frontier

Brown, Dee. *Wonderous Times on the Frontier.* Little Rock,
Ark: August House Publishers, 1991, or *Bury My Heart
at Wounded Knee,* or *The Gentle Tamers: Women of the Old
Wild West.* All of Mr. Brown's work lends sympathy and
humor to the lives of the settlers and Indians. Try any of
his books—you'll be glad you did.

Books About Native Americans

Deloria, Vine, Jr. *The World We Used to Live In: Remembering the Powers of the Medicine Men.* Golden, Colo.: Fulcrum Publishing, 2006. A collection of firsthand accounts about the powers of Indian medicine men, with insightful commentary by the author.

Foreman, Carolyn Thomas. *Indians Abroad, 1493–1928.* Norman: University of Oklahoma Press, 1948. Tells the stories of American Indians who traveled to Europe.

Goodbird, Edward, as told to Gilbert L. Wilson. *Goodbird the Indian.* New York: Fleming H. Revell Co., 1914. The autobiography of a Hidatsa Indian on the frontier. A chance to hear in one man's own words about the coming of the white settlers.

Hoxie, Frederick E. *Encyclopedia of North American Indians.* New York: Houghton Mifflin Company, 1996. A great source for basic information about Indians.

Matthews, Washington. *Grammar and Dictionary of the Language of the Hidatsa.* New York: Cramoisy Press, 1873. A dictionary of the Hidatsa Indians that was written in the late 1800s. My thanks to the University of North Dakota for sharing this dusty volume.

Philip, Neil (editor). *A Braid of Lives: Native American Childhood.* New York: Clarion Books, 2000. A chance to hear Indian children speak of their youth in their own words. You may recognize some things.

Books About Slavery

Franklin, John Hope, and Alfred A. Moss, Jr. *From Slavery to Freedom.* New York: Alfred A. Knopf, 1988. A very readable overview of the history of African Americans and slavery.

DICTIONARIUM
AMERICANNICUM

Words are the keys to knowledge.

—THADDEUS POPE

WARNING!

DON'T BE FOOLED BY THE FANCY TITLE

THIS IS A DICTIONARY

AND MAY PROVE

HAZARDOUS TO YOUR HEALTH.

CONTACT WITH THESE THINGS

HAS BEEN KNOWN TO CAUSE

EPIZOOTIC, MOUNTAIN FEVER

(SPOTTED AND OTHERWISE),

AND PROLONGED FAINTING SPELLS.

REPORT ANY

SUSPICIOUS RASHES

TO YOUR PHYSICIAN AT ONCE.

DON'T WAIT TILL IT'S TOO LATE.

A

accordion   The word may be familiar, but is its history? The accordion is a fairly recent invention, first appearing in Europe in the early 1800s. Dr. Buffalo Hilly's accordion would have been a novelty.

afeard   Afraid.

ain't   Contraction for *are not* or *am not*. If you're worried about proper usage, you shouldn't use it, for the word is a mark of being uneducated. That hasn't stopped a lot of people from using it over the years. There have even been times when this little contraction was in fashion among the upper classes.

airs   Not what you breathe. In this instance it refers to the act of pretending to be more important than you are.

Alleghenies   Allegheny Mountains, located in the
(al-uh-GAY-nees)   eastern United States and part of the

Appalachian Mountains, which marked the western edge of European expansion until the later 1700s.

Aphrodite
(aff-row-DIE-tee)

Greek goddess of love and beauty.

applejack

Liquor made from apples. It was an important drink on the frontier, where drinkable water was sometimes hard to come by.

apple-pie order

The best possible shape or condition.

a te dami
(ah theh dah-mee)

Translates as "three kings," although the literal translation is "fathers, three." It is from the Hidatsa language. The Hidatsa are an Indian tribe that lived on the upper Missouri River in the 1840s. They still live in the same general area, which today is part of North Dakota.

atwitter

Excited.

B

bandy　　To toss words about without thinking over what you're saying.

bang-up　　Really good, top-notch, or first-rate.

bankroll　　Money someone has. If you withdraw paper money from the *bank* and *roll* it into a cylindrical shape, you have a *bankroll*.

bile　　Anger. Today bile refers to a fluid made by your liver to help absorb fats. In Zeb's day it had a much different meaning, one that dated back to medieval times, when physicians believed there were four fluids that controlled a person's health and temperament. Back then bile was considered a fluid that made people easily angered.

bit　　A Spanish coin that was worth twelve and a half cents and was often used in the Old West.

biters　　Horses that bite.

Black Hawk   A chief of the Sauk tribe in Illinois. He fought with the British against the United States in the War of 1812, and in 1832 he took part in an uprising that became known as the Black Hawk War. The primary reason for this war? He and his followers refused to be pushed west of the Mississippi River by European settlers.

blackleg   Cheater or swindler.

blacksmith    Someone who forges iron. To forge something, you shape it by heating and hammering it. The word *blacksmith* comes from iron being called the black metal and a smith being someone who works with metal. On the frontier, blacksmiths did everything from making horseshoes to mending plows.

blimblam   A word that may have been made up by Mark Twain—at least, it appears in his fiction but not in any dictionary researched for this book. It seems to mean to talk noisily and endlessly.

blue streak A long, fast stream of words.

boiler deck On a steamboat, the deck above the boilers. The boilers heat (or boil) the water that powers the ship when turned to steam.

bonjour Translates as "hello" or "good day." It is
(bone-ZHUR) from the French language.

brush fence Fence made from cut brush. It is a quick way to build a fence and often the first type of fence that farmers threw up when settling in a wooded area.

buckboard Wagon with a seat mounted on springs.

buck the tiger The phrase means to try to win at the game of faro. The symbol for faro is a tiger, and gaming halls sometimes advertised that they played faro by placing a picture of a tiger out front.

buckshot　　Small lead pellets used in a gun.

buckskin　　Skin made from a buck (in this case, a male deer or antelope). It was a common material for clothing on the frontier.

bullyragging　　Threats.

bumpkin　　Someone who's unsophisticated.

bungle　　To make a dumb mistake.

bust-head liquor　　Really strong liquor. Drink too much of it and you'll feel as though your head has been busted.

C

cast iron　　Iron that has been heated to a liquid and poured into a cast or mold. Skillets (frying pans) are one of the more common items made from cast iron. Some people still cook with cast-iron pans.

catarrh
(kah-TAR)

The common cold. The term sounds educated, which may explain why Dr. Buffalo Hilly uses it. He wants to impress his audience.

chamber pot

Before indoor plumbing, people had to use outdoor bathrooms or outhouses. A chamber pot was a lidded pot that was kept indoors, usually in a bedroom, to save people a long, cold trip to an outhouse in the middle of the night.

chaw

A measurement that's about a mouthful in size and usually refers to chewing tobacco. Another way to say *chew*.

chock-full

So full that nothing more can be added. This usage may come from combining *choke* and *full*.

cipher
(SIGH-fur)

To do arithmetic.

clapboards

Narrow boards used as siding.

cob

A man.

combust

To burn. You may be more familiar with the noun form, *combustion*.

Conestoga
(con-eh-STOW-guh)

Wide wagon used to haul freight or belongings. It is usually pulled by a team of six horses. The wagon is named after a valley in Pennsylvania, where it was first built in the 1700s.

consarn

Mild cuss word used in place of *confound* or *damn*.

consumption

Disease that is called tuberculosis or TB today. It is caused by bacteria that infects the lungs. In 1849 it could have been fatal.

cooper   Craftsman who makes and repairs wooden barrels, casks, and tubs.

corn-shuck tick   Tick (or mattress) filled with corn shucks that rustle whenever you roll over.

corn squeezings   Liquor made from corn.

craw   Throat and stomach. The word is most often used to describe a wide spot in the throat of a bird where food collects. It's also used to describe a human throat, particularly if something is caught in it.

crockery   Bowls made of baked clay with covers and used to store food. The Tupperware of its day on the frontier.

crowbait   Worn-out horse that's so close to death, you can use it as bait to attract crows.

cubbing   Working as an apprentice. In the context of this story, it applies particularly to young men learning to be steamboat pilots.

cuss   May be short for *customer*. It's usually said in a humorous or mean-spirited way and refers to a man.

D

dang   Civilized way of saying *damn*.

darn   Another civilized way of saying *damn*.

dast   To dare.

dealing seconds   A way to cheat at cards by dealing out the second card from the top of the deck. The cheater stacks the deck by placing a card that he or she wants beneath the top card (in the *second* position) then dealing it out whenever it is needed. A slick cardsharp can deal seconds without anyone noticing.

deck passage Ticket that allows you to ride and sleep on the deck of a ship. It was a cheap way to travel back then.

deed A legal document showing ownership of something (in this case, the inn).

deuce Playing card with the number two on it. It's from the French word *deux*.

dickens Polite way to say *devil*.

dilly-dally Fancy way to say *dally*, which means to waste time.

dithers Trembles or shivers.

dotage Old age.

drat Mild way of saying *damn*.

dray Low two-wheeled cart that was used for

pulling heavy loads. Originally, the word described a sled used for dragging logs in the woods.

dromedary
(DROM-uh-dare-ee)

Another name for a camel. It comes from the ancient Greek language and means "running camel." The picture showing this animal is the very one that Chief Standing Tenbears wanted to take to his father.

du ska
(DOO shkuh)

Translates as "open it." The phrase is from the Hidatsa language. The Hidatsa are an Indian tribe that lived on the upper Missouri River in the 1840s. They still live in the same general area, which today is part of North Dakota.

E

egg

Not from a bird. This *egg* is a verb that means to push or agitate someone into action. It is usually formed with *on*.

epizootic   General illness or misery.
(ep-ih-zoe-OTT-ick)

F

fallback   Something you can resort to (or fall back
on) if you need help.

fandango   Silliness, playfulness, or foolishness. The
word's origin is Spanish. In that language
it is the name of a lively dance.

fantods   Irritable fidgets, occurring when you're
mad about something and can't sit still.

fare   Food.

faro   Card game of the Old West. It was the
most popular gambling game of its day but
is no longer played, mostly because it is
so easy for the dealer to cheat. The game
is played on a cloth that has pictures for

each card value (though not each suit) in a deck. Players set their bets atop the pictures. The name is a shortened spelling of *pharaoh,* the name for the ruler of ancient Egypt. At one time the cards used in the game may have included one with a picture of a pharaoh.

fess up   To confess.

five-card   Type of card game. Also called poker.

fisticuffs   Fistfight. Formed from *fist* and *cuff.* In this case *cuff* is a verb that means to hit someone.

fix   Difficult position or dilemma.

fixings   Food that goes along with the main dish of a meal.

flay   To skin something.

flimflam   Deception or trickery.

flinty   Something or someone who is stern.

flummoxed   Embarrassed, confused, or perplexed.

flush   A poker hand in which all cards are of the same suit but are not in consecutive order. For example, the two, five, seven, ten, and queen of hearts.

forge   Furnace that heats metal. Hot and glowing!

forty-rod   Liquor so strong that one sip can knock you forty rods back. A rod is a length equal to about 16½ feet. Forty rods would equal 660 feet, or slightly more than a city block. Strong stuff.

Free States   States where slavery was not allowed before the Civil War.

G

Galena   Wealthy Illinois town that was at the center of the lead mining district along the upper Mississippi River. Lead mining was the major business on the upper Mississippi for several decades in the early and middle 1800s.

garter   Band that holds up a stocking or sleeve. Quite stylish.

gibble-gabble   To chatter fast and foolishly. You may be more familiar with its shortened form, *gab*.

giddyup   Command to go faster, usually given to a horse.

goatee   Pointed beard that first became popular in the 1840s. It got the name because it looks like the beard of a male goat.

gold eagle   Ten-dollar gold piece that is also called a liberty head by coin collectors. It has a woman's portrait on one side, an eagle on the other.

goldurn   Polite way to say *goddamn*.

Good Book   The Bible.

goose flesh   Same as *goose bumps*, a term that describes what the skin of a plucked goose looks like.

gristmill   Mill that grinds corn into flour. In the 1800s, mills used stones, which were turned by gears, to do the grinding. Water wheels often powered the gears.

grog   Alcohol or liquor. Often it is mixed with water, lemon juice, and sugar, then served hot. A grog shop is a bar or tavern that serves this drink. The word comes from an Englishman, Admiral Vernon (of the 1700s), whose nickname was Old Grog because of a grogram cloak he liked to wear (a grogram is a coarse, stiff coat made of mohair and wool). The admiral had a special drink that he served to the men on his ships, and that drink became known by his nickname.

grubstake   Money or supplies used to start an undertaking. The word often referred to what a gold miner needed to start prospecting. If the grubstake was loaned to the prospector, the person making the loan was entitled to a share of all discoveries.

gumption   Energy or willingness to do something.

gut shot   Shot in the gut (stomach).

H

ha ka ta   Translates as "Halt!" or "Wait!" It is from the Hidatsa language. The Hidatsa are an Indian tribe that lived on the upper Missouri River in the 1840s. They still live in the same general area, which today is part of North Dakota.

hang fire   To be delayed. The phrase originally described an explosive charge that was slow in going off once its primer was lit or discharged. For this reason, the expression suggests a delay with some tension to it.

hankering   A want of something badly.

hawk   To sell something on the street by calling out to passersby.

high hat   Refers not only to a hat with a high crown but also to the fact that anyone who could afford such a hat would be well-off financially.

high roller   Someone who spends money freely.

high toned   Acting snobbish, as if you're important.

highwayman   Robber who steals from highway travelers.

hobnob   To be friendly and socialize with someone.

hogshead   Large wooden barrel that holds sixty-three gallons.

hogtie   To make something helpless. It comes from the way a hog's legs are tied together to make it unable to move.

hogwash   Something that doesn't make sense. Why would you wash a hog?

hold-out   Card that's held out of a deck for cheating purposes. The cheater hides it up a sleeve or down a boot and sneaks it into play during a game.

homespun   Describes clothing that is spun or made at home. Most people on the frontier made

their own clothes. They were usually made of linen and wool, then colored with natural dyes such as goldenrod for yellow, walnut bark and sumac for gray, and butternut hulls for brown.

Hudson Bay blanket Heavy wool blanket of bright colors that the Hudson Bay Company, a fur-trading company, gave to Indians in exchange for furs.

hullabaloo Loud commotion or excitement.

humble pie Something submissive or humiliated. The phrase comes from eating umble pie. Umbles are the edible inner parts of an animal, particularly deer, which were thought of as food fit only for lower classes.

humbug Someone who's not what he or she pretends to be.

hunker To squat down.

huzzah
(huh-ZAH)

Cheer or hurrah that was originally a sailor's greeting when friends came aboard the ship.

I

iota
(eye-OH-tuh)

Smallest possible thing.

J

Jackson, Andy

Seventh president of the United States. Before becoming president, he won fame as an Army general, earning the nickname Old Hickory for his discipline and determination. He waged war against the Creek Indians in the southern United States and in the War of 1812 defeated the British at New Orleans. The victory over the British made him a national hero.

jenny wren

A jenny is a female bird. A wren is a small brown bird that flits quickly about.

Joan of Arc   National heroine of the French. In 1429 she led an army against English invaders at the French city of Orleans and defeated them. She was viewed as a messenger of God by the French, which was why they let her lead troops into battle. The English viewed her as an agent of the devil and eventually had her burned at the stake as a witch. In the 1920s, almost five hundred years after her death, she was recognized by the Catholic Church as a saint.

jug bitten   Drunk. A jug is a large clay bottle often used to store liquor.

just deserts   In this phrase, *just* refers to what is right or proper. *Deserts* refers to something that is deserved, such as a reward or punishment. Zeb's definitely thinking punishment.

K

kingdom come   Old way of saying *heaven*, from the Bible.

King Louis   Name of eighteen French kings. An illus-
trious bunch.

kit and caboodle Collection of things or people.

L

la-di-da   Pretentious. Describes someone who pretends to be far more important or refined
than he or she is.

Lafayette   French general who fought on the side of
the colonists in the United States' Revolu-
tionary War.

lark   Bird known for its singing.

legging   Covering for the leg made of leather or
cloth.

levee   River landing where boats can dock.

lick   Tiny amount.

livery stable   Stable that cares for and rents out horses.

lodestone   Magnetic stone used in compasses that points north. For Ho-John, north is the direction of freedom.

looking glass   Mirror.

M

medicine bundle   A wrapping of skin or cloth that contains sacred objects such as an ancestor's skull, pipe, or robe. An Indian tribe might have many bundles, each owned by a keeper, who passes them on to a member of the next generation. A medicine bundle, similar to Christian religious shrines, bestows great honor and influence on the owner.

Methuselah
(Muh-THOO-zuh-luh)   Old guy from the Bible who is said to have lived 969 years and been the grandfather of Noah, who built the ark.

mettle   Courage or strength of spirit.

middling   Middle-size.

monkeyshine   Prank.

Mormons   Members of the Mormon religion. Dr.
Buffalo Hilly is making fun of them be-
cause they were run out of the state of
Missouri. Local citizens were afraid the
Mormons were trying to take over towns
such as Independence and Liberty. Not a
high point of religious tolerance.

mortify   To subdue or do away with. Those pinworms that Buffalo Hilly's talking about
don't stand a chance.

mountain fever   Any number of fevers that people come
down with while in the mountains. Colo-
rado tick fever and Rocky Mountain spotted fever are two examples.

mud clerk Steamboat clerk who is the purser's assistant. The name may have come from the clerk having to work on shore, which is often muddy.

muff To handle or deal with something poorly. Today you might hear it used when a baseball player drops a fly ball.

mumblety-peg Knife game. Players try to stick a knife
(MUM-bull-tee-peg) into the ground from different locations or distances. Losers have to pull their knives out of the ground with their teeth.

mumps Disease with symptoms such as a fever and major swelling of the cheeks. Today there is a vaccine that prevents it.

N

nabob Someone who is rich and important. The
(NAY-bob) word comes from India, where it was the name for the governor of a province.

nag
A horse that is old or in bad health.

Nantucket
Island off the coast of Massachusetts. It was once an important center for boats that hunted whales.

Napoleon
Emperor of France from 1804 to 1815. Famous for nearly conquering all of Europe and for being short.

nary
None at all.

O

oilcloth
Cloth treated with oil or paint and used to cover tables or shelves.

P

palaver
(puh-LAHV-er)
To talk in a misleading and cajoling way. The speaker is usually trying to convince the listener of something. It comes from a Portuguese word that means "to chatter."

parcel   To divide something into parts.

passel   Large group.

passenger   Type of pigeon that once lived in North
pigeon   America. Huge numbers of the bird nested

in the middle and eastern parts of the
United States. In 1840, John J. Audubon,
a famous bird painter, saw one flock of the
birds that was a mile wide and took three
hours to pass over him. He placed its number at more than a billion birds. The bird
was hunted to extinction as thousands were
shot to be sold in markets. The last passenger pigeons were seen in the wild in 1906.

Pawnee   Indian tribe of the Great Plains.

penny-ante   Small amount. Comes from a game of poker
that costs a penny to join.

pernickety   Overly concerned about details. Some-
(per-NICK-ih-tee) times spelled *persnickety*.

pigs of lead   Rough castings of lead that have the shape of a short rod and are easy to transport.

pike   Short for *turnpike*, which is a road you pay to use. *Turnpike* comes from combining the words *turn* and *pike*, the latter of which was a heavy spear used in the Middle Ages by the infantry. A revolving (or turning) frame with pikes attached to it was once used to control access to places such as a road. Today's turnstiles are a less pointy version.

pilot (riverboat)   One who steers a riverboat. It was a highly skilled job back then, for the Mississippi river was filled with snags and shallows.

pine for   To long for something you can't have.

pluck   Courage or willingness to fight for what you believe in.

pockmarked   Describes skin that has pits or marks left by smallpox or acne.

poke   Small bag or sack.

poleaxe (verb)   To be cut down by a poleax, which was a medieval battle-axe and quite wicked.

porridge   Food made by boiling grain until soft.

potshot   Shot taken from hiding or at an easy target. It's a slightly derogatory term, for such a shot is viewed as taking an unfair or un-sportsman-like advantage of whatever is being shot at. As such, it is a shot fitting only for someone trying to fill a cooking pot—in other words, a shot for the pot.

powwow   Meeting or social gathering. American Indians often hold them to celebrate important victories or occasions. Zeb isn't using the word quite accurately when he describes two people conferring.

poxes   Diseases (smallpox or chickenpox) that cause blisters or pimples. Smallpox is rare today because of vaccinations. Chickenpox remains common, although a recent vaccine may change that.

Prussia   Kingdom that became part of Germany.

pullet   Young hen.

purser   person on a ship who collects tickets from passengers.

Q

quicksilver Another name for mercury, which at room temperature is a silver liquid that's runny and toxic.

quill   Before ballpoint pens, people used quills to write. They were bird feathers sharpened on the end and dipped into ink.

R

rackabones   Horse so skinny that it doesn't look healthy —nothing but a *rack of bones*.

ragamuff   Zeb's mispronouncing *ragamuffin*, which is a child dressed in rags and needing a bath and good meal.

ragging   Tormenting or teasing.

rail   To disapprove of someone or something with strong, harsh words.

railroad   To be convicted of committing a crime without a fair trial or sometimes without a trial at all.

rapscallion
(rap-SKAL-yen)   Rascal. The word comes from modifying the word *rascal* and adding a fancy ending.

rawhide   To tease mercilessly. The word comes from the use of a rope made of rawhide to whip someone.

Red River   There are two Red Rivers of note in the United States. One flows north along the Minnesota–North Dakota border all the way into Canada. The other flows east along the Oklahoma-Texas border, then across Arkansas and Louisiana and eventually to the Mississippi River. It's this second Red River that Zeb is referring to.

redskin   An American Indian. The word is most often used in a mean-spirited way. The usage comes from the color of an American Indian's skin.

restorative   Something that restores your health.

rheumatic pains   Pain of the muscles and joints. Often
(roo-MAT-ick)   called arthritis.

riffraff   People with very poor reputations.

row   Noisy fight.

royal flush   A poker hand that goes ten, jack, queen, king, ace, with all cards being the same suit. It's the highest possible hand. If two players have a royal flush at the same time, they split the pot (or winnings).

S

San Carlos   Town on the Missouri River that today is known as St. Charles. Goose Nedeau calls it by its old Spanish name.

sapua sapua
(suh-POO-uh)   Translates as "seven, seven" (a pair of sevens). It is from the Hidatsa language. The Hidatsa are an Indian tribe that lived on the upper Missouri River in the 1840s. They still live in the same general area, which today is part of North Dakota.

sarsaparilla
(sass-puh-RILL-uh)   Sweet drink made from the dried root of the sassafras tree and flavoring from birch trees.

sawing wood   Snoring.

schoolmarm   Woman schoolteacher in a rural or small-town school.

Shanghai chicken *(shang-HIGH)*   Type of chicken popular on the frontier.

shebang   Everything that's under consideration.

shell out   To pay for something, used particularly if you feel you're paying too much for it.

shut   In this instance, to get clear or free of something.

sic   To urge one person (or animal) to attack or pursue someone else.

side-wheeler   Steamboat with paddle wheels on the sides of the boat instead of the back.

sight   Not only meaning what you can see, the word can also mean a large quantity.

skedaddle   To run away fast.
(skuh-DAD-uhl)

skinflint   Someone who's so cheap, he or she pinches pennies till they scream.

smack   Directly or sharply, often used in the phrase *smack in the middle.*

smithereens   Tiny bits.

smokehouse   Small cabin where fresh meat is hung to cure. The cabin is filled with a thick smoke that preserves and flavors the meat. In a time without refrigeration, this was an important way to prevent meat from spoiling.

soddies   Frontier houses built of sod. Used on the prairie, with lots of bugs for pets.

Spanish brown wash

Reddish brown wash or paint.

specs

Short for *spectacles,* which is another way of saying *eyeglasses.*

spell

In this case, the word refers to a period of time, not a magical incantation.

sphinx

Monster of ancient Egyptian and Greek legends. The Egyptian sphinx had a man's head and lion's body. The Greek sphinx in Thebes had a woman's head and lion's body and killed anyone who couldn't answer its riddle:

> *What is four-footed in the morning,*
> *two-footed at noon,*
> *three-footed in the evening?*

The answer is *man,* who in childhood creeps on hands and knees, in adulthood walks erect, and in old age uses a cane.

spitter Apple that is too sour to eat—one bite and you spit it out.

spittoon Bowl or urn for spitting in. When tobacco chewing was all the rage and men didn't mind what kind of juice was dribbling down their chins, chewers needed somewhere to spit when in polite company.

split-bottom chair Chair with a seat made from split logs.

squire A medieval manservant who carried a knight's shield and sword.

St. Jerome Patron saint of orphans. His full name is St. Jerome Emiliani. He lived in Italy (1481–1537) and devoted his life to the care of orphans.

St. Joe Short for St. Joseph, Missouri, a town on the Missouri River that was one of the starting points for settlers heading west.

staghorn knife   Knife with a handle made from a stag's horn (a stag is a male deer).

star-crossed   Describes something not favored by the stars—unlucky.

stateroom   A sleeping room on a steamboat. Each room is named after a different state of the union. They are generally small and cramped but luxurious when compared to deck passage, where people camp out on the open deck with livestock and one another.

steerage   If you don't have money for a stateroom (see above), you might be able to afford a ticket on steerage. It got its name from being near the boat's rudder, which *steers* the ship.

stove works   Factory that makes stoves.

straight   A poker hand where all the cards are consecutive (or in order) but of different suits.

An example would be the two of hearts, three of spades, four of diamonds, five of clubs, and six of hearts.

strap　　　　A strip of leather often used for whippings.

straw tick　　Crinkly mattress filled with straw.

stretcher　　In this case, a story that stretches the truth considerably.

T

tanner

Someone who tans animal hides to change them into leather. This is done by treating the hide with chemicals.

**tar and
feathering**

Frontier punishment. The person was covered with hot tar and then sprinkled with feathers that stuck to the tar. Very unhealthy and possibly fatal.

tarnation   Polite way of saying *damnation*.

taters   Potatoes.

telegraph   Before the telephone there was the telegraph. Invented in 1835 by Samuel Morse,
it was a machine that allowed people who
were far apart to communicate by sending
a series of clicks over electrical wires. By
1849 telegraph wires had spread as far
west as St. Louis, where they were briefly
halted until a way could be figured out to
string a line across the Mississippi River.

tenpenny nail   Nail that is three inches long. When this
nail was first made in the 1400s, you could
buy one hundred of them for ten pennies.
The price has gone up considerably since
then, but the name remains the same today.

ten pin   Early form of bowling.

Thebes Name of ancient Egyptian and Greek cities.

three R's The three fundamentals taught in frontier schools: reading, writing, and arithmetic. The phrase comes from saying the three words this way: *reading, 'riting, 'rithmetic*.

throw Bedcover or blanket.

tick mattress Fabric covering that is filled with straw, corn husks, or feathers for sleeping on.

to-do Activity, bother, or fuss.

trappings The appearance or outward sign of something.

travois
(truh-VOY) Sled used by Plains Indians. Comes from a French word that means "to travel." Pulled by ponies or dogs, the travois was the moving van of its day.

trey   The number three card in a deck of cards.

tribulations   Troubles or difficulties.

truck   Two different meanings are used by Zeb in
the story. First, *truck* can be small stuff of
little value. Second, it can mean to have a
close connection to something.

tsa kic ti   Translates as "very good." It is from the
(tsah kick TEE)   Hidatsa language. The Hidatsa are an Indian tribe that lived on the upper Missouri
River in the 1840s. They still live in the
same general area, which today is part of
North Dakota.

tsa ki ha   Translates as "quiet." It is from the Hidatsa
(tsah kee HAH)   language. The Hidatsa are an Indian tribe
that lived on the upper Missouri River
in the 1840s. They still live in the same
general area, which today is part of North
Dakota.

turnkey   Someone in charge of a prison's keys.

tyke   Small child.

V

varmint   Animal that is a nuisance.

Venus   Roman goddess of love and beauty.

victuals   Food.

vittles   Food again.

W

wampum   Money. The word originally referred to shells that Indians used as money.

war bonnet   Headdress worn by the men in some American Indian tribes. It is made up of feathers that circle the head and trail down the back.

wardrobe Upright trunk that is big enough to hang clothes inside. It used to do the same job that closets do in today's homes.

washbasin Bowl or basin to wash in. No indoor plumbing!

weather eye An eye that's quick to notice changes in anything, especially the weather.

wheat berry Dry seed of wheat.

whilst While.

whim-wham To have the jitters.

whistler Horse that makes a whistling sound when breathing hard. Not good.

whit Smallest thing you can imagine.

willies Jitters, often caused by something that frightens you.

works   Building where factory work is done.

wrangle   To get something you want by being persis-
                   tent.

Y

yarb and   Yarb is another word for *herb,* so this is a
root doctor   doctor who uses plant remedies.

yoke   Wooden frame that connects the heads of
                   two work animals, like oxen.